CLOSE TO HOME

NOLON KING

STERLING & STONE

CLOSE TO HOME

Chapter One

"I believe in knowing who you are, without ever limiting yourself to an idea of who you *have* to be."

Adam felt the corners of his mouth twitch. She had that power, the ability to speak to a part of him that he had no control over. Selena called, and it answered, every time.

Same for the reporter, Isla Porter. Her mouth twitched, too. Then she leaned forward, barely an inch, and said, "You use the word *believe*. Do you think that critics of your work have a point when they say your theories have no weight because you haven't been willing to make your research public?"

Another smile, wider this time. "You're fast. We're not even four questions in."

Selena laughed — *we're all friends here* — then let the laughter settle before she continued.

"Most people never discover who they were meant to be."

"Why is that?"

"You've heard the story about the man who loses his

keys but only looks for them under the streetlight, because that's where it's easiest to look?"

"Are you saying we're all looking in the wrong place?"

"It isn't your fault. You're trying so hard to mold yourself into an impossible image that someone else gave you. One that has nothing to do with you, and never will. We have to be brave enough to cast that false image aside and peek into the darkest part of ourselves. Believe that we have the grit to face the demons we fear might be lurking down there."

Selena leaned back in her seat, satisfied.

But Isla Porter wouldn't be. She gave Selena another smile, this one patient and ever so slightly patronizing. "You didn't answer the question."

She'd swallowed the hook that Selena had baited. Exactly like her agent Sam had coached her to do. The two of them spent weeks in practice interviews, honing sideways answers to every hard question Isla might ask.

Charm the masses and sell your books. The charts sell your show.

And if Selena's new show took off, she could do whatever she wanted, both with her career and her life.

The pilot was in post-production, and even without seeing a final edit, everyone from producers to executives agreed that the show was going to be huge. Selena had been successful as a clinical psychologist with a full roster of patients, then even more so as a first-time author, where she'd explored some original ideas about the nature of murder and the type of mind capable of ice-cold execution. But her fourth book, *How to Murder the Killer Inside You*, was the worldwide phenomenon that made Selena a pseudo-celebrity. Less than an hour or so after *Killer* cracked the NY Times Top 100, she'd been on the phone with Sam, discussing the offers pouring in. CBS won the bidding war on their pitch for a pop psychology show, *The*

Heartbeat of Murder, two days before the book hit number one.

Selena was standing on the bow of her life's ship, eyes fixed on a well-earned horizon. Even Isla Porter couldn't hope to throw her.

Adam couldn't have been prouder.

"It's key to start with the common denominators. The serial killer cycle has six distinct phases: Aura, Trolling, Wooing, Capture, Murder Totem, and Depression. In the Aura Phase, the lines of reality blur for the killer. This leads to his search for a victim. Wooing follows, the killer inviting his victim to come closer. Then Capture, where the victim is ensnared. The Murder Phase is, obviously, where the killer achieves his emotional climax. The Totem phase precedes Depression. As the thrill of the kill dissipates, the murderer will claim a souvenir, to remind himself of the moment when his fantasy felt most real. Then Depression either leads to the killer killing themselves, or it starts the cycle over."

Selena looked great. Maybe better than ever. Attention made her glow, and her glimmer aroused him. Adam glanced away from the Selena onscreen to the one sitting beside him on their bedroom couch.

Against the room's starkness — white walls, white furniture, white carpet — her dark pink lips were irresistible. Dirty blonde hair teased the tops of her naked shoulders, her snowy silk robe having slid further down her arms to reveal soft, salon-bronzed skin. The room's only rival for his attention was the oil painting over the bed — a blood-red rose, fully bloomed with too many petals to count.

Selena's smile wasn't as wide in person, but Adam found it even more arresting. On the television, sitting across from Isla, Selena wore a smart blouse, professional but scooped low in front. It was her natural style and Sam encouraged her to play it up, that people would love it.

They did, and Adam could certainly appreciate what they saw. He loved it, too. But he always preferred the version of Selena that was sitting next to him now. Simple and understated, putting on a show for no one. Her smile could still melt him, but there was something so beautifully honest in her right now that wasn't present in high-definition.

She said nothing, her eyes glued to the screen. Isla had finally arrived at the question that Selena had been waiting for her to ask.

"Will we ever learn the identity of your Patient X?"

Selena's laugh was born in Texas and could fill the state. It echoed through their room.

"There is no *Patient X*. Yes, I've based much of the last book on an individual, but that doesn't mean that this person is unique. There are others like him. And even if my patient was comfortable with divulging his identity, my responsibility here is more than the usual doctor-patient privilege. I won't endanger his progress for the sake of the public's curiosity."

"What about the public's safety?"

"I understand the desire to know more, so that we may stop future atrocities before they happen, but I strongly feel that the greater danger lies in our throttling the truth."

"Really, Ms. Nash, don't you think that—"

Selena muted the TV.

Adam said, "That's the part that I wanted to hear."

"You already know what I'm going to say."

He did. But— "I needed to hear it."

"You can just watch it later."

"I wanted us to watch it together."

Selena looked from the TV to Adam, then back to the

screen with a thin-lipped smile she would have never dared to flash on a national broadcast.

But the interview was over. The camera was panning across a long line of crazed fans waiting for Bookmarks the Spot to open, then to footage of a recent signing.

"Sorry. I'll rewind."

"It's fine," Adam said. "I'll just see it later. Do you wanna watch something else?"

"You know how much work I have to do."

"I'm not asking you to watch *The Godfather*."

Another smile, but this one looked like she meant it. She aimed the remote and turned on *The Thick Red Line*, a grisly true crime documentary they'd seen a few times before. It explored the case of Lily Templeton, a twenty-three-year-old barista who disappeared in 2009 without a trace, then turned up two years later in the bloodiest scene that anyone in the small South Dakota county that found her had ever seen. Lily's father is all over the documentary, and a less-than-reliable-narrator. The film actually showed some of the crime photos. It was the bloodiest real-life setting that Adam had ever seen, at least on TV.

The documentary had started in the middle of the worst of the crime scene, probably from where Adam stopped the last time. He didn't remember.

Selena nodded at the screen. "There's no way he did it. They just want us to think he did, because the producers know that makes good TV, and he's obviously an eccentric."

Now it was Adam's turn to smile. He'd heard her theories, not just on this true crime documentary, but on every one they'd watched together in nearly twenty years of marriage. But her passionate explanations were always an aphrodisiac.

"So who do you think did it?" Adam asked, even

though he knew. Goosebumps of anticipation made every hair on his body rise up. He loved their games, especially this one.

"It was the guy who delivered milk to the Hill of Beans. They were flirty with each other, and when she stopped flirting back, the relationship changed. He's charming and fun and far from the top of the suspect list, even though he shouldn't be."

"But he's married," Adam prodded, so that Selena would get to the next part.

She shot him a coy sideways look. "And I think his wife helped."

"Why? Why would she help him do something like that?"

Like she always did, Selena fixed her husband with a knowing stare.

But then she said nothing.

He wasn't quite sure if he was excited by Selena taking the game in a new direction, or unsettled that his wife wasn't playing.

Did that mean she was mad at him, or perhaps tired of the game?

Adam met her eyes, then returned his to the screen, settling into the silence between them to study the crime scene.

It was brutal enough to be beautiful, and so far beyond him.

That she could dip in and out of the mind of the monster who created such carnage — maybe even go deep enough to catch them, or save them — amazed him.

Then she ruined the moment.

"I wonder how many episodes of *Heartbeat* we'll have to shoot before I can dig into the Templeton case. They'll probably want to wait for sweeps. Still, can you—"

"Yes, I can imagine." They'd talked enough about Selena's new show and the career possibilities it would open up to last Adam for the rest of the year, if not the decade. She used to talk about *him* with that same enthusiasm. Not anymore. "You mind if we watch something else?"

The request was barely out of his mouth as Selena stood, clicked the TV off, set the remote on her nightstand, and walked toward their bathroom. At the threshold, she turned back and said, "You don't have to do that."

"I'm not doing anything."

"You're getting pissy every time I talk about the show."

"Occasionally I want to enjoy our time together without you thinking about how it fits into your version of world domination."

She laughed and came back over. Picked his hands up and squeezed them in hers.

"I'm sorry and I love you." A kiss on the cheek. "No one is more important. But please, it isn't fair to forget why all of this started. It wasn't my idea."

One more kiss, then Selena returned to the bathroom.

Adam stood there thinking, the same seed of a thought he'd been keeping buried for a while, finally cracking its shell and reaching through the soil for light.

No, it wasn't her idea. But she certainly didn't need to remind him yet again. Things were only going to get worse.

Once the show was live, there'd be more interviews. More appearances. More book signings.

Less time for him.

He never thought he'd see the day when she'd be bored with him. When she'd forget how much of her success was due to *him*.

He wondered what she'd think if he told her about the woman with the blood-red lipstick.

Chapter Two

Levi passed the ball to Pussabo, but the asshole was using all four of his eyes to stare into space instead of waiting for the pass.

"Look alive, Pussy!"

"Sorry," Pussabo said.

He ran after the ball and started awkwardly dribbling on his way back to the basket. But even right underneath it, without anyone to block him, Pussabo missed.

"Wow …" Elliot nodded in adoration, as if he genuinely meant it. "If you were trying to float like a butterfly or sting like a bee or whatever, you totally nailed it."

"Fuck you, Elliot," Pussabo said.

Levi ran after the ball, grabbed it, and started dribbling toward the basket.

Swish.

The game wasn't fun with only three people.

Five was perfect. Two-on-two with a ref. Levi and Dane were perfectly matched. Each claimed one of the feebs — Pussabo, who couldn't sink a basket if he had a century to aim, and Elliot, who preferred standing around with hands in his pockets and mouth flapping — then Levi's brother Corban reffed the foursome.

But Corban had been in a mood for a month or so, and Dane was apparently buried in homework.

"Float like a butterfly?" Levi looked at Elliot. "That's boxing, not basketball. Idiot."

Elliot shrugged. "I figured since Pussy is already dickless, I should keep all sports with balls out of my insults."

"How about I keep my balls out of your mother?" Pussabo asked.

"Gross, dude." Elliot scrunched his nose. "You put *your balls* up in my mother? I mean, good for you, getting those little Armenian raisins up in there and everything. I'm not really sure what that does for you, though. *Your* mom likes it from behind, but she doesn't have a thing for my balls, and they're too big to get all up there even if she did."

Levi laughed.

"Fuck you, Elliot!" Pussabo repeated. Then he added, "And I'm not Armenian!"

Behind Pussabo, Dane nodded at Levi as he walked up the drive.

"What took you so long?" Levi asked.

"The usual. But worse, because physics. What did I miss? Did Pussabo make a basket?" Dane turned around and looked at Pussabo, holding the ball. "Yo, Pussy, you know I love you."

"I made four."

"Out of like four hundred," Elliot added.

"Like twenty, asshole."

"Whatever, mystery meat."

"Fuck you, Elliot." Pussabo aimed and the ball and—
Swish.

"Congratulations." Dane turned back to Levi. "Mr.

Spencer assigned us a packet the size of your ego, and my dad said I couldn't come over until it was finished, even though it was like five nights' worth of work. But I was all *Yes, sir! Anything you say, sir!*"

Levi stood at attention and made the sign: *Heil Hitler!*

"Totally. But whatever. I mean, he's a dick about it, but he means well. And if he gets his way, then I get mine, too. Stanford is still close enough for us to hang out whenever, but far enough that my dad doesn't have to know when I'm here."

"Living the dream." Levi walked back to the game with Dane right beside him.

Elliot said, "I'm not sure if I want the guy who thinks he's God's gift, or the guy who can't bother to show up before it's time to go home. One of you can choose. Just don't ask Pussabo."

"I don't care who I play with," Pussabo said. "They'll be lucky. I'm totally feeling my game right now."

Elliot held out his hands for the ball. Pussabo threw it to him instead of taking another shot. Elliot hurled it at the basket without aim or intention.

Then he said, "Hey Dane, do you think that you're still going to be nerdy when you're in college, or will you finally be cool and learn to chill the fuck out? It'll make your dick bigger. And then chicks will want to get on it."

"Maybe chicks will want to get on it because I'm driving them to my mansion, and they want to give me head along the way, seeing as how they're so grateful for all the stuff I just bought them."

"Dude, you don't need Stanford for that," Elliot said.

"Yup," Levi agreed.

Pussabo shot and scored. "It doesn't hurt. And besides, Dane has a reason for wanting to go. You know he's not doing it just because."

Levi looked at Elliot, hoping he wouldn't go there, with something like, *Yeah, because his mommy went there.*

But instead he said, "Let's play!"

They did, the four of them easily falling into a game that was both fun and familiar.

Not just the rhythm of the ball in play, their words were dribbled and shot as well, rebounded and bounced all around. Insults and banter, born of boys being boys rather than animus.

Levi was the leader on the court, just like he was everywhere else.

Elliot had the most punchlines, but Levi's were usually sharper.

Pussabo was an optimist, but Levi lived on the sunny side anyway, since circumstances always seemed to smile his way.

Dane was smart and good-looking. People agreed that he was an excellent listener.

And Corban … well, Corban was a pain in the ass.

Swish.

"Nice shot," Elliot said to Levi as he jogged toward the ball. "Think Corban is going to be pouting about whatever the hell he's been all pissy about for much longer?"

"I dunno," Levi said, caring more about guarding Pussabo than anything Corban might or might not be doing.

"I'm just saying that maybe that's for the best," Elliot said. "He's a shitty ref, because he feels sorry for Pussabo all the time. Calls fouls when the problem is really just Pussy sucking. But since you assholes always split us up, that's a good thing for my game."

"You know what would be good for my game?" Dane said. "If you—"

A siren screamed in the distance.

Then another, and another, and another.

It sounded like a freight train getting torn from its track.

Dane stopped dribbling. "What the hell?"

"Maybe someone found Pussabo's giant porn stash, and since no one had seen that much eighties bush since the eighties, and maybe not even then, someone figured that there was a pervert among us and so they called the police. Then the police got there and saw all the semen. They called for backup—"

"Okay, Elliot," Dane tried.

"No, he's right," Levi said. "Pussabo loves eighties bush."

"I do not like eighties bush. I told you guys, I like Miley Siren."

Elliot made a face. "Gross. Miley Siren has been used like a car."

"All pornstars are used like cars!"

"Yeah," Elliot argued, "but Miley Siren has been used in every state."

"Yo!" A voice from the porch.

Levi looked over along with everyone else.

"You guys hear the sirens?" Corban asked.

Dane said, "You mean the ones that were just screaming? Yeah, we heard those."

Then Elliot: "Did anyone just see an echo?"

Levi said, "Did anyone just *hear* one? That joke probably wants us to get the hell off its lawn."

"Fuck you." Elliot punched him on the shoulder.

Levi grinned. Couldn't help pushing it despite the warning. "The rule of comedy is that jokes get *less* funny each time you tell them."

"*Guys,*" Corban said, stepping down onto the porch.

Levi turned to his twin. "What?"

But Corban didn't need to answer, because all of them had the Almond Alert installed on their phones, and the symphony of ringing and buzzing and the beats of some Drake bullshit from Pussabo's phone all screamed in unison.

That something was very wrong.

Chapter Three

Corban pedaled faster.

To hell with Levi and his friends.

They used to be my friends, too.

Until things finally blew up. If Levi had given a shit, then maybe everything wouldn't be so upside down now.

At least he had Kari.

She was on her way to Costa Bella right now, and Corban was hoping to beat her there. Her dad, Ollie — nice guy, but weird — got a lot of work on those tract homes.

Corban rounded another corner and eased off on his pedaling. The wind could do most of the work as he coasted downhill, eyeing the sprawling properties on either side.

His community, The Village, was at the top of the hills, so riding down was always a blast, and coming back up, a bitch and a half.

Corban slowed when he got to the Costa Bella bridge, where the gate would have been if crime was a problem in Almond Park, then followed the billowing column of black smoke down three curvy roads to the end of a cul-de-sac lined with McMansions, to where Kari was already waiting with the crowd.

The flames were out and a trio of fire engines idled. Corban could smell the sweat and the fear. Like barbecue and burning cake.

"What happened?"

Kari turned to him and his heart gave a hiccup in surprise. Her eyes were wide and wet, makeup smeared beneath them. Corban still wasn't used to these feelings. He hadn't been able to stop thinking about Kari for a couple of weeks now. The emotion ballooned in his chest and filled him up until he was ready to pop. He was all nerves at least half the time. Looking at her quiet tears, he wanted to reach out and wipe them away.

Or pull her toward him.

But Kari wiped them herself. Then she said, "Other than *fire*, I have no idea."

Corban nodded at the house. A large wreath nearly swallowed the top half of a door that was barely attached to a house. Everything around the door had become a charred husk. Unbelievable, considering the house had been so new, the paint probably only half-dry.

"It's one of the finished ones, huh?"

Kari nodded, then turned back to the house, staring.

Corban wondered if he should say something. Anything. Kari liked to think, and ever since he'd been spending more time with her than his brother, Corban had learned to listen. When she got going, she really got going. But sometimes she needed a prompt. Appreciated it, even. Death was sort of a thing for her, so surely she'd want to talk.

Or maybe he should grab her hand …

Corban stared at the house, blinking into the sooty air. Waiting.

"Good stuff is supposed to come from tragedy, right?" she finally asked.

Corban nodded.

"What good can possibly come of this? These houses are all brand new. That was someone's *dream*, Corban. Now it's gone. Just like that. Doesn't that make everything feel temporary to you?"

"Yeah. Totally."

"I bet that family wasn't all that different from mine. They moved to Almond Park because they could finally afford the house they wanted. And now their dream is dead!"

"Maybe their insurance is amazing, and now they'll get to live in a place that's even swankier."

Kari turned back to the house.

Corban wished she would say something.

He needed to hear her voice. Something about it loosened the constant squeeze of life's grip as it tried to force him through a round hole that his edges kept catching on. High school's typical hierarchy should have made their friendship impossible.

But when just-moved-to-Almond-Park Kari had shown up friendless on orientation day, she'd spent the morning giving Corban an earache, slowly drawing him out of his shell. For the past three years he'd thought of her as the extrovert to his introvert. Now he thought of her as the yin to his yang. Or at least that's what he wanted her to be.

"Think we'll see your dad?"

Kari shrugged.

Corban hoped so. She always lit up around her father. And right now she seemed as dead as the ashes of the burnt-out house.

Ollie was an odd guy. He had an intense stare, even though all of his words sounded like they were smiling. He wore his hair swept back with a part that would have looked at home on a Ken doll. He did and said the most random things (*I was born as a baby; sometimes I feel like sleeping in my sleep; my hair hurts*). But Corban couldn't help but like the guy.

So the rumors pissed him off. They weren't a *weird family.* They were close. They laughed a lot. They shared. Kari ate dinner with her parents almost every night. The Nashes hadn't done that since Levi and Corban were in middle school. Family dinners had dwindled to maybe twice a week.

It was dumb, but Corban missed them.

Ollie the oddball was married to the sweetest woman Corban had ever met. The kind of person who'd tend to a bird with a broken wing and worry about it for months after releasing it back into the wild.

If the school wanted a fucked up family to talk shit about, they could have started with his.

The crowd stirred, restless for news. Again he wanted to take Kari's hand. Still, he didn't.

Instead, he said, "My dad's house burned down when he was a kid. The house had faulty wiring. He said Grandpa should have noticed because some of the lights would dim when they switched from one appliance to another. Or for one thing to work they had to unplug something else. Fuses were always blowing. But they were all used to it."

"Were they home when it happened?"

"At the movies. But they lost everything. And it's not like now. I mean, you would still lose all of your shit, but pictures and stuff? That's all in the cloud."

"It would still feel like losing a limb, I bet. My stomach

hurts when I empty the trash on my computer; I'm not sure I could take losing everything I owned."

The coroner's van rounded the drive, coming to a slow stop in front of the charred shell before the murmuring crowd.

"Fuck." It hadn't even occurred to Corban that someone might've died in the fire.

Kari's eyes filled with tears again. If he offered to take her home, would she be grateful? Or did she want to be here, hard as it was?

The murmurs grew louder as the coroner got out of his van and slammed the door.

"Can you hear what they're saying?" Corban asked.

Kari shook her head.

"Want me to ask?"

"No. That's morbid."

"So … should we go?"

"No."

Soon the rumors were no longer whispers, and worse than Corban had imagined.

This family hadn't gone out to a movie.

They'd all been inside, watching one.

"Oh my god, Corban." Kari collapsed into his arms.

She had more to say, but tears were all that came out. Every word fell into a sob, soaking the front of his shirt as she buried her crying face into his chest.

And Corban couldn't stop himself from getting hard.

What's wrong with me?

Chapter Four

"Pass me the knife?" Selena nodded at the blade in Dane's hand and smiled at him.

"Sure thing." Dane slid it across the granite countertop, handle toward her. *Good boy* ...

She normally cooked on the other side of the kitchen, but Dane was sitting at the bar, and the TV was on in the living room behind him. The Costa Bella fire was awful. Levi and the rest of his friends had lost interest once they learned what the sirens meant and had retreated into the game room. Fine. She didn't mind Dane's company, and he was clearly struck by the tragedy. Why else would he have stayed downstairs to talk about it with her?

He was a junior like her sons, but had just turned eighteen, thanks to a repeated year back when his mother passed away. She wouldn't call him chatty, though he did like to talk. His words were measured, thoughtful. Selena had almost laughed to herself a few days ago when she caught herself thinking of them as *graceful*. It was such a pleasure to see him changing from an awkward teenage boy into an intelligent young man.

But today he was quiet. More than pensive, almost lost. Until he finally spoke.

"Do you think that death is just a door to something else?"

A good question. Selena smiled again. "What do you think, Dane?"

This time, he smiled back. Even if they hadn't been playing it long, this was still a game. Dane wasn't her patient, but it was fun to pretend that he was, with this marble counter between them.

"You first."

"Okay," Selena said. "I do have my doubts about an afterlife, but that doesn't mean that death isn't a door to *something else.*"

"Like?"

"I don't know. Something."

"But not heaven?"

She paused, then, "Definitely not heaven."

Dane nodded. Seemed to consider. "Why not?"

"Just seems to me that if there was really a heaven, why would we spend a lifetime trying to avoid it? I think that heaven gives people a reason to believe that there's something better waiting, so they don't have to do the hard work of reaching for it down here. I'd rather make my heaven on Earth." A beat, then, "You?"

"What if death is a chance to leave your body and see all of your life from a distance, to know whether you lived a true life, or one that was just what everyone expected of you? Then maybe if you did live righteously, not necessarily by helping others but by being true to yourself, you get another chance to come back and do it again."

Is that what you hope for your mother?

The next logical question, if Dane were a patient, but

it felt cruel to keep pushing when he was so clearly seeking comfort.

"So," she said instead, "you think reincarnation might be merit-based, and that achievement might be calculated around how honestly you lived your life?"

Dane's somber expression seemed to split in the middle. Then he grinned. "That sounds so professorial, but yeah, I suppose that's about right."

"And how long have you been thinking about this particular theory?"

Dane checked the time on his phone and grinned wider. "About a minute."

"Well that's—" *Holy shit.*

Dane turned around to see what she was staring at.

The anchors shifted from solemn to suppressed excitement — still respectfully sober, but there was a light in Colleen Little's eyes. Same for her co-anchor Martin Denison. News was breaking, and they were first to tell the world.

Or at least Almond Park.

"What is it?" Dane asked.

But Selena didn't answer. She kept looking at the screen, watching an Almond Park police officer pulling out a bright red scarf from the mailbox in front of the home's burned out husk, looking agitated as the cameraman caught him.

Martin said, "The police have confirmed that a woman's red scarf is the lone item inside the Andersons' family mailbox. But they are thus far unsure of what this might mean."

"Or they're unwilling to say," Colleen added.

"Or they're unwilling to say," Martin repeated, giving her a sage-like nod.

The talking heads kept talking, arguing about what the

scarf might mean. Selena had a suspicion, but it was nowhere near strong enough to voice. Not yet, and certainly not in front of Dane.

But he must have caught her expression. A twitch of her mouth, or maybe a glint in her eyes.

"What is it?"

"What do you mean?" Selena asked, as if she didn't already know.

Dane looked at her without speaking or blinking. His silence felt like a dare.

He finally said, "What are you thinking?"

"What makes you think that I'm thinking anything?"

And when did you start paying such close attention to me? How embarrassing to realize that Dane's observation felt both uncomfortable and inappropriately thrilling.

"Because you stopped talking like there had been a second fire, as soon as you saw that scarf on TV. You have to be thinking something. This is what you do, right? Do you think that someone might have set that fire on purpose to … you know, kill that family?"

Now Dane seemed worried, poor kid. She laughed, knowing he wasn't going to buy it, but trying anyway. "I wasn't thinking anything."

"Please," he said. "You don't have to tiptoe around me."

But Selena felt like she kinda sorta did. Surely this was the last thing the poor kid needed. Right now of all times, with an entire family dead.

At least that little boy won't grow up without a mother, because he's dead too.

It was an awful thought, and Selena swallowed it immediately. But surely the image had made its mark on her face.

She wondered if Dane caught it.

Of course he had. And the look in his eyes was there to prove it.

"A red scarf in the mailbox is … specific," Selena finally admitted.

"What do you mean?"

"Why would it be in there? I don't know one woman who would put one of their scarves — and that looked like a nice one — into a mailbox. To me, it's an obvious signal. Not necessarily a talisman, but at the very least a little bit of piss to mark his territory."

"His?"

"Yeah," Selena said without hesitation. "His."

"What if the dad was cheating on the mom? He kept telling his mistress that he was going to leave his wife. But of course he didn't, and was never going to. So, hell hath no fury, she burns the house to the ground."

"A female isn't likely to murder an entire family just to get revenge on the man. Don't get me wrong, woman are capable of evil, but that doesn't fit the MO."

"Maybe she thought he was alone. Or he was supposed to be. Maybe one of his lies was about a very particular schedule. Maybe Thursday was swim practice, and the kids never missed it. The wife took them, because that was her job."

He waited for her answer, expectant like a child.

Dane had always been unusually open for his age, at least with her, but now he spoke like a grown man.

"Even if his mistress burned down the house, a woman wouldn't have left that scarf. I just don't see it."

He shrugged. "You know best."

Selena wondered if she did.

The kid clearly needed an outlet. His father wasn't much of a listener from what she understood, and Dane liked to talk. The human need for expression ran deep, and too many teenagers vented in the wrong ways. He had a terrific head on his shoulders, so Selena wanted to encourage the conversation, even though it was raw. Besides, there was something missing there, something to fix. And that was the cream in her coffee.

Dane was in many ways a blend of her sons. He had Corban's depth and Levi's strength, but she connected with him differently than either of them. Different from anyone, really.

And the way he looked at her, so adoring, it wasn't like Selena could pretend she wasn't basking in its glow. It had always seemed so motherly. But now she wondered if it was. Nothing had changed except everything. She could no longer see him as a teenager — filled out in the shoulders, with perfect posture and a slightly squared jaw.

Selena looked into his eyes and said, "What are you thinking?"

She expected him to shrug again, maybe hesitate, but there was barely a pause. "About the difference between life and death."

Adam entered the living room and looked at the TV, his eyes going wide at the sight. As he turned toward the kitchen and saw Selena and Dane at the counter, his nose twitched, and so did his bottom lip at the corner.

"What about the difference?" Selena asked.

Dane's thick eyebrows bunched together. This time he took a moment.

"Both are beautiful. In their way."

Adam watched them intently, but he didn't interrupt.

"What do you mean?" Selena probed. "How is death beautiful?"

"Did you ever hear about the time Life and Death sat down to have a talk?"

Selena honestly wasn't sure if she had. "Tell me."

24

Adam was closer, trying not to be obvious, but his pissy face had already betrayed him. Couldn't he see that this wasn't about him right now? Dane was a motherless child, regardless of his age, and she was at the edge of helping him.

Adam could live without her coddling right now.

"Life asked Death why people loved Life so much, while everyone always hated him. Death said, *Because you are a beautiful lie and I am a painful truth.*" He paused, looked away before looking back, then continued. "But I don't think that's true. We both know that Life is a painful truth, no different from Death."

"Yes," Selena said. "I suppose it is."

Chapter Five

Levi assumed the position, rolled his shoulder, and let the baseball fly.

It clinked against the leaden milk bottle, but didn't manage to tip it, or the two underneath it.

Elliot said, "You, my friend, suck at Spill the Milk."

Levi retorted, "You, my friend, suck at existing."

"I don't give a shit if you want to waste all your money on stupid games." Elliot gestured down the row, from the dunk toss to the ring toss, with a rigged game of bingo in the middle. "But do we really have to waste all of our time?"

"One more, then I swear we're done."

Levi handed the carnie some cash, trading it for another handful of balls, a half-grin, and a lukewarm, "Good luck."

The annual Almond Festival was the town's biggest event. It lasted just two days, but everyone came out. Levi had loved it from the beginning: greasy corn dogs, sticky caramel popcorn, and throwing it all up after one too many rides on The Colossus. He wasn't seven anymore, but somehow the cheesy festival still carried a thread of excitement he couldn't explain.

Maybe it was the first fun he and Corban had experienced since Mom closed her practice to move here.

But right now they weren't riding The Colossus, or eating any funnel cake. Because Levi was determined to knock those milk bottles off of their goddamned pedestal. Elliot, Dane, and Pussabo all muttered impatiently, but they waited for him anyway. Corban and Kari stood off to the side, practically pouting. Levi had no idea why they were even there.

He threw another ball, hard enough to really feel it in his shoulder.

Again the ball *clinked* off of the bottle.

"You know this is rigged, right?" Dane said, as though he hadn't muttered it a dozen times already.

"Doesn't mean I can't do it anyway." Levi hurled the ball, missing the bottles entirely.

"Aren't you supposed to get better the longer you play?" Dane asked.

Corban laughed.

Fuck you, Corban.

"It's a good thing they didn't cancel the festival," Elliot said. "I would have hated to miss the beanbag toss and the lollipop tree. I totally forgot we were ten."

Pussabo took Levi's side. "Maybe he was feeling nostalgic."

"They were never going to cancel the festival," Dane said.

Corban disagreed. "Sure they would have."

Kari, nodding beside him, their hands too close said, "People are scared."

"Because there was a fire?" Dane asked.

"Because someone might have *set it,*" Kari said.

"The mom probably left a candle burning, or something." Dane looked over at Kari, and his tone was more cutting than it needed to be. "Or maybe Kari's dad did the electrical work."

"Fuck you, Dane." Then Kari turned to Corban. "We can go whenever you want to."

"Even if someone *did* set the fire," Levi said, "it's not like there's a dude running around loose with a flamethrower. Maybe the dad owed the mob money or something."

"Right." Elliot laughed. "Everyone knows how far Cosa Nostra is willing to take it in the dark alleys and McMansions of Almond Park."

Pussabo said, "It's not just about being scared. Some people think it's in bad taste to have a celebratory event in light of a tragedy."

"Some people like your parents? I've told you a hundred times, man." Elliot shook his head. "Their judgement lost all credibility the day they named you Pussabo. And they'll never get it back. Your name is a permanent stain."

"People are having fun." Levi gestured around the festival. "This gives them a way to forget, and the place to do it."

Again, his brother had to be an asshole: "Maybe we shouldn't be forgetting so fast."

"What should we do then, Corban?"

"Maybe delay it. Wait until we know more. Who knows what that detective guy is going to find out? The scarf shows it wasn't just an accident. It's spring in Almond Park. Who wears scarves?"

"Or puts them in their mailbox?" Kari added.

"Exactly," Corban finished.

"The show must go on," Levi said.

Corban bit his bottom lip, like he did when he was about to be a baby. "People *just* died. An entire family."

"Families die every day."

"Especially if you count what's happening on the inside," Elliot said.

Dane laughed. Then Pussabo joined him, even though he tried not to.

"It's not funny," Corban snarled.

"See, that's where you're wrong, Corban. That's the recipe for solid comedy. Tragedy plus time equals hilarity." Levi winked at his brother. "And that's why you're not funny."

"They died *yesterday*. And I don't think that being a dick is funny."

"Name a famous comedian who isn't a dick."

"Levi isn't wrong," Elliot said.

Corban shook his head and clenched his fists, stepping away from Kari, toward Levi. "How can you make judgments about people you don't even know?"

"Dad knows them."

"That doesn't mean you do."

"I will someday, because I'll be up on the stage with them. If you ever meet a famous comedian, it'll be thanks to a favor from someone in your family, and then that comedian will feel sorry for whichever one of us let you in the room, because they'll know we had to live our lives with someone who was so painfully far away from ever being funny."

As soon as the rant wound down, Levi wished he hadn't said it. He'd gone too far and he knew it.

Everyone else did, too. Because the group was now silent. As if the crowd of six was too timid to speak, everyone waiting for what might happen next.

Corban held Levi's stare. He tried not to blink but then finally did and turned to Kari. "You wanna go to the Wembley House?"

She nodded. "Better than here."

"Hey you guys, do you remember when Corban and Kari used to be fun?" Levi smirked at his own barb, to bury his irritation.

Because no, he didn't like Kari leaving with Corban at all.

"Whatever, Levi." Corban turned around and started walking away, with Kari a stride behind him.

A hundred insults crowded onto Levi's tongue, but he swallowed them all and let Corban leave with Kari. He turned back to his friends. Everyone looked serious, even Elliot.

He looked at Levi. "That sucks, man. What the hell happened with you two?"

Dane spoke before Levi could answer.

"He doesn't want to talk about it."

Levi could speak for himself, but Dane was right. And bitching about Corban wouldn't be wise, because eventually they would make up, then everything would go back to normal. He shouldn't say stupid shit that he would have a hard time taking back later.

Although maybe he already had.

His fuse had been so short lately. The thing he was best at — finding the sunny side of just about anything, the same skill that made his father the author of so many smiles — seemed to be getting harder. As Levi inched closer to manhood, he didn't like who he was slowly becoming. Dad would be so disappointed.

"I was asking Levi," Elliot said.

"Dane's right." Levi gestured at The Colossus. "You guys ready to split?"

Elliot turned to the carnie. "Can you just take all of our money right now? That would be a lot more efficient."

Chapter Six

"When exactly did your brother become such an asshole?" Kari asked, the second they were out of earshot.

Corban didn't answer. Instead he said, "Thanks for coming to look at the house with me. Levi thinks it's stupid. He won't go with me even when we're getting along."

"Of course." Kari didn't press him about Levi, and Corban was grateful for it. Instead she nodded toward the old home, looming at the end of a long road. "The house is so pretty."

"It's from 1908," Corban told her, as though Kari was the only one in the city who didn't know, or he hadn't already told her a hundred times. "I wouldn't call it pretty so much as *ornate*. Late Queen Anne Victorian. It's the oldest building around."

"Is that why you want to be an architect? To make things that last?"

"I guess," Corban said. "Even if we managed to delay the inevitable war with our robot overlords, the longest we're going to live is like a hundred years or so. But a building can last a lot longer than that."

"And it can look really tacky in ten years. Like if you build a strip mall."

"People will live and work inside my buildings. And if I do a good job, maybe I can even make their lives a little better."

They stopped in front of the Wembley House. Kari looked from it to Corban. "You don't suppose there's anything new inside this year, do you?"

"Are you saying you don't want to go in?"

"I'm saying that I've seen it before, a few times now. And yeah, old chandeliers are pretty, and wow, that's a really curvy banister, but both of my parents are at the festival. So why not go back to my house? We've never been there alone."

The world stood still for a moment as Corban tried to figure out if Kari was serious.

"You want to go to your place?"

"Why not?" she asked.

Maybe because they never had and even though he wanted to, Corban hadn't been sure they ever would.

Maybe because if he really did get the girl of his dreams totally alone, perhaps even in her bedroom, he wouldn't know what to do.

Maybe because Corban had the wrong idea.

"What would you want to do?"

She took his hand and gave him her usual smile, but in a way that she had never offered it before. "Stuff."

And then they were walking. *Fast.* A single skip faster and they would be at a run. Corban would have galloped, if he thought it wouldn't scare Kari off.

When they got there, she fumbled with her keys in the front door, visibly nervous.

This isn't happening.

She opened the door and the air conditioning kissed

him, cooling his sweating skin, overheated from the hot walk in the sweetest heat.

Kari took his hand, and Corban knew that his life was about to change.

"Kari?" her father called from what sounded like the other side of the house. "Is that you?"

"Shit," she whispered. "Fuck. Sorry."

"What should we do? Should we leave?" There was a terrible clatter, something like a drawer full of flatware falling on gravel, followed by a cascade of barely audible mumbles. "What is that?"

Kari shrugged. "You know my dad."

But Corban wondered if he did. If *anyone* did.

"Should we go?"

It was too late. There was the loud tromping of feet on linoleum, and then Ollie appeared in the living room. He often looked odd or off or disheveled or something. But tonight he looked wild. His usually too-still eyes were dancing. His body seemed to be fighting not to twitch.

"Kari. Corban."

"Hey, Dad."

"You guys aren't at the festival?"

"It was stupid. We decided to come home."

For the first time that night, Corban was glad that he was no longer holding Kari's hand, especially with the way Ollie was eyeing him. "Did you and Corban go to the Wembley House?"

"Yep. Same as last year," Kari said, before Corban could. "But Levi and Company were all being jerks, so we figured we'd come back here and watch TV or something."

"My mom was looking forward to having the house to herself tonight," Corban offered, before Ollie could wonder why they wouldn't be watching TV at the Nash place, seeing as how it had three times as many, and each of them was twice the size. "We can go back to the festival, Mr. Harris. We don't want to be in anyone's way."

"It's Ollie, Corban, for the last time. And it's fine. I'm travailing right now."

"*Travailing?*" Corban repeated.

"He means he's working hard at something," Kari translated. "He's *in his space.*"

"Oh," Corban said. "Cool."

"So, we're going outside to sit on the porch. Okay, Dad?"

Ollie looked at Kari like he didn't really hear her, said, "Sure, sure, sure," then turned around while the *sures* were still coming out of his mouth and ambled out, quickly gathering speed as he left the room.

"Sorry," Kari said, shaking her head.

"That your dad's home?"

"That he exists."

The banging was back. Drawers opening and closing, cabinets slamming, things getting dragged across the floor.

"What *is* that?" Corban asked.

"You think I know, just because I live here?"

Corban laughed. "No, I guess you wouldn't."

He always asked Kari about her father, same as all of her friends. The only difference between Corban and the rest of them was that he didn't talk shit about Ollie behind Kari's back. But he sure heard the whispers, including the ones that came from his brother and their friends.

Levi said that Ollie had the "insane look of a pedophile set loose inside an orphanage."

Dane disagreed, often stating that Kari's father didn't strike him as weird, so much as shifty.

Pussabo thought he might have something wrong with

him, but that he deserved the benefit of the doubt, especially seeing that he was Kari's father.

Elliot said, "People are strange, when you're a stranger. Faces look ugly, when you're alone."

Corban agreed with Pussabo most, but not completely. Corban didn't think that benefit of the doubt was necessary. Everyone was being narrow-minded. Ollie was eccentric. But that didn't make him a liar. It didn't make him dangerous. It made the man interesting.

It was entirely possible that Ollie Harris was playing a game with the world.

Kari's mother Cynthia appeared and asked him if he would like something to drink, like always. But this time when he said sure, and she went to get him some chocolate milk, she poured it into a wine glass.

Cynthia explained as she handed it to Corban. "We're drinking everything out of wine glasses now. Wine, Pepsi, chocolate milk, water. All of it. Ollie's idea."

Kari's mother rolled her eyes to let Corban know she was in on the joke, but there was something cool about that. She understood her husband's sense of humor deeply enough that it had become part of her DNA.

"He's so fucking weird," Kari often said, though she also liked to play along, and probably a lot more than she would ever admit to Corban.

But Corban would take Ollie's weird over his own father's, every time.

It wasn't even the jokes that irked Corban so deeply, it was how pleased with himself he always was. Corban had never known anyone who laughed at their own jokes more, except for maybe Levi, and that was only because he was Dad's Mini-Me.

Levi would probably grow up and cheat on his wife,

too. Then maybe his son would also have to keep it a secret. And—

"What are you thinking?"

But Corban couldn't tell Kari that. "Just wondering what your dad is doing this time."

"Wanna play the guessing game? I'll go first. I think he's looking for the entrance to Narnia. Your turn."

But Corban was having a hard time coming up with a guess.

Because he was wondering what his own father might be doing instead.

Chapter Seven

Selena drew sharp black lines across each of her last three ideas, deep and dark, over and over, as if to punish them for revealing her ineptitude.

She had to get this right. Her career had been steady, but it was about to get explosive. She'd been lucky enough to land Sam Atkins as her agent. The man had been right about everything so far. And despite some rather lofty promises, he had yet to come up short on a single one.

But some of Selena's success so far had been straight-up luck and she knew it. *How to Murder the Killer Inside You* was a bucket of popcorn at best. Her research was based on a single case study, and one she wouldn't publicly divulge. What the book lacked in research, she made up for with personality. How ironic that her first book to get almost universally panned by her peers was also the first to sell more than a million copies.

Selena moved more copies of *Killer Inside You* in any given day than her most well-received book did in a year.

But this next book *had* to be better. A perfect blend of the research and thought that gave her early body of work so much praise, infused with the personality that leveraged her worldview into what promised to be must-see TV.

Selena was grateful for Sam, and that he'd sold the pitch on her single-sentence *what if?*

But she had no idea that he could do that at the time. If she'd realized how much pull he had, she would never have let the brain fart leave her mouth.

What if I wrote a book about how to kill the serial killer inside you?

Selena didn't even get a second sentence. She had one, a whole explanation ready to go. She would have admitted that she only had a single case study, and that the idea was unproven, though it was something she'd been thinking about deeply for a while. It would take time, but it could be a remarkable book if done right.

But Sam said, "Sold!" like a hard stop at the end of a sentence.

And now, half the time, Selena regretted ever uttering that sentence. The rest of the time she looked around at what that book had brought her and felt just enough gratitude to want even more. Full of herself, but still hungry.

She looked down at the page and started to write, flush with an idea.

A trio of soft knocks on her office door announced Adam's entry — he didn't even give her a chance to ask who was there. "Hey. Am I bothering you? I don't want to interrupt."

Am I bothering you?

He had to be kidding.

She was in her office with the door closed. Of course he was bothering her, and of course he wanted to interrupt.

"What is it, Adam?"

"No one's home. We have a couple of hours. I thought maybe we could open a bottle or something."

"No one's home and I have a couple of hours. I need to get something done."

"You've gotten plenty done. You've been in here most of the day."

"I'm trying to map out the next several years of work. That takes a lot of thought."

"Maybe you could think better with this?"

He smiled and produced a bottle of pinot grigio like a magic trick.

"Adam ..." And now she felt bad. "I can't."

He blinked, bit his bottom lip, and took a step back. Then he looked around her office for a moment as if lost, before walking over to her desk and setting the bottle atop it.

He wasn't going to leave.

"Adam, I really have work to do."

"You always have work to do."

"That's because I have a job. Several of them, remember? And all of them require a hundred percent of *me*."

"Exactly."

"Exactly what?"

"This conversation bores you just as much as it does me. You're working too much. Again. Like always—"

"I'm doing it for our family. Just look around—"

"No, Selena. You do it because the spotlight is a nipple and you can't stop sucking on it."

Now he was pissed, his chest heaving, his upper lip curled into a snarl.

That was better than him biting on it.

"You don't have to get pissed. Why don't you just go into *your* office and turn this entire conversation into shit I never said so that some other comedian can pretend to be more clever than they really are?"

"That's a great idea, Selena. Maybe I could write a joke about a mom in the spotlight who's happiest when her family's in the dark?"

"Oh, that's great, Adam. Why are you writing for other comedians when you should be writing for Lifetime?"

Adam grabbed the bottle of wine and pretended like he was going to leave. They both knew he wouldn't. He made it one step before turning back.

"It doesn't always have to be like this."

"You mean interrupting me when I'm trying to finish the work that pays our mortgage? Or do you mean coming in here and pouting because I don't have time to play with you?"

Silence. The kind she hated most. Neither one of them were about to back down now. They were either going to open that bottle, or have this out in her office. Probably both.

"Have you heard the one about the asshole husband who couldn't be a little more patient with his doctor?" Adam smiled, thin but there.

And now she felt guilty.

Why was it always like this?

Why was he the one who couldn't understand the simple things, and yet *she* ended up feeling guilty?

Adam wanted to enjoy all the benefits of her success. But still he interrupted. Still tried to make light of every situation. Still made her feel like she had three children instead of two.

It was the same fight on repeat, and she was finished with it.

She wasn't obsessed with her work; Selena was determined to get things right. Do the best possible job. Reach for every rung above her so that she could *climb, climb, climb,* while carrying her family on her back.

She wasn't choosing career over family, she was using the first to improve the second.

Why should she have to feel guilty?

"I'm sorry," Adam continued. "Take your time. The bottle should breathe anyway. We'll toast when you're done."

She could've taken the victory. But it didn't feel like one. It felt like kicking a puppy who'd already rolled over and shown her its throat.

Selena sighed. "It's fine. My flow is already broken."

Adam smiled again, timid this time, not really sure if what Selena had said was good or bad.

He crossed her office to a small liquor cart in the corner, one of her favorite pieces, bought two days after her thirtieth birthday at an estate sale three doors down from their starter home. Adam opened the bottle and poured them each a glass.

Neither spoke until several sips had been taken. Then, finally, "What is it, Adam?"

"What's what?"

"If you want to talk about something, just tell me. You don't have to interrupt me while I'm working."

"You used to thank me for interrupting your work. Sometimes on top of the desk."

Adam glanced at the uncluttered surface. Did he really think …?

"Things change. People grow up. Neither of us is in our twenties anymore."

"I'm not asking you to fuck me on the desk, Selena. I'm asking you to share a bottle of wine, on a very rare Friday night when our house is empty."

"And I'm asking you to understand when I'm working, and to not bother me before I'm finished. It's easy to tell when I'm working versus when I'm not, because when I'm working the door is always closed. I shouldn't have to lock it, nor should I have to explain that to you. *Yet again.*"

Her words were still measured, and her tone perfectly even. Adam's too. But it wasn't going to stay this way much longer.

"You know what I've been wondering about a lot lately?" No pause, it wasn't like he wanted her answer or was willing to wait for it. Or like she wanted to guess. "I've been wondering why you always seem to have time for the things that are important to you, regardless of how important they might be to the rest of your family."

"What are you trying to say, Adam?"

"Do you really not understand? I'm asking for a little attention from my wife, once or twice a month. That's too hard? You *still* have work to do? Okay, fine. I get it. But you sure do seem to be frivolous with your affections if they aren't directed at me."

"Is this about Levi and Corban? *Again?* Jesus Christ, Adam. You favor Levi over Corban, and I coddle Corban too much. Agreed. Not much we can do about it now, since they're both out of the house in a year. Damage done."

"*Damage done?* I doubt you would say that about a client."

"I have before." Selena narrowed her eyes. Now she was pissed.

Him too. Something horrible flashed across his face. He exhaled through his nose. Gripped the wine bottle by its neck as if it were a weapon. Then he stepped toward her.

"Don't push me, Selena."

She took a step toward him. "Or what?"

43

They faced each other for a moment, their chests heaving, sweat beading both of their brows.

Selena blinked. If he was going to derail her anyway, she might as well get something out of it. She licked her lips and fell three steps back toward the desk, lifting her skirt and spreading her legs as she sat on it, black panties now showing.

"Is this what you want? You wanna fuck me before the boys get home?" She watched his eyes dilate, then closed her legs and gave him an evil little smile. "Or should I turn on *The Thick Red Line* and you can beat off to that?"

Adam was already at the desk, grabbing her by the arm and squeezing.

And then he was turning her around.

Her cheek flattened against the desk as he pushed her forward.

Her fingers bit into the wood.

Selena's panties flew down from her waist to her ankles in a violent swish.

Adam's hand was flat on her back, and then he was inside her.

He grunted and she screamed.

He pulled her hair and she growled back at him to *imagine the blood.*

He moaned and Selena moaned harder, louder and louder until each of them finished.

Then she gathered her panties and gave them to Adam, bunching them into his hands. "Your trophy."

He smiled, and she took that moment to nudge him toward the door.

"You need a shower. And I need to finish what I was doing."

This time, he took the hint. Hallelujah.

Chapter Eight

Adam finished rinsing his hair, then stood under the scalding water for another minute or so.

The heat was both almost too much to take and a salve.

He wasn't even sure why he was so bothered. His agitation usually faded after sex, but here he was still, standing in the shower, trying to figure out why the itch in the back of his head wouldn't go away.

Selena had gone back to work almost immediately, and her office door remained closed.

He'd been hoping for a little post-coital conversation, but she wasn't in the mood. The sex was great, like it usually was, but the aftermath was empty. As alluring as she'd been with Adam inside her, Selena was all business once done.

"Your trophy," she'd said, like a teacher handing out participation awards.

And sure, he got it. Selena had work to do. But really, what couldn't wait until tomorrow? It wasn't like Sam had given her a deadline. She made a big deal about needing thinking time, expecting the world to revolve around the axis of her mind.

He worked to deadlines, and didn't get a choice. If Anna Lies got booked on *The Tonight Show*, he didn't get the luxury of twiddling his pen for days. Those jokes had to be on the page, punched up, and over to Anna's inbox hours after he got the text. No matter the comic, the message was usually the same:

Hey second place. It's a good thing you can write shit, since you sure as hell can't deliver it. I've got some gig where I need to look funnier than I am, and preferably smarter. Can you drop everything you're doing and let me take credit for your work? I'll pay you a shit ton per word, but it's still pennies compared to what I make for existing. The sooner the better. I'd like time to practice. It has to sound natural.

At least his name meant something. If a script wasn't funny, studios might send Adam a pass. But that work wasn't consistent, and living outside of Hollywood kept him out of the game, and away from his dream job. Almond Park was Selena's idea. She's the one who insisted *writers can write anywhere.*

Not every kind of writer.

If Adam lived in Hollywood, he might be Judd Apatow. In Almond Park, he could only be Mr. Selena Nash.

He got out of the shower, drying off as he glanced at the mirror. His eyes were tired and he needed a haircut. Still, he looked good for his age. Despite the seven extra pounds. But maybe his age was the problem.

Adam thought about Dane, and the agitation was back.

He had never really liked Dane much, but the boy had really started to bother Adam in the last few months. He was always a needy little shit, hanging around in the kitchen too long, and spending way too much time at their house. Levi and Corban both liked him a lot. Selena doted on him in her way. So Adam eventually got used to him.

But something about the way Selena treated Dane lately had been different, and Adam just couldn't ignore it.

He wished he'd had the balls to bring it up in their almost-argument back in her office. That eventual blowup was a matter of *when*, not *if*. He could feel it brewing. Or maybe something else just as ugly.

He imagined what would have happened if he had done more than fish, if he had actually said what was on his mind: *Are you thinking about fucking that kid?*

He was probably being paranoid. The boy had lost his mother at a very young age. His father was kind of a dick. It was natural for him to gravitate toward a real family.

Adam put on his boxers and a black tee with bright white lettering:

I'm a writer so that the voices in my head have something productive to do.

Selena thought the T-shirt was funny. She wouldn't laugh, but maybe she'd smile.

Adam grabbed his tablet and digital pencil, then started to write.

Loose bits, as he didn't have a current commission. Not that it mattered, funny was funny, and while he liked to have plenty in the bank, right now the coffers were mostly empty.

Because Adam wasn't feeling especially funny.

He couldn't stop thinking about Selena, and what she might be thinking about him.

She always asked, *What are you writing?* even when she didn't really want to know.

If she didn't think the joke was funny, he would see it all over her face.

And if you're trying to be funny, the last thing you

want to do is *care* what people think of the joke. Because humor is born in the black and the blue, and you mustn't rob it of color. There was a freedom in ghosting the punchlines. If Wayne Hanger said something offensive, he got the glory and the shit. No one wondered if Adam Nash really thought something so awful.

But Selena did. Right now, that kept Adam from writing.

The pencil was moving, but the wrong words had darkened his page.

Dangerous words that needed to be erased.

The pencil kept moving as Adam thought about Dane, wondering if the kid was an issue or if he was growing old and paranoid. What if the problem he was sensing with Selena was really about him? Maybe he was fucking up in some way. Maybe she knew about the girl with the blood-red lipstick before he'd been ready to tell her.

Adam looked down at his work, sickened and aroused.

He couldn't delete the words without reading them first.

She's lying naked, face down in a pool of her own blood. It's beautiful, the way the crimson kisses her body. The pool continues to spread. The blood is fresh enough to leave its taste in the air. I lick my lips and swallow. Then I kiss her flesh, everywhere. My face is covered in her blood.

I turn her around to stare at the front of her body. The woman in blood-red lipstick. My obsession. The perfect eyes in the perfect face on the perfect head and body. Oh, the body. I am inside it, and inside you. I live for those final few moments together, when our pulses will be pounding as one.

Then, like always, Adam deleted the first paragraph and added the second to his archive, protecting the worst of his thoughts.

He'd been following the woman in blood-red lipstick

for a while now, and writing about her for nearly as long. His usual pattern had yet to fail him. But this was the longest it had ever been. Selena usually noticed by now. But she had never been this preoccupied.

Or so … unavailable.

The woman in lipstick was there whenever Adam wanted to see her. Or at least on Tuesdays and Thursdays, though only in the afternoons, and on one weekend day until closing, usually Sunday. Those seven extra pounds, all dairy, and every one of them gained after he'd started going to see her. Selena hadn't noticed that either.

For a moment, while he'd been fucking his wife on her desk, he'd pretended *she* was the woman with the blood-red lipstick.

Adam looked down at his tablet and considered erasing the rest. Maybe deleting them all. What good was his word porn doing him, sitting like liquid crystal evidence? Sure, he changed the passcode regularly. But what if one of the boys guessed it? There were ways to crack a tablet too, and if Selena was suspicious that he was hiding something from her, it wasn't unthinkable that she'd do whatever it took to figure it out. Maybe even get that little shit Dane to help her. The nerdy kid probably knew a dozen apps that would do it.

Adam tried to write something else, working himself into a sweat trying to shove aside the thoughts of her crimson lips, red streaks smeared on her alabaster skin, her naked body dripping with blood.

But still they lingered. And still the words refused to come.

He set his tablet on the nightstand and traded it for the remote.

He turned on Netflix, scrolled to *The Thick Red Line*, and forwarded to his favorite part.

Lily Templeton had a lot in common with the girl in the blood-red lipstick. Every time he watched this documentary, every time he saw Lily covered in blood, Adam imagined *her*.

But neither the girl in lipstick nor Lily Templeton was anything like Selena.

His wife filled him with a different sort of fantasy.

Even after all these years, he was obsessed. That those feelings seemed to be fading filled him with an arctic sadness. And Adam knew only one way to warm it.

Chapter Nine

Levi was leveling up, loving it, and letting everyone know they were losers. "Wow. It's like you're all competing to see who can make me feel better about myself."

"I didn't even know the game would let you do that," Dane said.

Pussabo clutched his controller like it might try and escape. He leaned forward, grimacing, almost grunting. His eyebrows bunched and his nostrils flared.

Elliot pointed. "Pussy looks like he's going to shit!"

"I told you not to call me Pussy!" Then, "Eat it Levi!"

Levi's character exploded into a trillion tiny pixels and Pussabo started laughing.

"Way to go Pussabo!" Elliot clapped, genuinely impressed.

Pussabo said, "How do you like my Pussy Bomb now?"

Elliot turned to Pussabo, puzzled. "I don't think anyone has *ever* liked your Pussy Bomb. And I thought you didn't want anyone to call you that? You literally just said, 'I told you not to call me Pussy!'"

"It's different if I'm saying it myself. Like black people and the N-word."

"Wait," Elliot said, deadly serious. "You're not black?"

"Fuck you! I told you I'm not black."

"But you don't know for sure, right?" Elliot pressed.

Dane said, "Leave him alone, Elliot."

Pussabo wouldn't tell anyone what his name meant, or where his family came from, and the more they asked the more he clammed up.

"Our ancestors moved around a lot," he would say, and then nothing more.

Dane found this a source of bottomless curiosity, as did Levi and Corban to a lesser degree. Elliot saw it as Christmas with unlimited presents.

"Are we done yet?" Levi looked from the screen to his friends.

"What?" Dane said. "You lost, so you don't want to play anymore?

"No. I lost, so the game won't be fun anymore, at least not for the next couple of turns. Pussy's gonna be a dick about his win, and this room isn't big enough for Elliot's bullshit."

Elliot looked around the giant room. From the short row of old-school video game cabinets — *Ms. Pac-Man*, *Elevator Action*, and *Bionic Commando* — to the air hockey and ping-pong tables, to the soda fountain. "Are you kidding?"

"Don't you want to go outside?" Levi asked the room. "We're up here too much and it's making us stupid."

"No. I want to stay here and play. I just won."

"Pussy's right," Elliot said. "He'll probably never get another this chance like this. We shouldn't take that away from him."

Dane said, "I think Elliot is allergic to the outdoors."

"I'm not allergic to going outside, I'm allergic to doing shit that isn't awesome. *HardCorps* is awesome. We go outside and I'll have to hear Pussabo bitch about losing his turn, and watch him miss another hundred shots."

"Good point," Levi said. "You know you we can't stay in the game room during the barbecue, right?"

"We have to go to that?" Elliot asked.

"You're going to be here anyway," Levi said.

"Yeah," Elliot nodded. "Up here in the game room."

"Why are you being an asshole? We're always hanging out in the game room. The barbecue will be fun. We can swim, and there's going to be tons of food, and—"

"There's going to be old people."

Dane looked at Elliot, clearly disgusted. "Don't be such a dick, dude. Levi's parents are probably going to spend a lot of money, you know how it'll go down. Think of it as an experience. You can come up here and play *HardCorp* any day of the week. We already do. Maybe Levi's mom and dad want to show off their son's well-mannered friends."

Elliot nodded at Pussabo while speaking to Levi. "You should definitely uninvite him, then, unless you're hoping to look good in front of the neighbors. Like maybe they'll think you're one of those people who sends fourteen cents a day to Africa."

"I've never even been to Africa," Pussabo protested.

"That you know of," Elliot reminded him.

"Leave him alone, Elliot," Dane said.

The doorbell rang.

But Elliot wasn't going quit. "Maybe that's Homeland Security. They got a tip on Pussabo."

"Shouldn't you get that?" Dane asked. "Your mom is working in her office."

"No. I'm sure it's just Amazon. She and my dad order crap, like, every day."

The doorbell rang again. Twice this time.

"Shit. Okay, yeah, now I gotta get it before she comes out of her office, pissed as a bitch."

Levi ran downstairs, fast as he could. His hand was around the knob a split second before the third ring.

He opened the door to a rumpled man in a pressed suit.

"Yeah?" Levi said.

"Hi. My name is Detective Rodney Sharpe, with the Almond Park Police Department." The man opened his wallet and showed Levi his badge. "I was hoping I might speak with your mother. Is she home?"

"Yeah, but she doesn't like to be disturbed while she's working."

"I understand," he said to Levi like he was an adult who had to be negotiated with, "but can you please do me a big favor, and let her know I'm here? I won't be long, and I think she'll want to help me."

He opened his wallet again, and this time handed Levi a card.

"Sure thing." Levi opened the door all the way after taking it, then gestured the detective inside. "I'll get her."

The moment Levi told his mother that a detective wanted to ask her some questions, she practically leaped from her seat to invite him in for coffee.

While she fussed with the French press and made small talk with Sharpe, Levi made himself a chai latte from the Keurig, then a small snack plate from the fridge, and a larger one for the guys after that to buy himself even more time to listen. If the detective wanted to talk to his mom about the fire, that meant the police were thinking *serial killer*. Here, in Almond Park.

A pointed look from his mother told Levi that his attempt at eavesdropping wasn't going to fly. So he gathered the food and trudged upstairs, as slow as he reasonably could. But his mom and the detective nursed an awkward silence until he was out of earshot. He hurried back to the game room.

"Holy shit, you guys, you're not going to believe what's happening downstairs." Levi looked over to Elliot before he could deliver his punchline. "Shut up, I'm serious."

"What's going on?" Pussabo asked.

"There's a detective downstairs and he asked to talk to my mom."

Elliot couldn't help himself. "About how hot she is?"

"Fucking Elliot," Dane said.

"They must've found another scarf. There's no other reason they'd want to talk to my mom."

"Shit …" No punchline from Elliot this time.

"There can't be a serial killer in Almond Park," Pussabo said.

"Where are they talking?" Dane asked.

"In the kitchen."

"Don't you want to know what they're saying?" Dane looked from Levi to Elliot and Pussabo. "Aren't you curious?"

"I'm curious," Elliot said.

"I'm curious," Pussabo agreed.

"It's not that easy. This is my mom's jam, you guys. Even if the detective is just asking her a few questions over coffee, she's probably going to act like she's on TV. She's going to go on and on about—"

"So don't you think she'll want an audience?" Dane interrupted.

"*Maybe*. But you never know. And if she doesn't want anyone around while she's talking to the detective, which is definitely the feeling I got while I was down there, then she's going to be *pissed*."

"Then I volunteer as tribute," Dane said.

And so he did.

Chapter Ten

This was getting big, fast.

One of the reasons Selena had pushed for their family's move to Almond Park was that it felt so much different living out here than in the city. She lived and breathed true crime, wanted to understand it. *Needed* to understand it. But from a distance.

But now it had followed her home.

At least that's what it looked like.

"There's no chance it was an accident?" Selena pushed the plunger down on the coffee. Decaf, per the detective's request.

"Sure, there's a chance. But it's hard to believe. The entire family was found poisoned. Right into their water supply. And—"

"And there's no accounting for that second scarf."

"Exactly."

Selena tried not to smile, tried to hide the rush of excitement at the idea that she might be the first to take a crack at a new serial killer. "Cream, sugar, agave? Anything?"

"Just black." Sharpe smiled and Selena slid his coffee across the counter.

She hoped her glee wasn't showing on her face — it was so horribly inappropriate — but she couldn't help thinking how happy Sam was going to be. They could push back some of the episodes they'd already shot, as people would be hungry for an expert's opinion on a breaking serial killer case. If the murders got national coverage, which they very well might, she would be *the* expert. Her instincts were crackling right from the start ... from the moment she saw that first scarf.

"So," Selena said with cool professionalism. The police didn't like to work with experts who fostered sensationalism; it made their job so much harder. "You're here because you don't have any leads, but the second scarf is too big a coincidence to ignore."

"Right." The detective blew steam from the lip of his mug, then took a sip. "What do you think?"

Having a potential new case — one she could really sink her teeth into — made Selena feel like someone had just given her fresh batteries. The details didn't fit a normal serial killer profile. The modus operandi for the killings were completely different. There didn't seem to be any connection between the two families. Or the scarves.

This stuff was all so obvious. As she theorized to the detective, she couldn't help secretly imagining the TV potential of the case. Being right in the middle of it as it unfolded. This thing could go in any direction. A movie was the obvious start, but studios had been playing that game since the eighties. A season-long anthology series on Netflix or one of the other streaming companies might be better. Something like *The Thick Red Line*.

Should she hire her own documentary crew now? It would be so much better to get on-the-ground reactions in real time rather than in the aftermath. Surely that had never been done before.

But then again, the world had never really seen a psychologist like Selena Nash.

It almost felt like Fate was on her payroll, doing everything possible to make her a star. The timing was *perfect*.

Sharpe cut her off as she launched into her theory about the six phases of the serial killer's emotional cycle. "But serial killers are usually smart, right?"

"That's a misconception. The good serial killers are the smart ones."

The mug stopped halfway to his mouth. "The *good* serial killers?"

Selena laughed: *Silly me*.

"I mean the ones we remember. The ones we talk about. The ones who get books written, and movies made. There's never going to be a TV show about a guy who randomly murders people and gets caught almost immediately. There's no character to a crime like that, so there's no reason for anyone to care. But the killers who plan and plot and perfect their delinquencies, keeping themselves from discovery for years, if not forever? Those are the impressive ones."

Sharpe listened intently, like she'd just recaptured his interest.

"The average IQ is around one hundred, depending on which test is given. The average serial killer hovers below ninety-five. That sort of killer will probably strangle or stab or shoot their victims. No finesse at all. Next step up are the bomb makers and planners. Most come from unstable homes, obviously. But you always want to look for the kids who wet the bed or started fires. The ones who didn't just kill small animals, but tortured them with no remorse."

Sharpe's expression hadn't shifted; he still seemed interested. So Selena went on with the lecture.

"Setting a fire and poisoning a family are two very different crimes, tied together only by the scarves. This isn't a cheap thrill. Neither one of these crimes is reactionary. Both took planning and execution. So this isn't a person with anger issues. Or at least that's not all there is to it. This is obviously someone smart."

"Do you think the killer lives in Almond Park?"

Selena had been waiting for him to ask. She narrowed her eyes at the detective. Leaned closer. "*I do.* I had a suspicion after the first one, of course, because getting into a house seems pretty intimate. But now there's been two, one here and another at Valley Estates. It seems almost personal. It *feels* personal."

The detective considered. "You mean like a vendetta?"

"I don't know what I mean. *Yet.*"

Selena could no longer pretend that she wasn't playing for the cameras that would soon be following her everywhere, documenting her brilliant cat-and-mouse game with the killer.

They spoke of motives and hallmarks and sprees, but despite its darker shade it had still turned to small talk. Sharpe promised to stay in touch, and asked Selena to contact him if she had any more insights into the killer's mind.

She walked him to the door, then returned to the kitchen, where she heard a quiet squeak from the living room. The sound of sneakers on a hardwood floor. She peeked around the doorjamb to find Dane standing awkwardly near the bookshelf, pretending to look for something to read.

He'd been eavesdropping.

He turned, as if surprised to realize she was there. "Hi, Mrs. Nash. I was just—"

"—curious about the murders." She smiled. "You understand that you can't talk about anything you might have *accidentally* overheard?"

Dane flashed her a smile of relief. "Of course. I just ... I want to better understand what you do."

Selena walked to the wine rack, pulled out a bottle of pinot, and poured herself a generous glass, all without saying a word, curious to see how far this might go and knowing it couldn't possibly be far.

Dane was only a kid. But he was also curious. She had always been a teacher for him, ever since the boys first brought him home. There was no reason she couldn't also instruct him in the back-and-forth between a man and a woman. It didn't have to be anything untoward.

She looked at Dane. He was still looking at her.

"The show is over and you're still here." She took a sip. "Your friends are all upstairs."

"I don't really feel like being bored, Mrs. Nash."

"Call me Selena." She smiled and took another, longer sip. "Are you saying that my son is boring?"

"Not at all. But they're all upstairs playing *HardCorp* and telling the same old jokes. Especially Elliot. Down here I'm learning something new. With you."

"What sorts of things are you learning?"

"It's like we talked about before. The thin line between life and death. You spend so much of your time there. I bet it gets hard to breathe sometimes. I bet it feels good to talk out loud, especially with someone who's interested in what you have to say."

"And why is this so interesting to you?"

Dane shrugged and leaned away from the counter. He looked thoughtful, not unsure of what he was going to say so much as perhaps questioning whether he should actually say it.

"Go on …" she prompted.

He hesitated, then seemed to force the words from his mouth, as if he had to get them all out before regret came to claim or retrieve them.

"I've been thinking about it. As a career. I know it will drive my dad nuts. He really wants me to go to Stanford, and that's not really why I want to go there. But every time Levi or Corban talks about your work, or this sort of stuff comes up, I can't stop thinking about it."

"You're thinking of becoming a homicide detective?" She deliberately misunderstood. Wanted to hear him explain why he was interested in what *she* did.

"I guess I don't really know much about it yet. Maybe a criminal psychologist, or a profiler. I don't know about writing books, like you do. But I know that I'm interested … and that you're interesting."

Selena felt herself flush. Not because she was sexually attracted to Dane. But because he looked at her with a little bit of awe in his eyes. He listened to her more deeply than Adam had recently. Maybe ever. He wanted to know what she thought. He admired her intellect.

She recognized that it was her ego talking. But surely there was nothing wrong in enjoying mentoring him?

"Are you at all scared that there's a killer in Almond Park?" he asked.

She imagined that the killer knew that Selena Nash lived in their tiny town. She was a celebrity here. He had to realize she'd be consulted by the police. No doubt he was taking extra precautions to make sure he stayed ahead of her.

Maybe that was why this all felt so personal.

"A little," Selena admitted. "But no, I'm not usually afraid of the killers."

"Have you ever met one before … I mean in real life?"

"Of course," Selena said. "All kinds."

"Do you think you would know it if you saw one?"

"I do."

She was about to deliver her latest theory, one that was only now brewing in the nooks of her mind — probably nothing, but definitely fun to discuss with the right person — when Adam entered the kitchen.

He eyed them from the other side of the room as though they were blocking his path to the fridge. He opened it, then closed it a moment later. Nodded at Selena as if to say, *don't let me interrupt.* But she didn't buy it. He always meant to interrupt.

Dane said nothing, but the boy didn't look uncomfortable, like most teenagers would. He really was growing up. He looked … poised. Like he knew what was coming and was ready.

Selena let the silence continue, seeing if her husband would give up his charade of nonchalance or if he'd keep it going until she called his bluff.

Adam pulled a bottle from the wine rack and a glass from the cabinet, then brought them both to where Selena and Dane were clustered, giving them each a thin-lipped smile.

He grabbed the bottle by its throat and poured himself a splash and a half. Just enough to down in a swallow.

Then he set his empty wine glass on the counter and said, "So, what are you two talking about?"

Chapter Eleven

Adam watched Selena leave the kitchen without a word, taking both the bottle and glass with her.

He turned away from Dane, selected a second bottle of pinot from the rack, and showed it to him.

"You want a glass?"

"No, thank you. I'm not old enough to drink."

Adam looked at him sideways. "You're telling me you've never had a drink? Come on, you're eighteen now, right?"

"The law says you can't drink until you're twenty-one in California. I think it's the law in all fifty states."

Adam filled his wine glass, all the way this time. "You don't seem like someone who is especially beholden to the law. None of you boys do, including mine. Well, except for Pussabo. I could see him as sort of a narc."

Adam laughed, keeping things friendly.

Dane laughed, too. But it was obvious the kid didn't mean it. When you wrote jokes for a living, it was easy to see when someone was being polite, or whatever that was.

Maybe there wasn't anything happening with Selena.

Maybe Adam was being paranoid. It was more than likely. Still, something about Dane had been bothering him for a while now. And it was frustrating that he hadn't been able to put his finger on it yet.

"Your friends are all upstairs. Is *HardCorps* getting old? Or is there something down here that you can't get up there?"

Dane looked Adam dead in the eye and spoke with barely any expression. "Sure, I could stay upstairs and listen to Elliot shit all over Pussabo, or I could come down here and listen to what Selena was saying to the detective. Honestly, it wasn't much of a choice."

Adam could actually understand that. Still …

"Was it weird?"

Dane raised an eyebrow. "Weird?"

"Yeah," Adam said. "Weird … having to sit there and wait for your turn."

"I wasn't waiting for my turn, Adam. I was just curious. About the killer."

"It's Mr. Nash. And did you hear what you were hoping to, Dane?"

He took a moment to think, then licked his lips, looking like he wanted water but wasn't about to ask. "I'm not sure, exactly. Someone's killing families in Almond Park, and Mrs. Nash is really smart about this stuff, and I've been thinking about maybe taking some criminal psych classes in college. And besides …"

Adam gave him a moment to finish, but he clearly wasn't going to.

"Besides what?"

The boy looked down at the floor before he continued.

"Ever since my mom died, my dad …" His voice cracked. "We'll never be a family. Not like you guys. Hanging out here is the closest I'm ever going to get."

Adam felt slapped. Surprisingly touched. Of all the things he'd expected from Dane, honesty wasn't one of them. He didn't want it.

"I don't remember my mom," Dane went on. "I look at the pictures of her when I was little and it's like looking at someone else's family. But I'd like to think she'd be a lot like Mrs. Nash."

There it was, like a knife twisting in his guts. Now he couldn't feel like anything but a prick for thinking something illicit was taking place between this kid and his wife. Like he'd projected his jealousy of Selena's success and his resentment that she seemed to be losing interest in him onto a teenage boy who missed his mom.

But he couldn't shake the feeling that something was off.

They shared a stare.

Adam took a long sip of his wine, buying time to study the kid sitting on the other side of his kitchen counter.

Was he a broken boy in need of a mother? Or a manipulative fuckstick who needed a fist in his face?

Maybe Dane was both.

Either way, this was his chance to have a conversation with the kid, without Selena or the boys around. A chance to be better, and try harder. Get out of his idiot head and all the shadows inside it. Talk to the kid. Maybe even—

"YO!" Levi boomed from two rooms over, just after the usual *THUMP!* from his jumping the final few stairs.

Seconds later, without enough time for Adam to finish his thought, Levi appeared in the kitchen, with Elliot and Pussabo trailing behind him.

"Hey Dad!" Levi said, surprised to see him. "Is Dane teaching you to be a dork? Hey Dane, did you tell him all about the boring crap that no one has ever asked or cared about, but that you always want to go on and on about anyway?" Levi looked at his father. "Did he, Dad?"

Adam smiled and tried to make nice. "I think I was the one who might have been giving Dane a hard time."

Dane seemed surprised. He smiled at Adam, warmly enough that he felt even worse for suspecting the kid. Not only was he missing a mother, Dane might've been wishing for a father he could respect, too. Had Adam's inability to get past his instinctive annoyance with Dane kept him from recognizing a chance to be a positive influence on a boy who just wanted someone to look up to?

Levi eyed the exchange and looked like he might have a question. But then he said, "So, Dane, are you coming out to get trounced by me and Pussabo?"

"That isn't going to happen. Pussabo's been practicing."

"I have," Pussabo confirmed.

"Practicing what?" Elliot asked.

Adam looked at Levi. "Where's your brother?"

Levi shrugged. "Probably off somewhere getting rejected by Kari."

"Be nice," Adam said.

"He hasn't been nice to me in a month." Levi glared at Adam like that was his fault. "But sure. You're right. I don't have to point out that he has no game and never will, and can't even get with a girl that he spends every second with. Especially when he isn't here to awkwardly defend himself."

Adam blinked. When had the rift between his boys gotten so big? Selena might've been right about there being a deeper problem than the usual sibling rivalry. And that made him feel even more like the asshole. Not only was he maybe letting Dane down, he was blowing his own shot at fatherhood. He'd lost his connection with Corban, and now he feared he might be losing it with Levi, too. The twin who was just like him. Idolized his father, despite the fact that he was a failed comic whose career was practically a hobby compared to their mother's.

Goddammit.

"Alright. Let's play." Dane stood from his barstool, scooted it in, then turned back to Adam. "Thank you for taking the time to talk to me, Mr. Nash. I really appreciate it."

Adam looked at Dane. He seemed so sincere.

The words just *fell* out of Adam's mouth.

"My pleasure, Dane. Anytime."

The boys moved in a herd toward the door. Almost out of earshot, but close enough that Adam could still color the blanks, Elliot sang, "*Thank you for taking the time to talk to me, Mr. Nash. I really appreciate it.*"

The front door closed, and Adam was alone.

Finally.

For a moment, he wondered if this was how Selena felt when she shut herself in her office. Relieved to set aside her family's demands. The idea that she might feel about Adam like Adam felt about Dane made him want to puke.

He'd spent the past few days stewing in jealousy, resentment and frustration at every level. The more frustrated he felt, the stronger his obsession became.

He'd never been able to stop the unrelenting stream of violent images, but Adam thought he'd learned to keep them in the back of his head until he was ready to dive in. Whenever he thought about the woman with the blood-red lipstick around his children, he felt a shame so intense that it sucked all the pleasure right out of his thoughts.

But now Adam was alone with her in his head, and already hardening.

He walked upstairs, wondering what she was doing right now, and hating himself.

This was the kind of hate he was used to. The kind that had always been there, ever since these ugly thoughts started building their nest in his head.

The obsession was destroying his family. Maybe it had been all along, and he never noticed before. The boys were older. Maybe they were picking things up on a subconscious level. Or they always had. Perhaps now it was louder, and Adam's thoughts were radioactive.

But how could he stop them when nothing had ever worked before?

Control was not the same as cessation. The images started as snowfall, but they were always an avalanche at the end.

Adam wished that he'd thought to bring the bottle upstairs. A few swallows might dull these throbbing thoughts. The house was finally quiet, but his mind refused to stop screaming.

The woman in lipstick. Limbs akimbo and blood like pomegranate syrup drizzled all over her naked body.

He didn't want to want it.

But there was so much blood, and Adam couldn't deny his arousal. Or his self-loathing.

He wanted to be normal, but he never would be. He was trapped in the cage of his perverted, murderous thoughts. Life was pulling him taut, and Adam was terrified that he was going to snap.

Fascination fed his disgust.

Disgust fed his slipping self-control.

And that fed his own loathing, which intensified his need for release.

His craving for murder.

Adam couldn't do what would eventually have to be done.

It wasn't time and he wasn't yet ready.

So he closed the bathroom door and did the only thing he could do for now.

Chapter Twelve

Kari kept on talking, with barely a breath between her thoughts. Corban listened like he had for the past several minutes as they sat outside on the porch, where rustling leaves were the only other sound.

"… So it's officially murder. No one is even trying to pretend that it isn't anymore. My mom won't even watch the news. She hates how they're always trying to whip everyone into a needless frenzy. Did you know that the first newspaper was commissioned by Julius Caesar?" Kari didn't wait for his answer. "It was a daily list of announcements, *carved into stone or metal.* Can you believe that? You probably had to get it right the first time. No delete, and definitely no app for that. I bet they still had fake news, though. I wonder what Caesar would think about all of this."

Corban didn't answer that either. He hated talking about any of this, but Kari wanted to and that was fine with him, so long as he could mostly listen.

She chose that moment to notice his discomfort. "What's wrong?"

He shrugged. It wasn't just that he didn't really want to talk about what were now being called the Almond Park Killings. Corban got plenty of that at home whether he wanted it or not.

He and Kari were alone at her house, and the last time that happened, they'd had a plan, before her father interrupted them. But now that plan was apparently a memory. Kari was hooked on rumors and hearsay.

"Nothing's wrong, it's just—"

"I sound like your mom?"

"Not exactly," Corban said. "But speaking of your mom, is it true that she isn't home?"

"Nope. She's out with her friends. She's *always* out with her friends."

"And your dad?"

"He's working." She laughed. "What are you *actually* asking, Corban?"

His heart was beating too fast. Why did this have to be so hard?

Kari was being playful, inviting him to play back. All he had to do was make a move and she'd surely move right along with him. He had been trying to maneuver her off the porch and into her bedroom for almost forty-five minutes. If he leaned over and kissed her now, he would bet every dollar in his bank account that she would kiss him right back.

But still Corban remained a statue.

Or maybe even a coward.

Levi would never have hesitated. His brother wasn't just confident, he had swagger. If Levi wanted Kari half as much as Corban did, he would have already slept with her, before telling his brother all the sordid details.

Levi had done it with four different girls, for a total of

twenty-three encounters, not including hummers and handis. But Corban was still a virgin.

Keeping score, it was four to zero. And like always, Corban was the zero.

He wanted to kiss Kari. Felt desperate to do it.

And now he finally would.

But he couldn't. Not yet.

He steeled himself, looked at Kari. She had to know what he was thinking. His hand was sitting on the bench, palm up, hungry for her breast.

He licked his lips, he was a second away.

Corban leaned forward and—

The front door slammed.

Kari jerked away from Corban and looked inside the house.

"What is it?"

"Someone's home. Probably my dad. I bet my mom's never slammed a door like that in her life."

"Is he mad about something?"

Kari shook her head. "I don't think so. Maybe he's in a hurry."

"Should we go inside?"

"No. He probably doesn't know we're here, and he might be leaving again, if he came back for something he forgot."

"Okay, cool."

But Corban couldn't relax. His heart was beating even harder, but for a different reason now. And Kari seemed distracted, if not altogether oblivious.

"Is he yelling?" Corban asked.

"It sure sounds like it. Maybe he *is* mad. And in that case, let's definitely stay outside."

Less than a minute later, Kari's father was right on the other side of the wall, pacing back and forth on the phone.

It sounded like three different calls. The first one was all mumbles and mutters. Neither Corban nor Kerry could make out a word. The next conversation came loud, Ollie yelling something about Lakeway Estates and liability. The last sounded frantic, upset but subdued. Corban listened hard, but he couldn't make out enough to have any idea what was going on.

They stared into each other's eyes, perfectly silent, while Corban craved Kari's lips.

They were red, but he was yellow.

No one had spoken in minutes by the time they barely heard the front door close, whispering shut as if in defeat.

Corban knew exactly how it felt.

Chapter Thirteen

Levi laughed. "It feels fucking amazing. What else do you want me to tell you? How many ways can I explain it?"

Dane shrugged. "Maybe if any of your prior explanations were anywhere near satisfactory, I wouldn't still be asking."

"You're eighteen years old, dude, and not bad looking. At least ten percent of the girls at Wembley would be willing to fuck you. Just don't let them get to know you, because then most of them will change their minds for sure."

"Forget it, then."

Levi didn't want to forget it. He liked telling his friends about his conquests. He wouldn't be the only among them with experience much longer, and Dane would be the first to go. Levi was surprised that he hadn't already. Besides, Dane always asked the best questions, and not just to set up a punchline, like Elliot did.

"You don't have to forget it," Levi said. "It's just not an easy question to answer. Sex doesn't just feel *one way*. It depends on my mood, and who I'm doing it with. What if

I were to ask you what eating was like? What would you say?"

Without thinking, Dane said, "I'd have to talk about autophagia."

"Autowhat?"

"Eating one's own body."

Levi grimaced. "What the hell, dude?"

"You'd know if you didn't sleep through health class every day. Elliot brought it up when Mr. D was talking about eating disorders."

That was definitely Elliot. "Why would you talk about that?"

"As an example of how much difference there could be between two people's experience of eating. Sufferers feel a tremendous sense of arousal before they start eating themselves—"

"Speaking from personal experience?" Levi joked, hoping to derail that train of thought.

"—but then there's intense pleasure," Dane continued. Because sometimes he just couldn't resist being a dick. "Once the act is finished, the feeling of arousal is replaced with a deep sense of guilt or regret."

No shit. Who wouldn't regret taking a bite out of themselves?

Dane looked at him expectantly. Like he wanted a serious response. What was he supposed to say?

So no surprise, Levi went with a joke. "Here's a tip: don't bring up autophagia until after the girl has sucked your dick."

Dane laughed, but more like he thought Levi expected it. "So you never feel guilty?"

"About what?"

"Sex."

"Nope."

"Not even with Lacy?"

"Why would I feel guilty about Lacy?" Levi asked. "She wants it even more than I do. And she hates her husband."

"She's still married. And you're still helping her cheat."

"I'm sorry, Officer Russell." Levi held his hands in front of him, ready for cuffs.

Dane forced another laugh.

Levi was bored with this conversation. He stood and stretched. "Want to go for a walk?"

On their way out the back door, they stopped to check out the setup for the barbecue. Lights were strung and the grill was gleaming under the bright nightlights spilling down from the giant garage. Dad put heat lamps out in case the party ran long, and set up the bar that would be stocked with a generous selection of alcohol that Levi would try to sneak a drink or two from while his parents were busy chatting up the neighbors. The only things missing were the popcorn machine they would bring down from the game room, the mountains of food that would be delivered in the morning, and the hundred or so people that the Nashes would be hosting.

"So," Dane asked, "if you pretend that Elliot won't be a giant douche, are you looking forward to the party?"

"The food will be good."

"That's not an answer, Levi."

He sighed. "Our parents hate it when Corban and I fight, and it's never really been this bad. That means I'm going to have to play pretend, and I hate that shit. Makes me too tired to kick your ass in *HardCorp*. Meanwhile, I'll have to watch my mom being obnoxious and trying to make sure that everyone knows exactly how awesome she is and my dad pouting because she's hogging the spotlight.

Oh, and I'll have to watch Corban being all awkward with Kari."

"Do you still have a thing—"

"Yeah, but whatever."

"And Elliot and Pussabo still aren't allowed to know?"

"I don't want to hear Elliot's shit, and Pussabo can't even keep his own secrets."

"Yeah, I didn't need to hear how he tried waxing his junk."

"No one did." Levi snickered. "Especially not the girl he was trying to impress. Speedos ought to be illegal. But if either of those two fuckers finds out, then it's only a matter of time before they tell my brother, and then I'll have to deal with all of his crybaby bullshit."

"And you're still not going to say anything to Kari?"

"Corban's still my *brother*."

"But it's not like Kari and Corban are together," Dane said, repeating his usual argument. "If you're going to do anything, then you need to do it now before they are. Then it will be too late. Kari has the right to decide between you. It's not—"

"That's what gets me," Levi said. "She and Corban have nothing in common."

"They have a lot in common, man. They're always talking about stuff they've read. When's the last time you opened a book?"

"Well, we like to talk about what we watch. And Corban is *bored* by TV. Seriously, since when is he too good for TV?"

"You guys have the same DNA."

"He's an introvert and Kari is an extrovert, like me. She and I talk. Corban just stands around listening. He barely adds anything to the conversation."

"Maybe Kari wants to be heard. You're not the best listener."

Levi gave Dane a dirty look.

"It's true. The two of you would be talking all over each other."

"At least we'd be having conversations. We'd also look good together."

"That's a terrible reason to want to be with someone. And not to point out the obvious, but you'd look exactly the same as they would."

Since when was Dane on his brother's side? "Corban slouches and he's a shit dresser."

Dane rolled his eyes. "Whatever happened between you two is stupid. You're obviously going to get over it, so why not just do it now and stop making everything shitty for the rest of us?"

"You don't understand." No one did. Because none of them were twins. They'd never get what it was like to have a brother who *got* you. And then stopped.

"How can I, if you won't tell me what happened?"

"I told you, it's between me and Corban."

"Then find another girl. It's not like you've had a problem with that in the past."

But he couldn't. Because he wanted Kari. In spite of the fact that she was the only girl in the world right now that he couldn't have. Or was that why he wanted her?

"Some couples are just right together. Look at my parents. Sure, they can be annoying, but even their fights are fun to watch. It's like they're good at it. They're both good at everything. My mom just needs everyone to know it."

"You're really hard on her, dude."

Levi looked down at Dane's crotch. "*You're* really hard on her."

79

"Gross. That's your mom."

"You're the one who's always like, *Oh, Mrs. Nash, will you please be my new mommy and spank me?*"

"Dude."

The steel in Dane's tone told Levi that he'd gone too far. "Sorry, man. Really."

A beat, then, "It's cool."

"I didn't mean that."

"I know." Dane smiled. *We're cool.*

"I am hard on my mom. I don't mean to be, but you don't have to live with her."

Another look. "I wish I had a mom a quarter as great as her."

"I know. I'm sorry."

The silence was long and the loud wind made it feel longer. Levi needed to break it. And he needed to make up for the potshots he'd taken at Dane.

And so he finally spoke.

"Wanna know what happened between me and Corban?"

Chapter Fourteen

Adam looked around his backyard and felt an almost-overwhelming wave of pride.

Everywhere he cast his eyes, people were smiling.

He tolerated Selena's barbecues more than he actually liked them. She loved being a big deal in Almond Park. Said that there was no reward in having a life full of riches if you couldn't share them with the people around you. And life had been good to the Nashes.

But the barbecue wasn't just about sharing in their family's abundance.

Selena was meticulous in cultivating their family's image. The way things *looked* often determined the way people *felt* about them. Selena made it clear to Adam that maintaining an air of decency and respect was essential to the world not knowing what was constantly boiling like lava beneath his skin.

Backyard events like this barbecue helped to build the picture of a perfect family, and that was exactly what he needed — what *they* needed — to keep the world off his trail.

But Adam thought it made them look like one of those families whose picture comes with your new wallet.

Still, he enjoyed them for the most part, even though he suspected that Selena would throw the parties even if she wasn't trying to protect him. The food was always fantastic. In addition to the usual spread, Selena found a guy who'd brought his own mobile kitchen and was making fresh tacos on the far side of the guest house. She wanted fish, but couldn't get the guy to budge. So it was carne and pollo asada.

Adam had to admit, it did give him hope that if he could convince everyone else he was normal, one day he might be. And she was *always* in a great mood at these things. She usually made eyes at him all day, delighting in the dirt underneath both of their nails, deep enough that no one could see, and here they were right in front of everyone. Sex afterward was always hot and raw and more than once.

"I just can't believe this is happening here," said June Mays. She'd been at the press conference this morning, where the police had confirmed that the two killings were linked. "It must be someone new."

"It's terrible," Adam agreed. He'd been saying it all day. Because what else could he say? "Truly awful."

But with every repetition, his urge to say what he really thought grew stronger, until he was biting back all but the simplest responses and swallowing half-formed monologues dripping with desire and death.

By the time meat was coming off the grill, the pool was filled with splashing, and at least half of the guests who could legally drink were tipsy, including the hosts, and Adam found that his tongue was finally loosening. Selena's, too.

"You really think it could be a serial killer?" Leonard

Murphy, who made his money making blinds in Manila and lived three houses down the street, looked at Selena in stark disbelief.

Everyone nearby quieted, looking to Selena. Like she was about to share the Serial Killer Gospel with them.

"I said it could be," Selena repeated. "There is something very specific about a scarf. That's what I'm most curious about ... these scarves. There's something there, and it's big. I bet someone here has an idea."

Selena turned to Abigail Granger. Until last week, Abigail had shared the 9:30 a.m. class at Yoga Bear with the mom who burned in the fire. "Did Molly like scarves? I mean, any more than the rest of us?"

Abigail covered her mouth.

"I'm ... I ..." She stopped, stammered, clearly uncomfortable. "I'm not sure," she finally finished.

Selena wasn't usually so obvious. But it sure could get ugly when she was.

Adam looked around, noting the handful of last-minute additions, people from town rather than just their neighborhood. More than usual. And several, including Abigail Granger, were friends with the deceased.

Selena had spent the early afternoon flitting from cluster to cluster like a gossiping little fly, gathering connections and looping them together.

What did people know about the victims?
How were the families connected?
Did the children know each other?
Were they in some kind of trouble?
What kinds of rumors had people heard?
Who had access to the houses?

Selena had so many theories, and loved to voice them out loud. So what if she ruffled a few feathers? She could always blame it on the alcohol. He'd guessed from the way the world blurred around the edges that he'd had more than a bottle of wine himself by the time she finally pulled him aside.

She squeezed his hand tight. Maybe *too* excited. Her eyes were dancing. "I think I've got it."

"Got what?" Like he didn't know.

"Ollie. Ollie Harris, Kari's father."

"No." Adam shook his head. "Stop it, Selena."

"I'm serious. Don't you at least want to know what I found out?"

He did, but this conversation wasn't smart. Not here, not now, and not with Ollie Harris waiting in line for a taco a few yards away.

"Can we talk about this later? Or somewhere else?"

"We're the hosts. If we disappear inside, people will come looking for us."

Adam translated that as: *I'm important, people will miss me if I leave the party.*

"No one is listening to us, and even if they tried, The Stray Bullets are loud enough to drown us out."

"Still …" Adam said, glancing around.

On one side of the pool, Levi, Dane, Elliot, and Pussabo played a game of pickup. On the other side, Corban and Kari sat on lawn chairs, each of them holding a book — Corban's on a Kindle and Kari's made of paper — with several pounds of snacks sitting neatly between them.

To Adam, the pool looked like a demilitarized zone.

Resigned, he said, "Fine. Tell me."

"I should make you wait for pretending like you don't want to know, but I'd rather get back to the party. Get a refill." Selena raised her mostly empty glass, swished the swallow at the bottom, then she downed it before delivering her theory.

"Ollie is the only one with access to both families. He recently did the electrical on both houses, and was the most recent contractor ..."

But now Adam was disgusted. It wasn't that he doubted Selena wanting to find the killer. But did she not care how it would hurt Corban if she accused his girl-friend's father of murder based on gossip and a hunch?

Sad as it was to admit it, even Selena probably wouldn't deny that finding the killer was as much about saving lives as it was gathering material for her new show.

"You can't tell people this. Not without proof."

"But it makes sense. Don't you see that it makes sense?"

"No. I see that you promised things would get better. But instead you can't even enjoy a barbecue without making everything about you."

Adam tried to keep his voice cool, not wanting to come off as pissy or needy or defensive. He didn't want to come off as *any* of the things she would later hurl his way.

He smiled, to give the impression he was having a pleasant conversation with his wife. She smiled back.

Nothing to see here, folks. Everything is perfectly normal.

Adam wasn't simmering because Selena had been ignoring him, petty as that might be. There wasn't a hint of jealousy behind his annoyance. His wife wasn't an atten-tion whore, and neither of them had downed one too many.

"Look, I don't want to fight. I want to enjoy the after-noon, and put on our best faces like you're always wanting to. Without you interrogating the town ... or digging for gossip."

"I'm digging for——"

"Mrs. Nash? Mr. Nash?"

"Adam," he said, like always. He had known Dane's father for years. They'd been introduced many times, but for some reason, the man still insisted on calling them by their last names, and he reintroduced himself every single time they met.

Adam offered his hand. "It's good to see you, Brandon."

"I don't mean to interrupt."

The man had been close enough to see their forced smiles and gritted teeth. But like always, Brandon seemed oblivious.

He gave them a pleasant but battle-weary smile. "I just wanted to thank you both."

"For what?" Adam and Selena asked together.

"For everything. For being leaders in this community, but also for taking such great care of Dane. The two of you are a wonderful influence on him. He looks up to you both so much." Brandon turned to Selena. "Especially you, Mrs. Nash. I know how busy you are, but you make time to raise two fine boys and still pay attention to mine."

"It's my pleasure, Brandon. Really."

"Last month was especially helpful."

"Last month?" Adam said.

"It was nothing," Selena said, a little too fast.

"What happened last month?" Adam asked.

"Oh." Brandon smiled. "Dane and Levi got their wires crossed or something, and Dane came over to an empty house. Or mostly. Your wife was there, and entertained my boy after an especially hard day, even though no one was home and she sure didn't have to. He needs that kind of care, in a way I can't get him. You know … just … thank you."

"You're welcome." Then to Adam, Selena said, "Levi had detention. Corban waited with him, so Dane was there for an hour or so before the boys came home." And back to Dane's father. "It was nothing, really."

"It was, though …" Brandon took a moment, and it looked like he needed it. "It's hard … not just being the only parent around, but …" another moment "… but always wondering if maybe the wrong parent died."

"Brandon." Adam was surprised by how raw he suddenly felt. This was a man who seemed brittle enough to break right in front of them, a man who turned off the endings of sad movies because he couldn't bear them. "You know that's not true."

Selena said, "You have to be fair to yourself. It isn't your fault that Dane doesn't have both of his parents. And we're always happy to do what we can."

"Thank you," Brandon said again, then he fell into yet another long and yawning moment.

Adam couldn't take it. He said, "I think I'll go and check on our guests," then walked to the bar alone, leaving Selena standing dumbfounded behind him with Brandon.

Adam asked for two shots of Patron and a margarita. He swallowed the first shot, poured the second into his maggie, then slipped into the first available conversation he could find. Like the second and third and all the ones after that, Adam listened to the chatter, making slightly off-color jokes about the murders, and watching his audience shift on their feet amid twitters of anxious laughter.

He looked at his sons, disappointed to see that they had drifted even farther apart. Bad blood between them still. Levi's group was now in line waiting for tacos, while Corban and Kari ambled about the party's perimeter.

And then he saw Selena walking up to Dane.

The two of them were laughing.

Even from here he could see her bright red lipstick, and wondered if the shade was for Dane.

Of course it was.

Bloody murder swallowed his thoughts.

Chapter Fifteen

Selena looked at her patient, sprawled on the couch.

He looked almost at peace with his hands folded on his chest and his feet crossed at the ankles, bouncing ever so slightly. Selena hadn't had a full calendar in years, her load now reduced to a small handful of regular appointments, plus the occasional session with her longest-standing client.

"Are you still experiencing these compulsions?" she asked him.

"Yes," Adam said. "But I've learned to control them."

She wasn't supposed to be seeing him. Not like this. And her use of hypnosis to indulge his fantasies …

There wasn't an advisory board in the world who wouldn't see what they were doing as highly unethical, even though it had been happening for years. Exchanges like this were at the start of so many unsavory things.

"How have you learned to control them?"

"Just like you taught me." A half-smile formed at the corner of his lips.

"And what did I teach you?"

"So many things."

"Tell me one …"

"That we cannot truly change ourselves without losing ourselves, and so the only option is to control ourselves."

"Is battling your urges a strength or a weakness?"

"It feels like a weakness. Because I don't want anyone to control me. Not even myself."

"Imagine yourself as a child. Christmas is right around the corner. You can see all the boxes sitting beneath the tree, including the biggest one. It has your name on it, and you cannot wait to tear it open. Can you see that box, Adam?"

"Yes."

"Do you feel the excitement?"

"Yes." The elation on his face said that he meant it.

"Now it's two days until Christmas. Do you do entertain your mind with diversion, or fantasize about that box day and night? What increases desire?"

"Both. I do other things, but I can't stop thinking about what's inside."

"And what is in your box?"

"Everything."

"Go ahead and unwrap the box."

A moment passed, then Adam said, "I've unwrapped it."

"Now open it and tell me the first thing you see inside."

"*Her.*"

"Describe her."

"She's beautiful. Five foot six or so. Bright blue eyes and a smile that appears when she sees me. Her body is perfect, snug in her uniform. Her skin is too pale and she's always blushing. Her lipstick is the color of blood."

"Why is she in the box?"

"Because she is waiting for me."

"What is she waiting for you to do?"

"To take her."

"To take her how, Adam?"

"Sexually."

"Is that all?"

"She's waiting for me to take her humanity."

Selena let that settle, then after several seconds of silence said, "Let's talk about the blood."

Adam grinned like a little boy. Like he really had a box.

"It's thick. Hot. Wet."

"What do you do with it?"

"Mark myself with it. Everywhere."

Selena squirmed in her chair as Adam slid his hands over his crotch. Hematolagnia was the technical term for his fetish. He wasn't a vampirist, and the thought of drinking blood disgusted him, but he found its presence deeply arousing. Most people with Adam's condition would naturally be into BDSM and bloodplay, using blades to bloodlet their partners. Adam stayed inside his fantasies rather than acting them out, and Selena got him off, without the guilt.

Blood wasn't her fetish like it was his, but sex was never hotter than in the fantasy with Adam. So why was she feeling so impatient with him?

Because she had a new theory burning a hole in her brain.

And that's what she wanted to discuss.

No. This is his time. Don't make it about you.

She couldn't help it. "Do you fantasize about being the Almond Park Killer?"

Adam took a moment to answer. "No."

"Are you sure?"

Another moment, then, "Yes."

"Why?"

"He's not getting close enough."

"Why do you think that is?"

"Maybe he's not ready."

"What would he be waiting for?"

"Maybe he wants the time to be perfect."

"Perfect for what, Adam?"

"His masterpiece."

"And what would his masterpiece be?"

"Blood everywhere." Hands back on his crotch.

Selena crossed her legs. *Squeezed*. Leaned forward. "What do you think he——?"

"I don't want to talk about him."

"What would you like to talk about?"

"*The Thick Red Line*. It started that night."

"What started that night?"

He hesitated. She hated this part. But the part she loved came right after.

Finally, "Her."

"Tell me who she is," Selena said, without so much as a hint of the irritation scratching at her insides.

"She's beautiful."

Selena didn't want to hear that.

"And young."

Or that.

"She thinks I'm funny, and always laughs at my jokes. Even when they're bad."

And I bet it's a barista, and you overtip her every time.

Adam described the girl, sharing all the details that Selena didn't want to hear. Fine if he wanted to think of this girl when he fucked her, covered in blood or not. It still felt good for her. But she didn't need the play by play on her tits and ass.

His prior fixation had blood-red hair, and Adam was *obsessed*. He even begged Selena to dye her hair that shade. She did, hated it, and kept it for one of the longest months of her life. That was five years ago. She should be grateful that it had taken him so long to cycle through to another obsession.

Now it sounded like she would be changing her shade of lipstick.

"It's *so red*. Every time I see it I wonder if everyone else sees blood on her lips, too? It's so sexy. I just want to lick them. I want to lick *her*."

Selena swallowed, tried not to be bothered, reminded herself that this was a small price to pay for all they had.

Her man had fantasies. It was her personal and professional job to indulge them.

And it was best for Adam not to know.

Because he was not the dormant killer that he believed himself to be. She had *allowed him* to think that he was. Led him to the conclusion because she had to.

Yes, there was a time when Selena believed that Adam had murderous urges. But soon after his treatment started she realized that his impulses were merely a blood fetish. Her husband didn't have a murderous bone in his body.

But the dominion she held over Adam's mind when he believed that she was helping him to suppress the worst of his urges and become the decent man he couldn't otherwise be, and the awe in which he held her — it would all be gone if she told him the truth. So she let it continue.

Adam's breathing sped up and his hands fisted around his erection. He was almost ready.

"I want to lick the blood off every inch of her body."

She should have stopped there. Torn his clothes off. Bled off all that excitement and anger by fucking him on her couch.

But something in her couldn't resist pushing him. Proving that her husband wasn't a psychopath.

"Why haven't you killed her?"

"Because that would be wrong."

"*Why* would it be wrong?"

"Stealing her life just to give mine a thrill, taking her from her friends and family forever." Adam shook his head, looking visibly upset even with his eyes still closed. "I just couldn't do it."

Psychopaths were emotionally crippled. Adam was not. He felt good after helping people, and always wanted to do his best. He was kind and considerate most of the time. He felt deeply, which was one of the many reasons that he was funny, even if she didn't always give him the props he deserved. Adam was motivated to do good things and avoid the bad, probably more than most people. The man clearly had a conscience. Psychopaths could never be happy, because happiness is emotional and they were a vacuum.

Adam wore his emotions like a winter coat.

He was a nice guy with a creepy fetish. Not that Selena was judging.

"But then," Adam said, with something ugly catching in his throat. "Sometimes I think that maybe I could."

Chapter Sixteen

No one spoke on the way to dinner. Selena didn't care. She was relieved to be leaving tomorrow morning, and unnerved by Adam's admission during their session. She almost thought she'd misheard. *It doesn't mean anything.*

Then there was the silent tension that had the boys at each other's throats. It was easier to ignore when everyone was in a different room. But locked in a car with them as they took turns either ignoring or sniping at each other …

A few days of work would give her a chance to recharge.

She checked her phone as Adam pulled into the Tequila Sunrise parking lot, just in case Sharpe had sent an update. She'd chosen the restaurant for its separate bar, where she could meet the detective on the down-low.

After a short wait, a redheaded waitress led them to their table. Adam had his eyes head-to-toe all over her, and he wasn't being discreet. Levi was oblivious, but Corban noticed for sure. He looked at his father in what might have been disgust, then over at Selena in what was probably sympathy.

Better that he assumed Adam was checking out the waitress than to know what his father actually fantasized about her.

She checked her phone as they sat. Still nothing from Sharpe.

Adam gave her a suspicious look.

"Sam is supposed to be sending me notes, but he hasn't yet," she improvised.

That earned her a pissy look. Fine with her. *Go back to ogling the waitress.*

Selena looked down at the water, grateful that Tequila Sunrise was one of the restaurants that served it first, because their waters were already on the table. She downed hers fast to make her upcoming exodus to the restroom more believable.

"Can we get nachos for appetizers?" Levi asked.

"The tableside guac is better," Corban said.

"We can get both. And these." Adam pointed to the short rib quesadillas. His favorite.

"That's a lot of appetizers," Selena said, resisting the temptation to check her phone again.

"So, Dad," Levi said, "do you think they're going to cancel any of the upcoming summer stuff?"

"No," Selena said. "Definitely not."

"I agree with your mother."

"They might," Corban said.

Levi slapped his menu on the table and glared at his brother. "Of course you'd think that."

Selena and Adam traded a glance. If she didn't intervene, would he? Or would he allow the boys to work it out?

She drank more of her water.

Corban said, "What's that even supposed to mean?"

"You know what it's supposed to mean." Levi glared harder.

"I really don't. Maybe you should try to articulate yourself better."

Selena had no idea either, but was grateful for the distraction. She pulled out her phone and checked for a text. Nothing yet. But Adam saw her slipping it back into her purse.

She pretended not to see his frown. They could fight later. Right now, she didn't want Corban to know. He *couldn't* know. Because it would crush him. He liked Kari a lot.

So did Selena. But that didn't mean she was about to protect a murderer. It would be irresponsible to keep what she learned from the detective, especially after he specifically asked her to share any information that she might come across. And yes, he made the same request of everyone, but she was their little town's most well-respected authority.

"What is it between you two lately?" Adam finally asked. And good for him.

Selena swallowed the rest of her water.

Levi looked at his brother. "Ask him."

Corban turned to Adam. "You don't want to know."

Her phone buzzed. Finally. Selena looked down and saw a text from the detective: *in the bar*.

She said, "All three of those sound great. Go ahead and order if they get here before I'm back. And you can order me the Number Two. I'm going to the restroom."

Levi laughed. Adam smiled. Corban rolled his eyes.

Adam put his hand on Selena's. "Stay. Just until we order. The waiter will have questions, and you can be particular."

"I won't be particular tonight."

"Tell us about your trip," he pressed. "You're going to be on live TV, right? That's a big deal."

"It sure is. And that's why I tried to talk about it at home, and then again on the way to dinner. Now I really have to go to the bathroom." Selena snatched her hand away from Adam and stood, glaring down at him. "I'll be right back."

With far more visible irritation than the situation called for, Selena turned and marched toward the bathroom, stopping for a furtive rendezvous at the bar.

Sharpe was sitting at the far end, alone. Selena walked right over and stood beside him.

The detective looked down at the empty seat. "You're not gonna sit?"

"My husband is likely to come and investigate any minute. I'll explain it all to him later, but for now we need to hurry."

"Okay then," Sharpe said, casting his eyes back at the restaurant. "How can I help you?"

"Ollie Harris. You should look into—"

"You think we haven't looked into Ollie Harris? He was doing work for both families. Do you have anything more than that?"

"Ollie worked on a lot of the houses in the development, but he had to go back a second time to those two houses, to replace shoddy parts because the original contractor was careless or cutting corners."

Sharpe was interested. "Anything else?"

Instead of the thrill she expected, Selena's chest felt hollow, as if her heart were surrounded by a vast space. Corban would never forgive her if he knew what she told the detective, and the reward for her betrayal was almost nonexistent.

"Thanks for the tip, Mrs. Nash."

And for wasting my time, his tone suggested.

This hadn't gone how she expected. She had imagined

his gratitude. She even mentally catalogued everything he was wearing, from the wool on his shoulders to the light blue cotton socks, preparing for the day she would have to describe meeting with him.

But the detective might as well have been shaking his head.

And in that moment she found herself missing Dane. Imagined him leaning forward in his seat, fingers gripping whatever he might be holding tighter. Obvious interest coloring his face, a cascade of questions.

"I'll call you when I have something more substantial," Selena said.

When.

"I'll let you get back to your family."

Sharpe smiled, but Selena didn't like what she saw behind it.

Condescension, annoyance, and the realization that Selena Nash was a disappointment.

Chapter Seventeen

Adam spit, rinsed, and dropped his toothbrush in the holder.

Selena was slipping into her nightgown in the bedroom, but he could see her clearly in the mirror. She wasn't putting on a show for him. In fact, she seemed indifferent to his presence. That was his fault, and he would make it right.

Tomorrow was a big day. Selena loved being on television, and couldn't wait to have a show of her own. But that didn't mean the experience wasn't always nerve-wracking. That part was easier for him than it was for her, and it was sometimes easy to get lost in the truth that what was simple for one person might be hell for another. Not that going to L.A. and appearing on *Whispers* would be hell for Selena. But her insides would be burning until that first minute. Then everything would be okay. It always was.

But tonight, more than a half-day away from when she'd be sitting across from Isla Porter yet again, Selena was obviously nervous. Stressed at the restaurant. She ran off to the bathroom *twice*, despite usually being an *I'll wait until we get home* sorta girl.

Adam had been telling himself that Selena was off, but it took him the seven minutes driving home to realize that *he* was the one who'd lost his center. Things were happening fast for all of them, and he seemed to be having some sort of problem with that. Tomorrow he'd write and write and write, keep that pen moving on the page until he figured out more of it. He knew where it started, with feeling more ignored than he wanted, or deserved to be.

Selena had been waiting for a call from Sam, because she was *always* waiting for a call from him before a scheduled appearance. It was almost a ritual. But there'd been a moment at the restaurant when he'd felt a flare of genuine anger, a sudden trill of rage as Selena kept checking her phone and making excuses to run off. He'd been sure it was Dane, even though that didn't make any sense.

He felt like an asshole on the way home, and tried in tiny ways to make it up to her. So far, nothing worked. Not that holding the door open was much of an effort. But he had to figure it out, and fast. Because there was something else that was almost a ritual, something they always did before Selena got on a plane, or would be gone for more than a day, and he wanted to lose himself in their sacrament.

Adam didn't want to fight. He wanted to fuck.

"Are you nervous?" he asked, stepping into the bedroom.

"Not exactly. You know how it is."

He did. Once upon a time, Adam imagined that he might eventually live his professional life from the other side of a talk-show host's desk. "I wonder how nervous Isla is right now."

"Isla isn't thinking about me."

"Oh," Adam said, "I didn't mean that she's thinking about you. I just wonder if she's nervous because of all those choices on the Cheesecake Factory's menu. Seriously, who needs all those options? It's a lot of pressure."

Perfect delivery. Thoroughly unexpected.

Selena laughed and some of the ice melted between them.

"Do you know what you're going to say?" he asked.

"I didn't get the questions ahead of time, but I don't need them. They can start asking me whatever and I'll get going. I won't even really know what I'm saying until I'm watching it later."

"But you have a good idea of the questions they're going to ask, so you have some answers semi-prepared, right?"

Selena shrugged. "I guess."

"I could help. You know, draft a few lines for you."

"Oh, you don't have to do that. It's late."

"It's not that late. And I don't mind. I work late all the time. We could do it together, in bed."

"Really, that's okay. I already have all my talking points from Sam. I don't need anything more in my head."

"These aren't talking points, Selena. They're jokes."

"I know how to be funny, but thank you."

"Anna Lies is hilarious even when in mourning, but she still has no problem paying me to punch up her stuff. This is what I'm good at. Remember, I almost had a talk show."

She sighed. "You didn't *almost* have a talk show."

He inhaled and exhaled. But again, Adam didn't want to fight. Not about that, and not right now.

He was offering to do something nice, trying to find something that the two of them could reconnect over. A marriage couldn't survive on hate sex and murder talk alone.

"I'm just offering to help."

"Thank you," she said, like she actually meant it. "That's very sweet. But I'm driving to L.A. for a professional interview. Turns out, I'm a professional. I know exactly what I'm doing, because this is what I do."

It's what Wayne Hanger does, too. And he still hires me for help.

But he wasn't about to name drop. Again.

"Is there anything I can do?"

"Thank you, honey." This time Selena didn't sound like she meant it at all. "But I'm fine. I just want to go to bed."

The discussion was over but far from resolved.

Adam got into bed and waited, grabbing his tablet to read so he wouldn't cross his arms, lifting his eyes from the screen to study Selena whenever he was reasonably sure that she wasn't aware.

He wanted to make sure that everything was okay before she pulled down her covers and got into bed. He wanted to fix this mess he'd made of the evening.

And yes, Adam wanted sex.

Unfortunately, Selena's body language had closed and locked that door.

He opened his *EW* magazine app, and started reading for real. Maybe that would ease his agitation, help to convince him that their exchange hadn't bothered him nearly as much as it did.

But no, whether Adam wanted to admit it or not, he was irritated. And looking at Selena was making it worse.

Because she wasn't looking at him. She hadn't really seen him for days. Not like he needed her to.

It had been days since her eyes said she wanted to fuck him. Now he was tense and in need of release. The last time had been in her office, hard and fast and just the interruption she needed, though only one of them would admit it.

Then nothing since then. Not even after his session, and that was a first.

They *always* fucked after therapy. Even if it didn't happen in the office — in the early days it didn't, when Selena still pretended to nurse her decorum — it happened soon after. But that day they were interrupted by a text from Sam. She'd gotten distracted, and stayed that way until well after bedtime, leaving Adam to fall asleep with cum on his stomach.

She got into bed and looked over at Adam. "What are you reading?"

"Something you might care about, actually." He turned the tablet so that Selena could see the screen. "Looks like some John Treadwell project is getting picked up by Netflix. Sam still represents him, right?"

"Yes. And apparently things are going well. More proof. Sam delivers, so we should do what he says."

"I've never had a problem believing that he'll deliver, and from where I'm lying, we're doing what he says all the time."

"Good night, Adam."

Selena kissed him on the cheek, then turned and flipped off her light, leaving Adam alone with one bulb burning and a cock at half-mast, and about to start hurting.

A throbbing ache, all that blood leaving his brain to settle below.

So Adam closed his eyes and pictured it somewhere else.

Covering her body. The woman in the blood-red lipstick, naked in death.

In his mind she was smiling. Like him, she loved all the

blood, even if it meant leaving this earth, even if she had to become nothing to make him feel like a god.

This time, Adam didn't just fall into a sticky sleep while picturing the woman in lipstick lying in a lake of crimson. This time he fell into a heavy slumber while imagining his hands around her throat.

Chapter Eighteen

Adam hated this dream the most. The one about his first love.

The first woman he'd ever stalked.

A high school sophomore to his lowly freshman, Charlotte would've been out of his league even if they'd been the same age. Blonde curls pinned atop her head, exposing a pale and slender neck as she took notes one desk in front of him. Shiny white bra straps peeking out when she wore his favorite blouse, the silky red one that slipped him an extra inch of shoulder. Black leggings clinging to the curve of her ass — the male half of the class gave her their full attention every time the teacher called her to the board.

And her scent ... sweet, with a hint of spice. Adam spent a couple of hours pretending to shop for his mother's birthday, demanding to smell everything at the perfume counter until he found that scent. Vivacité.

He sprayed it on his pillow every night before jerking himself to sleep with fantasies of his lips on the back of her neck, of her turning around and kissing him back, right there in Civics.

His little sister caught him. Threatened to tell Mom and Dad he was wearing girl's perfume, until he paid the brat a month's allowance for her silence.

In the dream, he could smell her even though he hung back half a block, following her home from school after choir practice. He always walked on the other side of the street, so she wouldn't realize that she was being stalked, even if she turned around.

He followed her past the gas station where she sometimes stopped to buy candy — Lemonheads were her favorite.

Past the burger joint that he'd vowed he would take her on their first date.

Past the park where she and her friends sometimes did homework on the weekends. Where Adam had started doing his homework every Saturday, hoping to catch a glimpse of her.

She was alone now, just like she'd been that day.

He was trying to work up the nerve to cross the street and catch up before she passed the frozen yogurt place, to ask her if he could buy her some. Just like he'd done on that sweet afternoon.

But he couldn't, not yet, because the sway of her ass as she walked gave him a hard-on that wouldn't go away, no matter how fiercely he commanded it to.

So he kept following, hands jammed in his pockets, as she passed the yogurt place.

And the convenience store.

And the dog park.

She stopped at the light, two blocks from her house. Looked over her shoulder and frowned at him.

Why'd she have to look? That was where it all went wrong.

Adam stepped into the deli, pretended to read the

menu over the counter, like he always did. Counted to thirty in his head, then stepped outside again.

She was crossing the street. Not heading north, toward her house. Toward him.

She'd figured it out.

Shit.

He ducked into Harthrop's Music and hurried past the racks of sheet music, grabbing something as he turned to face a wall display, appearing to contemplate guitar strings while watching her approach the store through the plate glass window. His heart raced with the fear of being caught, and goddammit if his dick didn't get even harder.

He ached for her to know how he felt about her, and the fact that she was probably going to think him the worst kind of creep didn't matter one bit to his fucking hard-on.

She'd made it halfway across the street.

Adam couldn't breathe. Couldn't move. Couldn't stop hating himself for what was about to happen.

The way her hips moved as she stepped off the curb mesmerized him, just like they had that day.

He saw the car jump the curb and his heart screamed *NO*, just like it had that day.

The blue Beemer slammed into her body with a squealing of tires, catapulting the girl through the window with a horrendous crash of shattered glass.

Just like it had that day.

In the dream, he didn't have to run to her; he was already there, kneeling on blood-soaked carpet beside the toppled shelf that her limp body had slammed into.

Her dead weight in his arms.

Her pale eyes staring unseeing into his.

Her blood everywhere, hot and slick as it oozed over his hands, seeped into his shirt, soaked into the stiff fabric of his jeans and coated around his still-hard dick.

He screamed himself awake, the last spasms of an orgasm sliming his boxers even as the dream left his cheeks wet with tears.

It was his fault Charlotte had died. She never would've crossed the street if she hadn't caught him stalking her like an animal.

No, *he* was the animal. What kind of asshole would be hard while the woman he loved bled out all over his lap?

Charlotte had shown him the sickness that lurked in his soul.

He'd thought Selena would heal him.

But what if he couldn't be saved?

Chapter Nineteen

It was a beautiful spring Saturday, and summer felt seconds away.

Corban and Kari were biking to the river, the thin gash of rock and water that separated Almond Park from the rest of Baker County. It sounded so much grander than it was. Same for the nickname given to the tiny inlet where the two of them were headed now. Gallows Point. No one knew where the name came from or why it had stuck around, but it was older than the city, and probably Baker, too.

Corban had theorized that one or more of the seven children who originally grew up in the Wembley House called it that, because that was the sort of thing that kids were always doing, and then the name just stuck. Maybe when Reginald Wembley became the city's second mayor.

"Do you think your mom might stay until next week?"

"Nah," Corban said, jumping a scree of rocks. He landed hard on the other side and pedaled faster. "She's been gone for two days doing interviews and taking meetings."

"Do you miss her?"

"Yeah, I guess. Though it's nice not to have my parents being all moody around each other."

"That's still weird?" Kari slowed down, encouraging Corban to do the same beside her.

"And getting weirder."

"Oh …"

Kari didn't end her sentence, because what else could she say? She'd tried, but Corban never took the conversational ball.

She found another way to finish. "And Levi's still being a dick?"

"Yep."

He didn't want to talk about that either.

But that was fine. They were almost there. And if things went down like he'd imagined once they reached the Gallows, they wouldn't be talking much anyway. It was time to start shifting the mood, and the silence was nice for that.

"You know what the problem is," Kari said a second later, "you won't admit how much you care, even though you care a lot, and so the fight never ends."

She slowed again, and now they were barely coasting. Corban didn't want to hear whatever Kari was about to say. He wanted to get to the Gallows and maybe undress her.

"I get it, Corban. It's easier to act like you don't miss your brother. But we both know that's bullshit."

"What are you trying to say, Kari?"

"What happened between you guys? And why won't you tell me?"

Corban didn't know how to answer, because although he'd expected something, it hadn't been that. He'd already told her he didn't want to talk about Levi. And until seconds ago, Kari had respected that.

But now the question was sitting like a stink between them.

He swung off his bike, now walking it down to the Gallows. A step ahead of Kari, so she couldn't see him fight to keep control of his face.

Kari stopped walking. "I'm serious, Corban."

Corban stopped walking, too. He turned back to Kari. "Why are you doing this?"

"Why are *you* doing this?" She shook her head with genuine confusion. "I hate what's happening between you guys, and not just because I feel sorry for you both. I don't like either of you as much as I did a month ago. And I don't want to stop liking you."

Kari looked like she was trying not to cry. Holding her gaze was horrible.

But Corban did it anyway.

"If there's a reason, fine. I'll support you. But I have to understand. Otherwise, I can't be with you. Is that what you want?"

"No."

"Then tell me, Corban. What happened between you and Levi?"

Finally, begrudgingly, "My dad is cheating on my mom."

"*What?*" Then, "What does that have to do with Levi?"

"I found something my dad wrote. I wasn't even snooping, really, I swear — stop looking at me like that, because I didn't do anything wrong and I wasn't invading his privacy. I know how you feel about that, and that's not what this is. Anyway, there was this file and there was some sick shit in it about her naked body and how he wanted to be inside it and all kinds of crap. A bunch of paragraphs like that, over and over and over and ov—"

"I get it. What made it sick?"

"I don't know … the detail? That he used the word *young* a bunch of times."

"Gross. How young?"

"I don't think young like that, it didn't feel that way. But it was graphic, and she's definitely not my mom. There was just something obsessive about it. Like he's in love, but not with her so much as the idea of her? Or her body? But it wasn't even that. I don't know, it was hard to explain. It just—"

"Pissed you off. I can see that. I'm sorry. So what about Levi?"

"I told him and he was an asshole about it. He defended our dad, of course. But then he got mad at me. Said that I shouldn't have been snooping, and asked me how I would have liked it if Dad had been looking on my computer and reading my private shit."

"He has a point."

"Do you want to hear this or not?"

"Sorry."

"Levi refused to read it. I practically begged him. I *did* beg him. But he wouldn't budge. He said that was a line he wouldn't cross, and that he couldn't believe that I had. He asked me all kinds of questions, like whether or not Dad actually confessed to any sort of cheating, or whether it was just descriptions of naked chicks. He said it would make sense that our dad liked word porn, and made a whole joke about it. But he wasn't getting it, and couldn't unless he read it, which he wouldn't do, no matter what."

"Look, I totally want to understand, but why are you sure that your dad is cheating on your mom? Would you have thought that if you came across his porn folder and saw a video he liked with some guy giving it to the babysitter?"

"It's not the same."

"What's the difference?"

"This came from him. From his mind. This is his specific fantasy."

"His *fantasy*."

"It's about a real person."

"How do you know?"

Corban drew a breath. This was frustrating. "Because of the detail. It's very first-person."

"Your dad is a writer."

"He writes jokes that aren't even that funny, and the character in this narrative was obviously him."

"So maybe your dad is cheating on your mom. I'm sorry if that's true. That really sucks. But why should that ruin your relationship with Levi? And why can't you just talk to your dad?"

"Because I don't know if I want to. Even if I did, Levi forbid me."

"He *forbid* you?"

"Yeah, I guess. He said that if I talked to our dad about it then it would only hurt everyone. But that wasn't the worst part."

Kari waited for him to force the words through clenched teeth.

"We both said a lot of shit. About how our mom prefers me and our dad prefers him and the feelings are all mutual." Corban bit his bottom lip to keep from crying.

Kari took his hands. "Oh, Corban."

They stared into each other's eyes.

He was hungry to make his move, and had been forever.

But maybe now he was starving.

Not that he wanted to take advantage of Kari feeling sorry for him. This wasn't that at all.

The river was gleaming, and the sun was shining, together with the clouds, and everything seemed to agree: *Kiss her, Corban.*

And so he did, first taking her by the hands without daring to break away from her eyes, then slowly drifting in to kiss her.

Kari kissed him back, wet and long and harder than he expected, pushing her face aggressively into his.

Buzz.

And then they were on the dirt, rolling around, their tongues tasting each other.

Her hand was under his shirt, but only for a moment, and then it was already in his pants.

Buzz. Buzz.

That felt like an invitation, so Corban's hand went up her shirt.

She liked it there, pressed herself into it.

Buzz. Buzz.

Buzz.

He could feel her trying not to react to the buzzing in her jacket pocket, but now Corban's was buzzing too.

Buzz. Buzz.

She kissed him harder, wrapped her hand around his shaft.

Corban whimpered without meaning to, then leaned back as she scrambled between his legs.

Buzz. Buzz. Buzz.

Buzz. Buzz. Buzz.

They stopped. They looked. They had no other choice.

Kari's hand left his pants. His heart was pounding.

Buzz.

Buzz. Buzz.

Buzz. Buzz. Buzz.

Their phones were blowing up for a reason.

The Almond Alert. Another family found, all of them dead at their picnic.

And the mother had a bright blue scarf with yellow bees tied around her neck.

Chapter Twenty

Adam held Selena's hand, the two of them sitting on the couch, holding court while everyone in the room gathered around the TV to watch her interview with Isla Porter. Even the twins and their friends seemed excited.

Onscreen, Selena seemed to consider Isla's question, then crossed her legs and said, "There is zero doubt in my mind that we are looking at a serial killer."

"And what makes you so sure?" Isla asked.

"It's not the three dead families. It's the three scarves. It wouldn't have been easy to convince me that these were *accidents*. Even alone they feel like murder, but once we're adding totems into the mix, I don't see how anyone could doubt that there's a serial killer involved."

As Adam expected, and surely just as Selena had wanted her to, Isla asked her to explain what she meant by the word *totem*. With every interview, Selena was getting better and better at taking control of the conversation.

"Your mom looks huge on TV," Elliot said, probably to Levi since Corban was on the other side of the room, extra close to Kari.

"Thanks, Elliot," Selena said, though she was smiling at the kid and clearly took no offense.

"I don't mean you look *big*, Mrs. Nash," Elliot tried to correct himself. "Like, you're not fat. You just look really giant on the screen … compared to how you are … sitting on the couch right now."

"I understand." Selena smiled at Elliot, trying not to laugh as he blushed.

"At least we're not in the game room," Pussabo added, not so helpfully. "Then she'd be even bigger."

The game room had the biggest TV in the house, with more than a hundred inches of 4K, but that space belonged to the kids — not just Levi and Corban, but their friends too — so Selena and Adam only entered when absolutely necessary. The cleaning crew came every other Friday, and that was enough to know that parental intervention wasn't needed.

"You've been advising the Almond Creek Police Department. Is that correct?"

"Yes." Selena nodded onscreen. "I'm not working with them in any official capacity, but I am a concerned neighbor with an understanding of a serial killer's mind, so they've naturally been asking me questions."

"And one of your *concerned neighbor* conversations was about the third scarf, correct?"

"That is correct."

"And it took place just after its discovery. Is that right, too?"

"It is." Selena nodded.

"Would you like to tell us about that?"

"The scarves are an interesting choice of totem, because up until the third one they were especially difficult to trace. Either scarf could have easily fit into either woman's closet. There was nothing especially unique about them. But the third was different."

"And what was different?" Isla asked, even though her bright eyes said that she already knew.

"It was the bees," Selena said, emphatic. "The mother at the third scene, Julia Hendricks, *hated bees*. And everyone knew it. She was allergic and had almost died twice. She hated the sight of them. That's a scarf she never would have bought, or had in her closet. That meant it was clearly there to get attention, and tied around the victim's neck *after* her death. If attention was true for the third scarf, then it was surely true for the other two as well."

Onscreen, Selena leaned back in her chair, clearly pleased with her answer.

Adam squeezed her hand and whispered in her ear, "You're doing great!"

Selena smiled, her eyes still fixed on her onscreen self as Adam surveyed the room.

Corban and Kari were so close, they looked almost conspiratorial. They weren't holding hands, but they might as well have been as they sat in the oversized chair off to the side of the loveseat, barely big enough to seat the two of them.

Levi was half-watching the TV, but the rest of the time his gaze was on his brother and Kari, whenever it seemed like he could steal a withering glance. Adam hated to see them fighting over a girl, but at least now he was starting to understand why they'd been at each other so much. It was almost a relief. Such a normal teenage thing.

And in no way his fault.

Blood was thicker than water, especially for a Nash. They weren't just brothers, they were twins. They were—

Then he saw it.

Something that shouldn't be boiling his blood like it was.

Dane, watching him. Staring without any clue that he was being inappropriate. He smiled.

Despite the anger inside him, Adam smiled back.

Then he turned to the TV, a deliberate dismissal to let the boy know he didn't care.

Adam wanted to jump up from the couch, yank the little asshole to his feet, and beat him bloody. Every instinct he had screamed that Dane was a threat.

But he didn't know why.

Dane's smile was pleasant enough.

And now he seemed glued to the TV like everyone else.

Selena's interview ended and the room erupted in applause. Beaming, she stood and made a little bow with a joking flourish of her hand.

"Awesome job, Mom!" Corban shouted.

Kari echoed, "Yeah, that was great!"

"You kicked ass, Mom!"

"That was amazing, even as big as you were." Elliot chuckled uncomfortably.

Dane said, "You were mesmerizing."

Mesmerizing?

Is he undressing her with his eyes?

He might be. That little fucker was practically leering.

Except he wasn't so little. Dane was bigger than Adam and had been for more than a year. Maybe two. At least he was taller. Adam was still wider than Dane in the shoulders, and would make him feel it when he eventually pressed one of them into his pulsing throat, just long enough to make him start choking before Adam cut it and—

Enough. He'd never had so much trouble controlling his murderous fantasies. And they'd never been focused on

119

another male. He needed to stop this long enough to figure out what was wrong with him.

He forced himself to smile at Selena. "I'm so proud of you, honey. You owned the interview. If my calculations are correct, Sam should be over the moon."

She laughed.

He took a breath, and then a second deeper one. But the desire to tear Dane apart got more intense, not less.

Something was wrong. This wasn't like before.

This wasn't how the thoughts usually came. They felt more urgent. More dangerous. He had to speak with Selena.

But how could he tell her about this? About who he was thinking of? Or why he was thinking it?

Things would get ugly fast. Sure, Dane was eighteen. But he was a junior like the boys, and Selena would defend him on the basis of his youth.

She turned to Dane, practically glowing. "Mesmerizing, huh? I don't know that I've ever been called mesmerizing before."

"You have," Dane said. "Alicia Ayers from *First Murder on The Left* called you mesmerizing in episode ninety-three. I'm just agreeing with her. She's almost as interesting as you."

"Is that what you do? Collect women who interest you?" Adam regretted the words as the room went silent and everyone looked at him like he'd grown a second head.

He was out of control and even his kids could see it. But he couldn't stop himself.

"Don't we all?" Dane said, completely unfazed. "I collect everything that interests me."

"And what are your interests, specifically?"

Dane looked thoughtful in his silence, as if deeply considering his answer. "Everything interesting."

He didn't *look* like he was trying to be a smartass. His face was honest and tranquil. Completely sincere.

Maybe he was wrong about Dane, but that didn't stop Adam from picturing himself turning the kid's face to blood pudding. By the time he was done punching it in, Dane's head would look like a bowl of tomato soup.

He shifted his thoughts to the girl with the blood-red lipstick instead.

That would help.

Her naked body, covered in blood.

"I'm sorry if I offended you in some way, Mr. Nash."

Everyone was looking at him. He forced a laugh from his throat. "Not at all, Dane. I'm just giving you a hard time." Then, he couldn't help but add, "Like you probably give your father."

This was surreal.

He wasn't taking any pleasure in cutting the kid down. He was feeling worse by the insult, and horrified by the anger lurking behind it all. Adam had lost it, seeing things that weren't there. He had to be imagining that glint of hostility under the surface that no one else seemed to notice. The hints that Dane wasn't the super nice guy he was pretending to be.

Something inside him coiled in oily knots.

Dane is up to something. He's too interested in Selena.

But the look on Levi's face made Adam stand down.

Levi was usually the one to jump in and join him in batting insults back and forth, but right now he was chewing on his lip with disappointment in his eyes. Adam and Dane were breathing the loudest, enough that everyone could hear them.

Selena was a statue, putting visible effort into doing nothing.

Adam had to apologize. Somehow make this right.

He opened his mouth to say he was sorry and more, but no one was paying attention, the room's focus having been jerked back to the TV by a newsflash.

Then the anchor finished the announcement — a break in what the press was now calling the Almond Park Killings — and Kari started to scream.

Chapter Twenty-One

Corban tried to hold her, but Kari was hysterical.

Sobbing, she ran outside for fresh air, but it didn't look like it was doing much good, despite her gasping and choking and sucking tiny sips of it through her teeth.

He wanted to tell her that everything was going to be okay, but given what they had just heard on the news, why would she believe him?

She finally swallowed a mouthful of snot, then sputtered, "He … he's being investigated …" More sobs, then, "What the fuck, Corban? What am I supposed to do?"

And then it was like her outside lost all of its insides and Kari collapsed against him, soaking his shirt with her tears.

"There's nothing tying him to the third murder. The news reported that. So they don't have anything. My mom would say that's circumstantial evidence."

"He's being investigated! And I found out at the same time as the rest of the world!" She gasped. Covered her mouth. "My mom! Oh my God, my mom! I have to call her."

Kari pulled away from Corban, fumbled in her pockets, then almost dropped her phone twice on its way to her ear.

Corban gently took it away.

"Hold on. You can't call your mom yet. She's probably freaking out too. Doing it on the phone together won't help either of you. Let me take you home."

Kari didn't fight, just started to whimper.

"It was an anonymous tip. My mom would also tell you that there's always a good chance that means it was a neighbor with a beef, or something worse. The best tips are rarely anonymous. Everything is going to be okay."

Corban remembered her father's strange behavior, but he wasn't about to bring it up now.

Ollie coming home and slamming doors.

Pacing inside while they were out on the porch, ranting and raving on the phone about Lakeway Estates, the site of the second killings.

But maybe she was thinking the same thing, because she finally said, "Do you think …?"

"No." Corban shook his head. "Of course not."

But maybe he did. His mom said that anything was possible, and this was definitely anything. Corban couldn't imagine, and was dying to ask her what she thought.

"But it doesn't matter, does it?" Kari looked up at him helplessly. "Even if he's innocent, no one will ever look at him the same again. Same for my mom."

Her lip trembled, she tried harder to hold it this time, but eventually Kari collapsed against its weight and fell forward into Corban's arms again.

He held her, knowing that she was right. Everything had changed. For Kari's father and everyone in his orbit.

Things would be different for her at home, and surely at his as well. Along with anywhere and everywhere Kari went in Almond Park. But Corban had no doubt about where her nightmare would play hardest, and where she would want to scream the loudest.

Kids could be cruel, and in the waters of Wembley High, the sharks were already circling.

Chapter Twenty-Two

Selena looked up from her notes as Corban entered her office, his eyes red and puffy, looking more like a child than he had in forever.

"Mom," he pleaded, "you have to make them take it back."

Her heart twinged as she saw the faith in his eyes that somehow she could fix this. She chose her words carefully.

"Detective Sharpe wouldn't question Ollie unless he had a good reason to."

"But you can explain to the cops that it's not him."

"It's not my place to—"

"Bullshit." Corban actually kicked her desk, his face crumpling. "That detective asked who you thought it was. He'd believe you."

Selena laced her fingers together and sat up straighter, readying her most reasonable tone. "You're asking me to risk my professional reputation to interfere with a police investigation, for the sake of a girl whose father might be guilty."

"Dad's right. You make everything about you."

"If Ollie's innocent, Detective Sharpe will let him go."

"By then, it'll be too late. Kari's life is ruined and you don't even care."

"Corban, I—"

But he bolted, slamming the door behind him.

He's only a kid. Someday he'll understand.

A part of her thought he already got it: that she'd sacrifice his girlfriend — or anyone else — if it meant grabbing another rung in her career.

But Selena had merely assembled the facts and passed them to Sharpe. How was it her fault if Ollie was in the wrong place at the wrong time?

Chapter Twenty-Three

"Want to hear another one?"

Selena knew he didn't before she looked up from the letter.

"Sure," Adam said anyway. Humoring her.

She looked down at the pile and picked another envelope from her desk at random. He could've left three letters ago if he'd just shown her the courtesy of at least acting excited for a minute or two, instead of letting her see he was bored — maybe even annoyed — with her success.

The letters were always interesting, and sometimes fun. Today there were plenty of both types. And it was nice to see them all in a pile. Her ratio of emails to letters was at least ten to one, but Selena could never get excited about the stuff she read on a screen.

Her P.O. Box got hit with a dozen letters the day after her interview. Yesterday, almost twenty. Today, thirty-one. They were all over the place so far, though that wasn't unusual. Selena had seen it all, read the creepiest confessions, from murderous thoughts to things that person wanted to do to her. Most of it excited her, even the letters telling Selena that she would go directly to hell with all the murderers she made excuses for. She'd never had so many all at once. Her career had finally reached escape velocity, headed straight for the stars.

She opened the envelope, plucked out the letter, and read it aloud.

Dear Ms. Selena Nash,

Thank you for the brave work you do to understand something that most people will never try to. I used to think I was crazy, because I could never get these thoughts outta my head. It was always the same. I would grab someone, in my mind she usually had dark curly hair in tight little ringlets. I would take her and put tape over her mouth so she couldn't scream. Then I could put the cuffs on her. I always do the tape first and the handcuffs second. I keep all of that stuff in a box in my closet. It's full of other kinds of toys, so no one will ever think anything if they look.

Selena looked up from the letter and gave him a wink. "Kinky."

Adam gave her a thin-lipped smile.

I first got the handcuffs before I ever had the thoughts, back when I was into this girl who was into that kind of stuff, the handcuffs I mean, and so we liked to play with them, but then things didn't work out with her and so I moved on and eventually I started wanting to use the cuffs on someone else, even if they didn't like it so much. I thought I could get them into one of my rooms and I could leave the tape on and same for the handcuffs and we could watch porn together. Maybe they would warm up after a while but probably not and if they don't then it will have to go violent. But if they were good then I give them a bath.

She looked up again. "This is still all one paragraph. The whole letter is *Dear Ms. Selena Nash,* and then allthewords."

"Is it over?"

She continued reading.

All of this is the stuff I can't talk about with anybody because nobody would ever understand me or even want to. I told two people and then I could never tell them again. Twice. Because sometimes you have to delete stuff. I delete stuff on my computer all the time. Sometimes there are crime scene photos and you can buy them and if they are really gross they are exciting too. I bet you see stuff like that all the time. I like all of that and the porn but not with the kids that's not for me. Anyway to tell the truth this is all the stuff I think about and like I said I can't really talk about it with anyone but maybe you could like me too. I have supplies if I ever meet you, and maybe you could like sex with me together. Or—

"Why are you reading this?"

"People's most intimate confessions? The heartbreaking, the brilliant, the daffy … you love this stuff."

"You should report this."

"There's nothing to report."

"How does that one end, the one you're reading now?"

"I don't know. You haven't let me finish it."

"I'm sure you have an idea."

"What am I supposed to do, Adam? Take it to the police?"

"Yes, Selena. Take it to the police."

"Why? You've never wanted me to do that before."

"It's never been so close to home."

"*That's* what you're worried about?" She laughed. "If I thought there was any danger, or that the police could do anything with any of these letters, then I would pass them forward. But we both know I'd only be wasting their time."

"Why don't you give them to Detective Sharpe?"

"Reading these letters isn't part of his job."

"It is if this has something to do with the murders."

"Do *you* think that any of these letters have anything to do with the murders, beyond—"

"Let's just drop it."

"I don't want to *just drop it*. You're obviously bothered and I want to know why."

Adam looked at her like she was crazy. "You know why."

"No. I've always gotten letters, and I've always read them out loud. You've never reacted like this before. Not even close. Sometimes they've even turned you on. It's reasonable for me to want to understand the difference. If I'm doing something wrong, don't you want me to know what that is so I don't do it again?"

"You know what it is because it's the same conversation every goddamned time. We're all happy for you, really we are, but we're also all a little sick of The Selena Show."

"Thank you for telling me that, Adam." She started pacing. "So … what? Are you and the boys having little pow-wows behind my back? Should I brace myself for an intervention?"

"No. But I can tell that what the boys want most is to be your sons, not your audience."

The moment settled. Selena was already feeling sorry. She took a breath and stopped pacing, then she half-smiled at Adam and walked over to take his hands.

"I really am sorry. I'm not trying to be negligent with you guys, or make this all about me. I'm just listening to Sam, and he says that it's time to capitalize on all of this. Everything is happening fast, and while I can't exactly stop the murders, or control what's going down in Almond Park, I can control how it affects our family. This isn't just about striking while the iron is hot. It's glowing red right now, and Sam doesn't think we're going to have to wait on the pilot, because within the next couple of days we're going to hear that they've ordered *at least* a half-season up front."

"I get all that. But I'm not talking about any one

specific thing that you're doing …" Adam drew a breath. "I just mean that you're making this — *all of this* — all about you."

That was fair. But Selena couldn't exactly argue that point.

Because she knew what he didn't.

This *was* all about her. And she had proof, or at least so much as such a thing was possible in a situation like this.

Something tightened in her gut. A very specific sort of hunger. She needed to see it for herself yet again.

"I'm really sorry," she said, squeezing his hands tighter. "I promise to try harder."

They stood in her office, holding hands. He obviously wanted to believe her, but the anger in his eyes still intensified.

"Okay," he finally said. "Thanks."

His fingers tightened around hers, and he leaned closer, like he was thinking of kissing her.

Absolutely not. She was not rewarding his pissy, jealous behavior with sex. "I've got more work to do. Sam needs—"

Adam dropped her hands like Selena was an open flame.

"Of course. Whatever Sam needs. We know what's most important."

She let him stomp out, and stayed in her office long enough after he left to make it seem like she was finishing something up, but each one of the eleven minutes spent behind the closed door felt close to an hour of waiting.

When she did leave her office, she didn't see Adam anywhere downstairs. Their bedroom was mercifully empty, so she went straight to her closet.

She dug through everything again, but they were still there, just like they were the last time she'd checked.

The red scarf, the green scarf, and most chillingly, the bright blue one with the yellow bees.

Selena couldn't believe she'd missed it after the first two scarves, though she had an excuse, seeing as how they were both solid colors and rather generic. But the third had been practically blinking in neon.

After that third scarf was discovered, and Selena realized just what she was seeing and what that might mean, she couldn't wait to get to her closet, not quite knowing if she was nervous or excited or terrified or all of the above.

But all of her scarves were there, so the killer hadn't been in her house so much as paying close attention.

To her.

Selena loved wearing scarves and had quite the supply. She never would have started it herself, but it began one night in her junior year of college while club-hopping with her roommate, Julie.

She and Julie were working the club with their usual goal — to have the time of their lives without spending a dime. It usually worked. When Selena and Julie put their minds to it, they could party hard for the cost of half a cab. This night, they met an Englishman visiting the States for three weeks. He'd worn the most hideous scarf that Selena had ever seen. It was almost ugly enough to be beautiful, like a bulldog. The Englishman defended it to no end, saying it was the very scarf that Doctor Who wore in the original series.

Julie giggled like a minx as she left the club with Doctor Who, then came back to their apartment Sunday afternoon, wearing the scarf but missing her bra. Julie gave the scarf to Selena.

It's magical. You should wear it when you want to get fucked all night like I did.

Julie still sent two scarves every year, one on her

birthday and another on Christmas. She hadn't missed even one over the years. So yes, Selena had a lot of scarves. But that one with the bees was too distinctive to ignore.

Now her heart was pounding.

Because she'd just noticed that the Doctor Who scarf — which had been hanging on a hook in her closet, so that she could see it whenever she opened the door, a reminder of those happy days and the friend she'd shared them with — was gone.

And after seven minutes of searching, each one more frantic than the last, Selena was certain. The Doctor Who scarf wasn't in her closet.

She thought hard.

Had she moved it, displaced it somehow while obsessing over the other three?

She hadn't, she was sure of it. Someone had taken it.

Someone was trying to get her attention.

She'd had that thought before, but this time it felt like a plane falling from the sky to land on her psyche.

Adam.

What if for all of these years, she had been wrong? What if he didn't have a simple, bloody fetish? What if he *was* a serial killer and her lack of attention had pushed him into the arms of his inner monster?

The hair on her arms was standing and her shoulders were pinched in knots. Her entire body felt stiff and heavy.

She had to talk to Adam.

So Selena closed her closet and went downstairs.

But he wasn't in the living room or the kitchen or his office or anywhere else in the house.

Adam was gone.

Chapter Twenty-Four

Selena couldn't sleep.

How could she? There was a murderer out there planting scarves at the scene of his crimes, and the three so far just happened to match scarves in her closet?

And now her favorite was missing, along with a husband who knew that scarf's story?

A husband who'd stormed out of the house in a near-rage?

He hadn't answered his phone. He wanted her to wonder. To worry that she'd unleashed something terrible on the world.

Maybe he wanted her to figure out that he'd finally made the leap to murderer.

She called again. No answer.

She dropped the phone on her nightstand with a thunk and turned over, blinking hard and hugging the pillow close.

To make it worse, tonight was game night for Levi and his friends. Usually it was hooting and cheering and the too-realistic cacophony of sudden violence as they hunted aliens or conquered monster bosses. But tonight, the faint moaning told her they were watching porn on the biggest screen possible, thinking they'd turned the volume down far enough that she wouldn't hear.

Teenage boys. Jesus.

She should say something. But right now, she couldn't stand to face her son. Not when she might have pushed his father over the edge of a very tall cliff.

So instead, she tossed and turned and worried and waited.

Another hour passed. It was inching toward midnight and Adam still wasn't home. Levi and his friends should be quieting down, but they weren't.

She turned around and buried her face in the pillow. Selena had worn all three scarves in public, and even though she only found one of the three on Google Images, that didn't mean there weren't more out there or that a picture of her in the bee scarf, which she wore while speaking at CrimeCon, wouldn't appear at any minute on Facebook, along with the headlines to follow. The kind that would make Sam want to kill her.

Serial Killer Expert Duped By Her Own Husband. Or worse, *Serial Killer Expert Covers For Husband's Murder Spree.*

Something like a machine gun mating with a laser tore through the house. The boys were back to their video games. She threw off the covers, swung her feet onto the hardwood floor, and marched toward the door. When she yanked it open—

Dane stood there, one foot on the top stair and the other in the hallway, frozen. Holding a bag of chips in one hand and a bowl of pretzels in the other.

"Mrs. Nash," he breathed.

"Selena." She felt a rush of warmth and wondered again where her husband might be, but not because she wished he'd come home right then. "What are you doing?"

He looked down at his hands, moving his eyes from the chips to the pretzels. "Snack run."

Another machine gun laser blast.

"It's way too loud, right?" Dane gave Selena an apologetic smile. "I'm sorry."

"Yes, it is." She glanced at his snacks. "You guys shouldn't be eating that crap this late. Why don't you come with me to the kitchen where I can't hear the world ending upstairs. I'll make you a plate, and you can tell the guys to keep it down for the rest of the night. Okay?"

Dane smiled. He took the final step into the hallway, then another three steps back as he gestured toward the stairs. "After you."

Selena could feel him behind her as he descended. Not quite like someone's breath on her neck, but close.

The way he had paused on the stairs, it was almost as if he was waiting for her.

But he couldn't have been. How could he have had any idea that she would even be leaving her room?

Her foot hit the floor at the bottom of the stairs and then he was there, right beside her, the two of them keeping pace on their way to the kitchen, striding in an uncomfortable, overheated silence.

Selena got a fresh loaf of bread and started to slice it. Then the meat and the mayo and cheese. She sliced tomatoes and cut the lettuce while he watched her, both of them breathing heavily enough to hear but neither speaking.

The tension made Selena want to scream. But if she broke it, what would come falling out? She needed to guide them back to a safer place. A place where she was the mother-figure and he was the boy in need of some TLC.

She put the last finished sandwich on a plate with the

others and slid it over to Dane. "Is everything okay? You seem ... upset, or something."

He gave her what looked like a hard-won smile. "Thanks for asking. I'm good."

"You don't sound good."

Another smile, but this one came easier. "Really, I'm fine. Just the usual bullshit."

"Stanford?"

He took a deep breath and nodded. "In part."

"Anything you want to talk about?"

Dane shook his head. "I'll take these upstairs and turn it down. Sorry we woke you."

"I wasn't sleeping anyway." Seconds of silence and fathoms of depth. "But I'm glad I got out of bed."

"Me too," he said.

More silence.

Selena tried to read his face, but she was a tourist without a map in whatever this was.

Watching her watch him, he asked, "What are you thinking?"

"That you seem disappointed."

"What would I be disappointed about?"

"You tell me?"

He sighed. He shrugged. He shifted. "I've just been thinking a lot."

A note of excitement, vibrating too long like an electric chord. "About what?"

"About the killings ... of course."

"What about the killings?"

"Do you agree with the police? Do you think that Kari's dad did it?"

Selena had to look away.

"You do, don't you?"

"I didn't say that." She swallowed, then forced herself to look back.

"You didn't have to. Maybe you're the one who is disappointed."

Another note. The music was getting sweeter.

"What would I be disappointed about?"

"Mr. Nash doesn't seem too crazy about your new career. Maybe all of this stuff makes you feel alive, but it's making him feel left out."

"Maybe you've been talking too much to Levi."

"Maybe Levi didn't tell me anything."

More silence. And then Selena surprised herself with a laugh, and said something she shouldn't. "You're right, in a way. He should know better, but right now he doesn't seem to realize—"

Her voice fell into a whisper. Considering what she was saying, anything louder seemed an atrocity. And she shouldn't be saying it to Dane. Selena could never admit this to Adam. Especially not if he was the killer and he was doing this to get her attention, to compete with her budding career. She absolutely could not do anything to make him think she *wanted* him to act on his violent desires.

But she had no one to talk to. No one who understood why she loved what she did.

At least Dane tried to get it.

"I love the puzzle part of this, piecing everything together and getting inside the killer's mind, but this time is different. Because it's right here in town, and it's directly affecting my career. Repeat this to Levi and I might just have to tie a scarf around *your* neck, but I practically want to write this guy a thank you letter."

"I would never—"

The front door slammed. Selena's heart pounded harder.

Adam's footsteps echoed through the silent house, a counterpoint to distant, muffled echo of the game room racket.

Then he appeared in the kitchen doorway. He looked from Selena to Dane, lip curling as if he could smell the intimacy between them.

There was nothing to do but go on the offensive, so Selena said, "Where have you been?"

Chapter Twenty-Five

Adam sat in his Porsche 356 outside The Inside Scoop, watching the woman in the blood-red lipstick, imagining all of the dark and delicious things he'd love to do to her.

He could see her through the window, but she couldn't see him. Soon she would. And like the last several times, she would brighten the second she saw him. He would wait for her back to be turned away from the door, then he would enter, jingling the bell above it as he did. She would turn around, see him, and smile.

But for now, he watched. He liked the face that she made when she was working hard to scoop the ice cream, though it was always better up close. He liked watching her sweep, and he liked watching her unguarded expression when she checked her phone.

Most of all, he loved this shift best. When she was alone, waiting for him without even knowing what she was doing.

The last customer left the Scoop empty, except for the smell of ice cream and her.

He got out, locked the Porsche, crossed the street,

waited a beat for the woman to turn around, then entered, jingling the bell as the door closed behind him.

She looked up, met his eyes, and smiled. "You always come in right when I turn around!"

"That's funny," he said.

He felt better. Instantly cooler, and not just because of the air conditioning's kiss.

"The usual?" she asked.

Adam surveyed the many flavors, licking his lips as though the ice cream enticed him.

"You know I always like to look first."

"Right," she smiled, "That's your usual."

Adam's gaze settled on a simple coffee-colored cream with what sounded like a complex name, and not especially good. He wanted to hear what she said about it anyway. "How about that one? Is that good?"

"The Vietnamese Coffee with Frosted Almonds and Peanut Butter Curry? It's excellent. But different for sure. It's made with creamy peanut butter. The crunch comes from the candied almonds and the hot curry."

"Will I like it?"

She laughed. Her lipstick was faded, it didn't look quite as bloody as usual, but even so, the crimson blush on her mouth was still there. "Probably not. You usually like things a little simpler. But I think it's delicious."

"How about that one?" Adam pointed to one that was a Grinch shade of green.

"That's our pineapple cilantro sorbet."

Adam made a face. "I can read what it's called, I'm just wondering if anyone meant to put those flavors together."

Another laugh. "It's actually really good. The pineapple is sour and sweet, and the cilantro is grassy."

"Grassy, that's just what I want from my ice cream."

"It tastes like summer," she said without missing a beat.

And now Adam wanted to taste her.

"What do you recommend? I want to be surprised, but not too surprised if you know what I mean."

"I think I do." Another smile, the widest since Adam rang the bell.

He eyed her, imagined his hands around her neck, squeezing.

He saw her covered in blood, watched as the viscous fluid dribbled from a cut in her throat — shallow, so he had plenty of time to lick it up.

"Are you in the mood for chocolate?"

Adam was in the mood for exactly one thing. Chocolate wasn't it.

"Yes! Chocolate sounds perfect. What do you suggest?"

A giant smile as she pointed. "That one!"

Adam looked. "Spicy chocolate. Why do you only recommend flavors that I feel like I'll need a hipster card to even sample? I'm not nearly cool enough for any of these. When I was a kid, we thought cookies and cream was fancy."

"You seem pretty cool to me, and if you like chocolate and you like spicy, then you really should love this."

"I like both of those things, I've just never thought of them together."

"Wanna give it a try?"

"Tell you what … why don't you put whatever flavor you want to in a sundae, but I'm really in the mood for hot fudge. The ice cream is really just the hot fudge delivery vehicle, so you choose. Two scoops, and each one should be different."

"Perfect," she said, and went to work.

His jeans were already tenting as he watched her bend forward, fingers shifting on the handle of the scoop as she worked it into the frozen-stiff ice cream.

He'd been waiting for this all day.

Adam needed help, and there was only one person in the world who could aid him.

But Selena wasn't available. It was her fault he'd gone this far, that he'd crossed the line from fantasizing to making contact with the woman he fantasized about. He felt completely out of control and unable to stop himself. It seemed as if the universe was conspiring with everything living inside him to shove him through these doors.

Now he might have to kill her.

"How is this?" She displayed his bowl, now filled with a pair of generous scoops.

"Perfect. Now remember, there's no such thing as too much fudge. And I'm happy to pay extra!"

"I remember, and you know I'll never make you pay extra."

There might have been an ever-so-subtle glance at the tip jar, or maybe he'd imagined it. Then she started adding toppings, finishing with a liberal drizzling of fudge.

Adam watched. He imagined the syrup as blood and the scoops as her breasts. He thought of her body, naked and sticky. Nipples erect, before he suckled the blood off her skin.

Adam didn't know if he wanted to fuck or kill her more, as she held his dessert out to him like a trophy.

"How is this?"

"Perfect," he said.

"Great. I'll ring you up."

If he didn't do something soon, then the worst was going to happen.

And it was going to happen to her.

This was how it started. He would picture someone dead, and then he would see himself killing them. If Selena didn't help him to vent, eventually he would. Last night, seeing her with Dane, something about that had poured gasoline on the fire of his fantasies. The urges were growing more powerful, and Adam was no longer sure that he wanted to stop them.

She asked him for six dollars and seventeen cents, her red, red lips parted even in silence. Adam paid with a ten and told her to keep the change, still grateful for the counter between them. He didn't dare to press up against it like his body was wanting him to, but he was glad it was a wall to hide his hard-on.

"Thank you, Adam."

"Thank you, Poppy."

He took the sundae, then spun around and strode to the door before she could witness his arousal. He made it safely to the other side, waved while looking over his shoulder — Adam had done this before — then crossed the street to his Porsche.

He dropped his ice cream in the garbage can next to his car, then got inside.

And he watched as Poppy reapplied her lipstick.

Chapter Twenty-Six

"Then what did you do?" Selena looked at Adam, lying on her couch. It was all she could do not to hit him.

"I sat in the car for a few more minutes."

"What was she doing?"

"She put on her lipstick, and then she did some cleaning up."

"Did you relieve yourself?"

"Yes."

"While watching her?"

"Yes."

"And what were you thinking of?"

"Me and her and all the blood."

Selena shifted in her seat. Yes, she was irritated, but this was more than that. She was *upset*. Adam was acting on his urges for the first time, unless he had not always been as forthcoming as she imagined. Throughout their history, he merely fetishized imagery. Same as anyone, except his colors were uglier. But *this* was a threat to their relationship.

She was a beautiful, successful woman. Yet her

husband was sitting across from the ice cream shop, beating off to some sorority girl, in that little car that looked like a goddamned bathtub.

Why? Why was Adam doing this all of a sudden? What had changed? This felt like more than his usual need for attention. What if she had misjudged him?

What if he was a killer?

That would destroy her career and there would be no coming back from that.

"What did you do to try to control your impulses? Did you do any of our exercises?"

"No," Adam admitted.

"Why not?"

"Because I didn't want to."

"You can't *not want to*, Adam. We're talking about murder."

"Bloody murder."

"Yes, bloody murder," Selena repeated.

She was sure that Adam caught her irritation. But it didn't make him frown, like it usually did. He looked smug, and that was frightening.

She didn't seem to be getting anywhere with him, and she wasn't sure what to try next. This was frontier. And if she'd been wrong, if he was truly a serial killer, the things they'd done before wouldn't work. She'd been able to guide him in the past because she understood how a blood fetish worked, and because he believed he needed her to control his desire.

Maybe his saying that he didn't want to control it was his way of leveling up on his cries for attention. His way of saying, *You're going to keep ignoring me? Fine, I'll show you.*

She tested the theory by standing fast and snapping her red notebook shut. "If you're not willing to do the exercises, I'm not sure why we're bothering with this."

He stared at her for a moment, mouth falling open again. "That's it?"

"What else do you want?"

He shrugged, then swung his feet off the couch and stood in a violent lurch. "I don't know. Maybe something more than the bare minimum."

I knew it. This was just another way to whine for attention. Like a puppy who pees on the carpet because no one will play with it.

"I'm sorry if you think sitting here for an hour listening to you talk about waxing on and off in your car while looking at some Twinkie is fun for me. I'm sorry if seeing your redheaded homewrecker making a tent in your pants isn't a thrill ride for me. And I'm sorry that I'm not dying to hear the same goddamned bloody fantasies that I've been listening to for the last twenty years!"

That last one might've gone too far — she hadn't meant to suggest that she *wanted* him to stop playing at being a serial killer and actually become one. But honestly, she was so sick of playing the same game with him over and over, she'd blurted it without a thought.

He stared at her like he couldn't believe what he was hearing.

And sure enough, his cock was swollen.

Selena looked down, couldn't help it.

He saw her do it and knew the look in her eyes.

She wanted to unzip him, pull him out, wrap her hands and then her lips around it.

She wanted him behind her, one hand on her neck, holding her down, the other exploring her wetness.

She wanted his tongue and then she wanted his cock.

Adam was snarling. Angry and aroused.

He was about to fuck her like an animal. They'd done that before. Plenty. But something about his eyes told her that this time would be different.

Selena knew she was right as he charged.

His hands were around her arm, squeezing as he marched her over to the desk.

He pushed her down, harder than usual, and this time he tore off her panties. His fingers were there just like she wanted, rougher than he'd ever been before. But she was wet enough to take it.

She lifted her head from the desk, ever so slightly, and Adam pushed it back down.

And then he filled her.

It was deep and seething and wonderful. She rocked her ass against him, moaning.

Selena groaned. "Are you thinking of her?"

Adam grunted. "Yes."

"And all the blood?"

"So much blood ..."

His pounding was relentless, piercing her through the eyes. She hated the thought of it stopping.

"What are you ... thinking about ... now ...? Her ... or me?"

"I'm thinking about both of you." *Grunt.* "Fucking you and seeing her blood."

That was new. He'd never made her part of the fantasy. She was surprised to find that the horror aroused her even more. She'd heard his fantasy so many times, she could easily imagine herself bent over a strange woman's couch, Adam's blood-smeared fingers digging into her hips as he celebrated his first real kill.

She'd known that fear could be an aphrodisiac, but she'd never experienced it.

"Do you want to hurt me?"

"No," he said, pressing down harder on her body, roughly thrusting, though this pain was delicious.

"But you want to hurt her?"

Rapid panting, then, "Yes."

This was exquisite — the ugly, the savage, the elegant, all of it flooding her mind.

"What are you … thinking about now?"

Heaves and grunts. Adam was close.

Selena was already gone. She vented an inhuman growl, low and guttural. *"What are you thinking about, Adam?"*

He made a sound like a charging hog, then panted, "Killing …"

And then he did something he'd never done before.

He wrapped his hands around her throat.

Chapter Twenty-Seven

Selena stepped closer to the one-way mirror as Detective Sharpe circled his suspect on the other side of it, making a full revolution around the metal table before he finally sat across from Ollie Harris. He leaned forward as he looked down at his pad full of notes. Again.

"So why were you going to check on Mrs. Wahlberg, if you didn't have an appointment with her?"

"I already told you."

"Tell me again."

And so he did. The words were all different, they had been every time, but the underlying story still sounded like the truth. Ollie's attention was all over the place, and he was clearly agitated. He wouldn't make eye contact with Sharpe, at least not for longer than a few seconds at a time. The detective obviously didn't trust him, but he had yet to catch the man in a lie.

Selena sighed and checked her phone again. She wanted to see this through, but so far there had been little to see. When they filmed the episode about Ollie as a suspect, they'd probably skip this part altogether and summarize Sharpe's discoveries.

She turned back to the interrogation, curious to see what the detective would do next, because what were you supposed to do when holding such a shitty hand? Ollie's link to the two families wasn't strong enough to make a legitimate case.

But Almond Park was on edge, and in need of someone to blame. Ollie was an excellent candidate. Weird enough for his own wacky show. Selena wondered who would eventually play him.

Sharpe said, "Hey, I gotta joke. Wanna hear it?"

Ollie blinked four times and then his neck twitched. "Probably not."

"How do you keep the neighbor kids from playing in your yard?" A long uncomfortable moment, then, "You fuck one of them."

Sharpe laughed, but Ollie didn't.

The detective finished laughing, and then loudly exhaled. "You do know what people say about you, don't you, Harris?"

Of course he did. He ignored them, because what else could he do? Protesting just made you look guiltier. Selena doubted that Sharpe was going to break Ollie by repeating rumors he'd probably been living with for years.

Ollie's words, his mannerisms, his tics, all of them broadcast that something was wrong with him. He was downright unsocial, too. When Selena had first invited the Harris family over for dinner, Ollie declined, saying that he had deipnophobia, or a morbid fear of dinner parties.

Her gut said that he was the killer, even though he wasn't displaying any of the typical signs. There was a certain magnetism to his personality, despite his quirks. If only she could put her finger on why he seemed so off.

Not just to stop the killings. It would also be a coup for her career. She was desperate for any sort of real life success that wasn't dependent on her research with Adam, and Fate had put this in her yard. That had to mean something, didn't it?

The interview ended with nothing conclusive. Selena stayed behind the glass until Sharpe returned for her thoughts.

"I don't know," Selena admitted.

The detective slowly nodded, thinking.

They promised to keep in touch, then Selena went out to her car.

When she'd first tipped him off about Ollie, his manner was skeptical or condescending or suspicious or something. He didn't seem all that impressed now, either. She might be losing her chance to participate in the investigation. And if the cops caught someone other than whoever she thought it might be, her credibility would take an unfortunate hit.

She drove home, thinking about Almond Park, and how much their city was changing. This would put it on the map. Give it an identity. Before it was just a place, one of the few in California where the opportunity hadn't mostly been snatched. But now it was the place where *that thing* happened. And everyone would know that Selena Nash called it home.

She tried to keep her thoughts in that lane as she drove, thinking about the inevitable book or film or television adaptation that would one day follow this story. The elements were too good, and having an expert mere inches from the killing lent the whole thing a Hollywood air.

Selena wondered who might play *her.* Connie Britton would be perfect.

Chapter Twenty-Eight

When Selena arrived at home, dinner was on the table. It was Adam's night to cook. Usually, he'd "cook" by taking the family out or bringing home takeout. But a few months ago, he'd subscribed to BistroBox, and he'd been experimenting with making gourmet meals with the pre-measured ingredients. Of course, Adam acted like he invented the recipes.

Selena and the rest of the family went along with it, mostly because they thought it was funny. But tonight, she had to make an effort.

"These are delicious," she said, biting into her Cajun shrimp taco.

"Thanks. It has paprika, ground yellow mustard, marinated peppers and tomatoes, oregano, with fresh carrot and celery slaw." Adam grinned, enjoying the role of gourmet chef. He turned to Levi. "Do you like it?"

"It's great, Dad. Thanks."

Adam looked at Corban, who said, "Congratulations, you're really great at reading the ingredients and following the directions on the box."

"Corban ..." Selena said.

He didn't say sorry, or anything.

Levi broke the awkward silence. "Hey Corban, if you're not too busy being a loser, would you mind passing the tortillas?"

And there it was again.

"Knock it off, Levi ..." It sounded like Adam was going to say more, but he trailed off into the same uncomfortable silence that had been hovering over the table.

Levi rolled his eyes and went back to eating. Corban looked a million miles away. He'd been alternating between sullen and despondent since Ollie had been identified as a suspect.

And, Selena thought, as something gnarled part of her into knots, *it's about to get a lot harder. For his family, and for Corban.*

She took the last bite of her taco, then wiped her hands and mouth as she looked around the table. "Why don't we have a little get-together this weekend? A small one?"

They all wore the same dubious expression for completely different reasons.

But at least they were listening.

"Not like the barbecue. Nothing like that." She waited a beat, then finished, "We could have Kari's family over."

The silence was heavy.

Corban looked down at his plate as he loudly swallowed. "Her dad has deipnophobia."

"What's that?" Adam asked.

"A morbid fear of dinner parties," he answered.

Adam looked at Selena. "He doesn't really have that, does he?"

"I don't think so."

Corban snorted. "And you know because ...?"

Selena shrugged, focused on Adam as the potentially

reasonable one. "Kari is important to Corban and Levi, so that makes her family important to us. We can show a little solidarity."

"I'll double up the next BistroBox order." Adam turned to Corban. "But only if this sounds good to you."

Corban nodded, refusing to meet anyone's eyes. Levi looked suspicious.

But Adam smiled at her. She could read the thoughts in his eyes. He was pleased with her, for wanting to spend more time with the family and for trying to do something nice for Corban.

Guilt gobbled at her insides. If he knew that she'd suggested it to get deeper insight into Ollie, in an informal environment where his guard might come down …

He'd hate her for it. They all would.

Chapter Twenty-Nine

Corban looked around their backyard, feeling a sort of awkward disgust.

"Sorry," he said to Kari.

"What are you sorry about?"

"Everything." He shrugged. "All of this."

"Your family invited my family over when everyone else is being weird. Isn't that a good thing?"

"Yeah, of course. But, you know, your dad, he's not comfortable with stuff like this, right?"

Kari laughed, a light little twitter. "Yeah, I know my dad. If you expected him to ever be comfortable in any situation, then you don't really know him well at all."

"I guess."

"After last week ... I just want to be with you. And my mom was so happy to be invited. She's been shut up in the house all week. She couldn't even go to the grocery store."

"I'm sorry about that."

"I'm sorry that everyone's whispering and staring when you hold hands with me between classes." She looked sad.

"If you stay with me, they're eventually going to hate you too."

"How bad do you think it's going to get? You know, at school?"

"If they'd just find another suspect, then everyone will feel sorry for me. Maybe I'll get enough pity votes to be homecoming queen."

Corban laughed. "You'll never be homecoming queen. You would have to kill Chelsea first."

"That can be arranged." Kari slammed a fist into her palm. "I know my dad is innocent. I just don't know how to prove it."

"If they don't …" He didn't even want to think about what would happen if Ollie went to jail. "No matter how bad it gets, I promise to stick with you, no matter what."

"I know."

"I won't let anything happen to you."

"I know."

And now he wanted to tell Kari that he loved her, but Corban could already hear the *I know* on her lips, and he wasn't sure he could stand to hear it. Not when he'd already told her he loved her once, and she hadn't said it back.

Corban nodded toward the adults, his father turning the meat on the grill while the other three sat around a small table shaded by an umbrella. They'd already consumed what appeared to be a vacation's worth of cocktails, and there was still more than an hour until dinner.

Everyone was laughing loud. Dad must be delivering some of his better one-liners.

"Where's your brother?" Kari asked out of the blue.

Corban shrugged. "Inside somewhere. Probably playing *HardCorp*. His way of pouting, since our parents said that he couldn't have any of his friends over while you guys were here. My mom said that this evening was about getting to know your family better."

"That was nice of her."

"Yeah, but he's still inside the house like an asshole."

"I think he's mad at me."

"He's mad at me."

"It isn't the same between us, either. We always used to joke around, and now it feels like he's always giving me dirty looks. Half the time when we talk, it feels like he's insulting me."

"That's because you're probably either standing next to me, or you're going to be later and he's trying to save time."

"Maybe you guys should make up."

An angry glance at his father, then Corban shook his head. "Maybe Levi should start caring a little more about this family, and the fact that our dad is a liar."

There was a long pause, as though Kari didn't really want to say the rest. But then she did. "You don't have all the facts. What you saw could have been out of context. Or who knows, maybe your parents have an open relationship or something. Like Will and Jada Pinkett Smith."

"They have an open relationship?"

"I'm sure I read that somewhere." Kari's voice dropped to a whisper. "Look. I'm sure you can guess that my parents are having a really hard time right now. Like, *really hard*. My dad is being even weirder than usual; last night he was wearing Teenage Mutant Ninja Turtle pajamas around the house. The kind with feet. I've never seen them before, but they were obviously old. So they're either from when he was a kid or he bought them at Goodwill or something. But they were his size. Sort of. I didn't want to ask. Anyway, my mom is just … *sad*. And it makes me sad."

She looked at Corban, and waited until he was fixed on her eyes.

Corban didn't know what to say to that, so he put his arm around her and gave her a quick sideways hug. She smiled up at him, looking so grateful it made him even madder that everyone had been so awful to her this week.

Levi came out a few minutes later. He shot about a hundred baskets or so, then drifted over to the adults, just moments behind Kari and Corban.

As they walked up, his mom was saying "… We just wanted to extend our support in what must be a difficult time."

A spark of irritation crackled through Corban as he recognized her hungry eyes. His mother was hunting. For what he wasn't sure. *I should've known this wasn't just about getting to know Kari's family better.*

Ollie didn't look anywhere near relaxed, but he was also nowhere near the nervous wreck that Corban expected. His legs were primly crossed, and he was slowly sipping at his glass of wine. Across from him, Kari's mom, Cynthia, finished her wine, then set it down on the table and emptied the bottle into it. Her eyes were glassy and her smile seemed wounded.

"People will think what people will think," she said, raising her freshly-filled glass to Corban's mom before taking another swallow. "This'll all blow over. But thank you … for all of this."

Adam turned from the grill to the group. "Right. Even if they don't catch this guy, it's summer. Someone's gonna leave a baby in their car at Provisions, and then Almond Park will have something else to talk about."

Silence. No one knew what to say to that. Then, Cynthia let out a wailing laugh, half-hysterical, half-distraught.

Corban turned to Kari. Sure enough, she looked as surprised as he felt.

Cynthia gulped more wine.

Ollie said, "I don't think people will stop talking about this for a while."

Adam glanced back at his meat, seemed to determine that it was perfect as is, then settled into the group. "You're probably right. But all you need for people to stop talking about Ollie Harris is for the situation to get *really* bad."

"I'm sorry?" Ollie looked up from his chair at Adam.

"Imagine that instead of these quiet, silent deaths, the killer really went to town. Made McNuggets out of the family. Left their eyeballs floating in the soup. I mean, gruesome shit. *Bloody.* Well, no one could ever think that was you, could they?"

"They could," said Ollie tightly.

Again, shockingly, Cynthia laughed. And then she finished her wine, reached for the bottle of red, refilled her glass, and turned the final swallow of white into a dark rosé.

"What if he set up a croquet game outside? But with limbs for the mallets and—"

"Adam."

"—heads for the balls."

Cynthia was still laughing, but this wasn't funny.

Ollie's big eyes were even bigger than normal.

Kari was dead-white, her mouth open.

Mom looked like she wanted to kill Dad.

And Levi was smiling. Corban wanted to smack him.

Dad looked wistful, like he always did just before a well-tailored punchline, then said, "Just imagine all the blood!"

But a punchline that was not.

"Adam ..." Mom repeated.

He turned to her with what would surely have been a sneer if they didn't have company. "What?"

"I think you might be making our guests uncomfortable."

He looked at Cynthia, still trying to stop the wracking laughs that were almost sobs.

"I doesn't look that way to me." Dad picked up his mostly empty bottle of beer, swallowed the rest of it, then set the empty at the end of an already impressive row. Corban wondered how many he'd had before their guests had arrived.

"Has anyone seen *Mars is On Fire*?" Kari asked. No one responded, even after she added, "It's really good."

Dad said, "So, who's ready to eat?"

Everybody was. Please let the show be over, Corban prayed. Unfortunately, there was an unrequested encore.

"Maybe I'm the killer," Adam said, grabbing at Cynthia's attention. "No one's found the body because we're eating it."

Mom turned white, gasping. Dad ignored her as he poured a red wine reduction over his very rare steak, "and here's the blood."

Cynthia shrieked like someone was tickling her and murdering her at the same time.

Ollie said, "Can we please stop talking about blood?"

Mom sighed, trying not to lose her shit. "You just ruined your steak."

"See," Adam grinned, nodding at Ollie's pallor. "No way anyone'll blame you if this gets bloody."

"Dad!" Corban was out of his seat.

Still grinning, Adam looked up at him. "Corban?"

"Sit down," Levi said. "Nobody wants to hear what you have to say."

Corban turned to his brother. "Without your posse

around, no one will ever want to hear what you have to say."

Mom looked from one to the other. "Boys."

Cynthia was trying not to laugh.

Kari was trying not to cry.

Corban was trying not to charge his brother and bash his head into the planter behind him.

They should be in this together, both of them working to bring their father back in line. To protect Kari, and her hurting family. And theirs.

But apparently it was every man for himself.

Chapter Thirty

Levi felt sick to his stomach.

He swiped through LiveLyfe like he'd been doing for the last hour, feeling worse by the minute.

Tomorrow would be miserable. Not for him, but definitely for Kari, and for his brother, if he kept holding her hand in front of everyone like he definitely would.

It wasn't the DMs asking for dirt.

It wasn't the speculation about whether or not Kari's dad was guilty.

It was the meme.

Someone had found a picture of a murdered family from an old newspaper article and put a caption across the top in a silly font that said, *Ollie was here!*

Levi had no doubt that it would go viral. If it hadn't already.

Corban had no idea — he wasn't on LiveLyfe and he hadn't been for a while.

And Levi doubted that he'd listen if Levi tried to warn him. Things were already bad between them before that bullshit at dinner with Kari's parents. Levi felt bad, because Corban was right, their father had definitely taken things too far. It hadn't been funny, even with Kari's mom laughing like a hyena beside him. But when Corban criticized Dad, it felt like he was picking at Levi too.

He hadn't been able to stop himself from lashing out. Even though he knew better.

Maybe if he apologized ...

Levi knocked on the door, but Corban ignored him. He knocked again. "Hey Corban, it's me."

From the other side of the door: "Congratulations."

Levi opened the door and stepped inside. "Hey."

"What do you want?"

"To talk."

"Text me."

"You haven't answered one of my texts in weeks."

Corban finally looked up. "Maybe that's because you're an asshole."

That wasn't completely unfair. Levi sighed. "Can we just talk for a minute?"

"Just go."

"*Go* as in my minute just started, or go as in you want me to leave right now?"

Corban looked at his brother, eyes alive with impatience. "Spit it out, Levi."

"I just want you to be prepared for tomorrow."

"Prepared for what?"

"People are talking, you know, about Kari's dad. Things are going to be rough for her tomorrow ... and you if you're with her."

"What is it you want me to do, Levi? Abandon her? Leave her to fend for herself against people like you?"

"I like Kari."

"Sure, you do. But that still wouldn't stop you. Not if

you thought you could get a laugh, or become *that* much more popular."

Corban wasn't making this easy, trying to pick a fight when that was the last thing Levi wanted right now. When he was genuinely trying to help.

"News travels fast whether we like it or not." Levi tried again, looked at his brother with pleading eyes, silently begging for him to listen and not make this any harder than it had to be. "Everyone knows that the police interrogated Ollie. So naturally, a lot of people think that he did it. And even those who don't might like to get in on the pranking. I'm just saying that—"

"He did work for two of the three families, so *of course they're going to question him.* But did they arrest him? *No.* Because he's innocent. Anyone who doesn't see that is an idiot."

"Okay, I hear you, but—"

"The problem is that you'd rather join in the fun than stick up for your friends."

"That's not true."

"It *is* true. Just look at last night. You were *laughing,* Levi. When Dad was saying all of that shit, you didn't say anything, and then when I did, you refused to back me up. Fuck you."

Levi left the room without another word, quietly closing the door behind him.

Because what else could he say, when everything inside him knew that his brother was right?

Chapter Thirty-One

Most of the other kids had already filed outside of Mrs. Ellison's physics class, but Kari was still inside.

Corban waited. It wasn't that he was impatient so much as worried about what might be happening to Kari, inside the classroom where he couldn't see. Mrs. Ellison for sure wasn't watching.

Sure enough, she came out last, still pretending that she wasn't being harassed, same as she had been all morning.

"I just don't understand why everyone gets to their junior year and turns into an idiot. Why is everybody fixated on the same two dozen colleges? It's stupid. Just because your grandmother hasn't heard of your school doesn't mean it's a shitty university that isn't worth the money. Seriously, people will spend their money on the stupidest things. Like degrees that don't mean anything. And everyone is always complaining about how they don't have any choices. Are you kidding me? We have more choices here than anywhere else in the world."

Corban didn't interrupt, just fell in beside her as she

headed to her next class. He'd made a point to walk her everywhere today. He'd vowed not to let anyone hurt her.

"You know how people move here from like everywhere on the planet? It's so that they can get a good education. They just need English and the willingness to work hard. Wherever anyone at this school ends up, *that's* not what's going to define them. I mean, the only people who ever give a shit about where you went to college are people who need you to give a shit about where they went, right?"

"Right."

"Juniors should just chill the fuck out. The best thing a junior can do is to know that senior year is right around the corner, and then the end is just after that. And the rest of your life. Junior year is a zit. Even the worst ones go away eventually."

He could feel the stares as they walked down the hallway. Kari had to feel them too.

Why didn't she care? How could she pretend this wasn't happening?

It had been relentless. All morning. The stares, the whispers, the names.

The printouts of Ollie's meme all over the school. Taken down by faculty, but not before Kari saw several.

The calls of *Olly-Olly-Oxen-Freak!*

The looks of shame-faced pity or worse from both teachers and students alike.

Demon Seed written in lipstick on her locker. And a black scarf with what looked like dried cum stuffed inside it. On top of a picture of Kari with her father, probably taken from LiveLyfe, where some primitive Photoshop work made Ollie look like he was leering more than he was. His speech bubble read, *Nice tits, Kari! Mind if I kill you?*

If Corban ever found out who'd done that one, he might murder someone himself.

But Kari kept talking, ignoring the long whispers and hurried stares.

They were almost to French. He would see her inside, then hurry to Language Arts.

Fifteen feet from the door, someone shouted, "Hey Spawn!"

Kari didn't turn around, making it the final few steps and only stopping with her hand on the classroom door.

"Hey Spawn! Offspring! Demon Seed!"

Kari clenched the knob in her white-knuckled fist. It looked like she might break it off the door. Corban didn't know what would happen when she turned around.

"It's Matthew Decker," he whispered. "Just ignore him."

"I know," Kari said, low through clenched teeth. "I'd know that asshole's voice anywhere. Because it always sounds like he's talking through the hole in his tiny little dick."

Corban wasn't even sure what that meant, and he didn't want to laugh with Decker staring daggers at the back of his head, but he couldn't help it. There was no way Decker could have heard her, though he surely knew where Kari had aimed whatever she said. But he tensed anyway, because the way things were going, anything seemed possible.

"Thanks for walking me to class." Kari reached up, kissed Corban on the cheek, opened the door and said, "You better hurry or you'll be late for LA."

She slipped inside the classroom, closing the door behind her.

Decker muttered, "Murderers are hot" as Corban passed him.

Unable to help it, Corban channeled his brother. "Too

bad your mom isn't. That's why I make her wear a paper bag."

He kept walking, knowing that he'd pay for that later. Decker wouldn't try anything now, with Mr. Weston watching the hall. But he'd be back, and probably with his idiot friends. And he couldn't count on Levi or the rest of the guys for help anymore.

He was on his own.

Language Arts wasn't too bad. Corban ignored all of the dickheads giving him eyes, pretended he couldn't hear their mutters and hisses, focusing on Mrs. Bradshaw's thoughts about *The Scarlet Letter*, while waiting for grace from the lunch bell.

As soon as it rang, Corban flew from the room. To his surprise, Kari waited in the hall.

"How'd you get here so fast?"

"Mrs. Dubois feels sorry for me. She took me aside a few minutes before class ended and asked me how I was feeling, if there was anything she could do, you know, stuff like that. Then she just let me go early. Said I shouldn't have to wait in the lunch line."

"I guess she doesn't know you brought your lunch?"

"I saw no reason to give it up. I really enjoyed those extra four minutes."

Corban smiled. Maybe he was worried for nothing. Sure, people were assholes, but Kari seemed to be doing just fine. He was stressing more than enough for the both of them, and maybe that was making things worse.

They went to the quad and ate alone in a corner, trading entrees like always. Corban gave Kari his shiitake-and-scallion lo mein in banana leaves, served around silky noodles. It was from Five-Star China, a place with food that was much better than their name, but still too fussy for lunch, according to Corban. He was thrilled to swap the dish for Cynthia's simple yet delicious BLT, in a wrap rather than bread.

Corban tried not to remember what life had been like not too long ago, when lunches were spent with Levi and the guys who used to be his best friends. Corban had always felt at least a little on the outside of the group. More so since he started hanging with Kari, as the two of them stuck to the edge together. But looking around, Corban didn't even see Levi or the gang.

They ignored the stares while finishing their lunch, then Corban and Kari tossed their garbage and walked toward the football field, where they usually meandered until the bell announced that it was time to finish their day.

They didn't make it far.

Olly-Olly-Oxen-Freak!

Spawn, spawn, look at her on the lawn!

Olly-Olly-Oxen-Freak! Olly-Olly-Oxen-Freak!

Demon seed!

Olly-Olly-Oxen-Freak!

Corban didn't even know where the chanting was coming from, other than everywhere. He didn't want to look.

Neither did Kari. She kept her eyes mostly ahead, cast only ever so slightly down, as they walked faster.

He took her hand. She squeezed it tight. The chanting continued.

It almost felt planned. Like a flash mob rehearsed by the lot of them.

The half-eaten peach came out of nowhere, hitting Kari in the face. He had no idea who'd thrown it. She yelped and swallowed what sounded like a possible breakdown.

Corban put his arm around Kari, pulling her toward

the main office, where he knew the cowards wouldn't dare to follow.

"It's going to be okay," Corban said, making a promise he couldn't possibly keep.

"I know," Kari lied. She was crying, and her left cheek was red and shiny.

He wiped some of the sticky juice off her cheek while staring into her eyes, neither of them speaking, nor needing to. Corban didn't need words to make his promise.

He would stick with Kari, see this through no matter what. Not just because it was the right thing to do, but because he was — no doubt about it — deeply in love with his best friend, a truth he could no longer deny.

Lunch ended and they each went their own way, planning to meet at the flagpole after school.

But Corban never made it.

He was halfway there when someone shoved him hard from behind.

On the ground, reeling from the shock and the scrapes to his palms, he looked up at a sneering Decker.

"Where's your bitch? If she off helping Daddy?"

That didn't even make any sense. Decker was an idiot.

But he was bigger and stronger than Corban, and the gathering crowd seemed to be on his side, hungry to see a fight.

Corban tried to stand, but Decker shoved him back down.

"Hey, Leftover Levi, I didn't say you could stand."

"I don't want to fight."

"Too bad I do." Decker grabbed him by the collar. "Tell you what ..." He looked around for the crowd, as if seeking their approval. "If you admit that her daddy did it, I'll let you go. If not, I'll punch you so hard, my mom will start making *you* wear the bag."

Decker tightened his grip, his lips curled into the cruelest smile.

From the corner of his eyes he saw Levi, standing at the edge of the crowd, alone.

Their gazes met, brother to brother.

Levi saw Decker and Corban and the crowd. Levi saw all of it.

But then he turned around and walked away, leaving his brother to die.

I tried to warn you.

Corban could hear Levi in his head.

The crowd was waiting.

He looked into Decker's eyes and in his steadiest voice said, "Ollie Harris is innocent, but Matthew Decker is definitely an asshole, and I feel sorry for his ugly whore of a mother."

And then Corban's face exploded in pain.

Chapter Thirty-Two

"You sure you don't want more ice?"

Cynthia looked at Corban in sympathy, like she wanted to reach out and touch his nose again.

"Thank you, Mrs. Harris, but that's okay. Really, it doesn't even hurt that much anymore. I'm sure it looks worse than it is."

"That's what you get for running too fast and not watching where you're going." It was the third time that Kari had found a way to naturally deliver the lie she needed her mom to believe.

Because this couldn't be about that. Not in her mother's current condition.

Under normal circumstances she would never have fallen for such a sham, but Kari's mom was an absolute mess.

She warned him before he came over, but Corban hadn't expected this. It was heartbreaking, and such a contrast with his own mother, who seemed so delighted by all of the disasters raining upon Almond Park. He thought of that farce of a dinner party a couple days before —

Cynthia's drinking and his father's nauseating onslaught of garbage — and wanted to shudder.

According to Kari, her mom had barely left the house, and she was clearly hanging by a thread. Kari made a pot of oolong, but Cynthia ignored it entirely for the bottle that she seemed determined to drink as fast as possible.

Kari glanced at Corban, worried. Her mother was too lost to notice.

"I don't have any friends anymore," Cynthia said, a second after a giant swallow.

"That's not true, Mom."

But it was. Kari told him the same thing herself on the bike ride here.

"This will all blow over," Kari added. "They'll find the killer and everyone in town will feel really bad about how they've treated Dad."

Another swallow, much closer to a gulp. "But how could I ever be friends with *them* again after this? After what they thought of your father? I just couldn't." She shook her head, haunted and furious. Another sip, this one small and nervous. "Everything's ruined forever."

"It's not *ruined forever*, you just have to—"

"It *is*, Kari." Cynthia stood. She gulped — no, *guzzled* — the rest of her wine, then headed for the kitchen, probably to open another bottle. "I can't *just* anything. Not today or tomorrow or ever again."

Cynthia cracked the bottle with a couple of twists of the corkscrew followed by a pop, without ever once looking down at the bottle. Same for the way she filled her glass. Extra impressive, considering she was already drunk.

"I'm ostracized."

Her words were starting to slur. *Ostracized* definitely had an added *H*. Kari squeezed his hand under the table, hard.

"What can we do, Mom?"

"You can't do anything! No one can do anything. Either your father did it and our lives are ruined, or he didn't do it and our lives are still ruined."

"Things will be okay if—"

"What do you know, Kari?"

Kari flinched.

"I'm sorry. I just—"

"My Bunco group canceled on me. *I made a beef enchilada dip.*" Her voice cracked, like the real tragedy was that her dip might go to waste.

"It will pass."

"You're not getting it," Cynthia said, sounding more upset by the word, "it *won't*. Once people decide, they don't change their minds."

"But Dad didn't do it!"

"That doesn't matter!" A long, horrible moment, where something died on Cynthia's face. Then, in a brittle voice that broke at the end, she added, "And what if he did?"

"Mom!" Kari gasped.

Corban held his breath. Poor Kari, having to see her mother fall apart like this. To have to be the strong one while her parents fell apart. It wasn't fair.

Cynthia drank more wine and laughed. "Of course he didn't do it."

Kari looked at Corban, helpless. He squeezed her hand.

We'll figure this out.

Cynthia's phone was sitting like a brick on the table. She picked it up and her thumb started dancing on the glass. Less than a minute later she paused. Her eyes turned dark. The line of her mouth receded.

"And there they are. My Bunco girls. Jeanine was hosting. Do you see this shit?" She showed Kari and Corban her screen. A group of nine women sitting around a kitchen counter, all of them smiling for their collective selfie. "*Do you fucking see it?*"

Corban had no idea what Kari's mom was talking about. He wondered if Kari did.

"They're all smiling?" Kari attempted.

"It's the goddamned hardwood floors." She took a huge swig of her wine, her throat working frantically as she tried to swallow the whole glass at once. "Installed by your father! The entire first floor. And that fucking cunt Jeanine still hasn't paid the bill! What? Is she waiting for Ollie to get hauled off so she can get them for free? While those other eight bitches all stand around gawking?"

But then she started laughing.

"It's fine!" She waved a hand like this was all nothing, then she looked at her daughter and Corban as though she were only seeing them now. "Of course this will all work itself out. I don't mean to worry either of you. Really, I'm fine."

The second *I'm fine* came out sounding tired, and barely intelligible.

"What can we do, Mom?"

Cynthia looked at Kari with eyes that had suddenly, and surprisingly, rediscovered their kindness. "Thank you, honey. You too, Corban. Thank you for being here for me, and for Kari.'

Corban blinked. "Of course, Mrs. Harris."

"Cynthia." She gave him a smile that looked a splinter from cracking.

She was mumbling something as they left the dining room and headed off to Kari's room.

"Is your mom going to be okay?"

"She'll be fine," Kari said, her uncertainty chilling. She was so pale, Corban wondered if the woman was in shock.

"I thought she didn't swear."

"That was literally the first time I've ever heard her."

"Wow."

"Yeah."

Kari closed her bedroom door and turned to Corban. "Will you stay with me?"

"You mean … in here?"

"Yes. I don't want to be alone. Especially if …"

She left the thought unfinished, like it was too horrible to voice.

"I'll stay." Corban wasn't about to let this opportunity pass. And he wasn't going to ask his parents and risk his father saying no, just to be a dick. "They won't even notice I'm gone."

Chapter Thirty-Three

"Let's watch a movie," Adam suggested again.

"I told you, I don't want to watch a movie," Selena said.

"Then can you talk to me? Maybe we can have a conversation instead of just glaring at each other?"

But Selena wasn't glaring. She wasn't even looking at him. Barely had all night.

"Let's go to your office."

"I don't feel like working either, Adam."

"It doesn't have to be work." He smiled suggestively, one eyebrow raised.

Her response was flat, clearly annoyed. "It's *always* work."

And then, silence.

It's always work. He hated the implication that *he* was work.

But he couldn't deny that what he wanted from her was inseparable from her work. He wanted — no, needed — her to keep him on the straight and narrow like she always swore that she would. She acted like he was barely worth her attention, when he was on the verge of his first kill. She was breaking the unspoken agreement that their marriage was built on. Without her, there was no release from his unspeakable urges.

It would be her fault if he killed.

"Wanna play a game?"

"Are you kidding? What, now you want to play *Scrabble*? Is that your response to my not wanting to work?"

"It's my response to you not wanting to give me a session, or watch a movie, or have a conversation, or do *anything with me.*"

"Okay." Selena stood from where she'd been reading in the nook, set her tablet on the table, and paced the room. "Let's talk. Detective Sharpe can't find anything linking Ollie to the murders, other than his access. He says that it's circumstantial, and not enough to charge someone. He's right. Even if they could bring Ollie in, it would never stick. As is, there is zero chance of a conviction."

"This isn't what I wanted to talk about."

"So," Selena continued. "What do you think is the best way to play this?"

"What?" He looked at her, exhausted. Was she really going to do this? Hold their marriage hostage to her career? "Play what?"

"If Ollie is the killer, and the police are able to prove it, then don't you think that people will wonder why I didn't see it? I mean, he was an acquaintance and I'm the supposed authority, and there he was right under my nose. If the killer is someone else, then that might be even worse."

Right. Because this wasn't about finding a serial killer. This was all about her, and whether or not she looked good to her target demographic.

But he played dumb. "Why is that?"

There was a long beat before Selena answered, and there was something strange on her face when she did. "Because I'm the one saying that he's guilty, so obviously my judgement is flawed."

"No one knows that you're saying he's guilty. Unless you go around telling people."

"I think there's more to the story."

"Of course you do."

"I think this is personal."

"With Ollie?" Adam asked.

"With the killer. Whoever it is."

"Personal with his victims?"

"Personal *with me*."

Because everything is about you. He bit the inside of his cheek to keep from saying it.

"I think the killer wants to rub this in my face," she continued. "Did you notice anything about the crime scenes?"

Unbelievable. "Like what?"

"Like something obvious."

"You're not being very clear."

"It's that obvious. I was hoping I didn't have to be. What do *you* know about the crime scene that the police might have missed?"

What in the hell was she going on about? She was clearly digging for something, acting like Adam played cards with the killer on Tuesdays. "I don't know what you want me to say."

Selena peered at him. "I guess I don't know either."

He'd never been more disgusted with her. She'd been guessing when she'd accused Ollie, and ruined his family's life in exactly the same way that she'd been trying to stop Adam from ruining theirs. She was clueless.

Worse, she didn't have a clue about him. She didn't

understand what was happening because she had stopped paying attention entirely.

Selena *assumed* that she understood him. But she was wrong, and there would be consequences.

He could feel them coming, whether he wanted them or not.

She was at her closet. The door was open and she was digging inside.

"Sam thinks that *The Heartbeat of Murder* might be the biggest thing on TV when it debuts. He could see us getting the cover of *Entertainment Weekly*." She straightened and chirped, "Have you seen my Doctor Who scarf anywhere? I can't seem to find it."

"No. I haven't seen your Doctor Who scarf."

"You sure you didn't take it?"

Adam looked up. Selena gave him the look she usually gave one of the boys when she was catching them in a lie.

"Why the fuck would I take your scarf?"

She finally blinked and turned back to the closet.

Adam stood to leave.

"Where are you going?" she asked.

"I don't know. But right now this bedroom isn't big enough for both of us."

He closed the door behind him, wondering when he would finally go all the way.

Maybe tonight.

Chapter Thirty-Four

Was there anything more pathetic than watching someone else play a video game thousands of miles away? Levi thought probably not, despite the 337,841 people watching *Shanghai* alongside him.

That thing in his gut was a cousin to loneliness, but it was born of something much worse.

He felt wretchedly guilty. It was tearing at his insides like a frothing, rabid beast, scratching and clawing and tormenting him so he wouldn't forget what he'd done.

Today Levi had taken it too far.

Except that was a massive understatement. He had done the one thing a twin should never do, and left Corban to the wolves. Levi wasn't sure if the sickness inside his stomach was because sometimes one twin could kinda sorta feel the other, or if he was alone in this miserable stew.

He couldn't know for sure, but Levi felt reasonably certain that they were both dying inside.

Levi left the game room and wandered the hall, passing Corban's room on his way to the kitchen.

He would come back later. Once he worked up the courage to apologize.

Because that's what he had to do.

He was inside out with sorry, and totally in the wrong.

He had no excuse.

Levi opened the fridge and stared inside it. He wasn't hungry, but he didn't know what to do with himself. After looking long enough to chill his face, he slammed it closed.

He and Corban used to be close, almost like one person split into two.

Back when they were little, they dreamed the same dreams and finished each other's sentences.

In middle school they became their own people, meaning they both figured out that Corban was sort of a nerd.

But Levi had always been there for him anyway, included him in the jokes and the fun, made sure he was one of the gang.

They had started to drift, but away and around rather than apart.

Then freshman year came, and Kari. Levi had been jealous. He could've gotten over it, probably, if not for the other bullshit. The stuff Corban found while snooping on their father.

He wouldn't listen to reason. He had been his nerdiest, angriest, pissiest self.

He made Levi furious.

They had nearly come to blows.

But that didn't excuse his leaving Corban to Matthew Decker, not when a few simple words would have stopped the bully.

He trudged back upstairs to the hallway. His gut felt like a family of porcupines was living inside it. There was no way to get past this other than apologize.

Levi forced himself to stop at Corban's door and knock. Then again after a moment without any answer.

He opened the door after the third knock and looked inside. "Corban?"

But Corban wasn't in his room.

Levi went back into the game room, then tried every other room in the house. Levi looked outside. Dad's car was gone. Maybe he was somewhere with Corban, though that seemed unlikely after the way things had been going.

He went back to Corban's bedroom, and this time he went in without knocking.

"CORBAN?"

Levi wasn't sure what to do. He'd spent most of the afternoon moping in his room, so he hadn't heard Corban come home from school. Shit. It was bad enough that things had gone wrong, but he told himself that he'd fix them. Apologize and make everything right. Now he couldn't.

Levi began snooping around Corban's room, feeling like a hypocrite for being angry at his brother for doing the same exact thing to their father.

Then he found a note from Kari to Corban, and of course he had to read it.

Chapter Thirty-Five

"Are you feeling any better?" Kari asked Corban, who was clutching his stomach.

"A little," he said.

But he wasn't. Not even a little.

Something was sitting in his stomach like crumbled cement, jagged and jabbing inside him.

Still, it was better than being at home, where everyone would be miserable in their own way. Sure, it was miserable here too, but at least it wasn't his misery. Or his family.

And Kari seemed to need him. She hadn't let go of his hand since they'd retreated to her room.

The room was quiet. Kari's usual conversation had gone mostly to crickets. And Corban felt content.

She squeezed his hand, then let it go. "I should really go check on my mom."

"Do you think your dad will come home? Or do you think he'll make it two nights in a row?"

Kari gave Corban the saddest shrug he'd ever seen.

"No idea. Mom told him to stay the fuck away from her, forever."

"Oh. You didn't tell me that."

No answer.

Kari swung her feet off the bed and stood. "He's hasn't even been charged, but my mom has already given up."

Corban swallowed, prayed he wasn't making a mistake. "Do you think your mom *really* believes that your dad could've done it?"

"She should know better." Kari glared at him. "Everyone should know better."

"He has an alibi for the third … one, doesn't he?"

"I'm not sure."

"If he—"

Kari shoved him backward, hard, and he lost his balance, landing on the bed. She crawled on his body and kissed him, her tongue insistent, breathing hard.

This wasn't how Corban had imagined it would be at all.

"Don't think," she said as she rushed to pull off her pants. Then her panties. "Don't make me think."

He tried to keep up with her as she undid his jeans and yanked them down. Struggled to unhook her bra as he felt cool air on his …

Then everything was heat and wetness and his hips moved without him telling them to.

Kari squeaked like he'd hurt her. She screwed her eyes shut and whispered, "Don't think."

Then she moved.

Shit.

It wasn't how he'd imagined it *at all*.

Afterward, they lay together in silence. He could've probably stayed that way forever. But in a few minutes, she said, "I need to go check on my mom."

Corban rolled over. He wanted to say *I love you.*

She was out of the bed, pulling on her pants. "I'll be right back."

Buckling up and getting ready to follow her, Corban said, "I'll come with you."

She smiled and held her hand out for his. The gesture was especially sweet considering that Kari would likely drop it in seconds, once they were around her mom.

But Cynthia wasn't in the kitchen, or the dining room, or the living room or den.

"I guess she's in her room. That means she's gonna be *sooooper* sad. And I should probably go in alone."

They stopped in front of her door. Kari looked at Corban, uncertain.

"Let me come," he said. "You'll be there for her, and I'll be there for you."

Corban looked at Kari like he loved her, and felt certain she knew what his eyes were implying.

"Okay." She exhaled, and in that moment everything felt fine. They would be okay.

Kari opened the door.

Dim light spilled on the husk of her mother's body. Cynthia's head was lolled to the side, skin like wax and eyes of dirty glass. Three orange bottles littered her nightstand. None had caps and one lay on its side. All looked empty enough from the doorway. No one needed a pulse to know the truth.

Kari screamed and this time Corban couldn't hold her.

Chapter Thirty-Six

"My mom was my favorite person in the world."

Corban fisted his hands in his lap, over and over, as he watched Kari try not to cry. Fail. Continue with the eulogy anyway.

"She loved to be happy ... deserved to be happy. She could make me laugh even when laughing was the last thing I wanted to do. Her friends all loved her, until they didn't."

Kari needed nearly a half-minute to recover from that one. She raked the empty pews with angry eyes as she gathered her breath. Corban thought that if she'd had laser vision, the whole church would be on fire.

She had been up there too long already. Kari was going to have a full breakdown if she didn't stop talking. She should have stepped down after *My mom, Cynthia, was my favorite person in the world.*

"I don't know how I am ever going to be okay again without her ..."

Kari was grieving onstage. This was no longer about her mom, this was about Kari.

"... I feel like I'm empty. There's a hole in my heart and I'll never—"

She shook her head, couldn't continue.

And then she broke down.

Corban was out of his seat, but Ollie was faster, leading his daughter down the stairs as she murmured, *"I'm sorry, Mommy ... I love you so much."*

The reception was better. Calmer. Still mostly empty.

Corban's so-called friends were all assholes. Levi hadn't shown. Same for Dane, Elliot, and Pussabo. To hell with them all. Dad hadn't come, either.

The one person he wished hadn't come — his mom — insisted on attending. She seemed fascinated by the whole thing, and he felt embarrassed that they were related. Not that she was smiling or doing anything inappropriate, but she kept finding subtle ways to pump people for more information about Ollie. He was pretty sure Ollie had noticed, too.

The final straw came when she put her arm around Kari and said, "I can't imagine what this must be like for you."

"Then stop pretending you can," Kari snapped, shaking off the condescending hug and fleeing outside.

Corban started to follow, but Mom grabbed his arm.

"What?"

"She'll be okay." Then, "Want me to help?"

"I wish you would stop helping."

He found Kari outside, sitting in the shade of an over-hang, hugging her knees. He walked over and sat cross-legged beside her.

"You're doing great."

She wiped her eyes and tried to smile. "Thanks."

He took her hand and she leaned on his shoulder. "It's really hard, holding your shit together, you know?"

"I know."

"And you know what else?"

"What?"

"Your mom is a lot to take sometimes."

A stab of guilt and a swallow. "I know."

"But she means well."

Corban nodded, but he wasn't sure he agreed.

"How's your dad doing?" he asked.

"I don't know. He's totally stopped talking. He's started carrying around a dead lightbulb, and I have no idea why."

"How do you know it's dead?"

"Because sometimes he sets it down. I shook it one time."

"Weird."

"Yeah."

Silence.

"But he still didn't do it," she said.

"I know."

"Even the police know he's innocent. But everyone thinks that since my mom killed herself she thought he was guilty, instead of—"

She couldn't finish the sentence. It didn't matter. They'd already talked the possibilities out, and there was nothing new to say. Not unless they could figure out who the killer might be. Give the police a new suspect.

Wait, what if they could do that?

He tamped down his excitement, kept it out of his voice. He didn't want to give her false hope. "I wonder if the killer has ever written to my mom."

Kari pulled away from him, blinking. "What?"

"She gets letters from killers all the time."

"That's terrible. Why are you telling me that?"

"Because maybe this one is close. What if he knows her, and wrote her a letter?"

"Why would the killer confess in a letter?"

"He probably wouldn't, but sometimes people slip up." And he didn't exactly feel like singing his mother's praises right now, but … "My mom's an expert on how serial killers think. She might be able to learn something from what he said that would be a clue."

"If your mom had a letter from the killer, wouldn't she already have taken it to the police?"

Guilty knuckles, right to the gut. There was a time when he'd have assumed the same thing. But she'd been talking nonstop about doing episodes about the killings on her new show. He wouldn't be surprised to find out that she'd kept something secret. To be the first. Or prove herself as the best.

But he couldn't confess that to Kari, it'd make her feel worse. So instead, he said, "She might not have realized it yet."

Kari looked at him like he was her hero, and he wondered if it was a mistake to offer her even the smallest of hopes.

"The killer might not have written my mom. But I'll ask her to take a second look."

"Thank you," she sighed, leaning her head on his shoulder again.

It was up to him. He needed to get his mother to consider the possibility that she — one of the world's top serial killer experts — had somehow failed to notice that the murderer she was tracking had sent her a letter.

What if she refused to look through her fan mail again?

It was possible. When Selena Nash had a theory, she was right until proven otherwise.

If she wouldn't do this for Kari, then he'd steal the letters and look for himself.

Chapter Thirty-Seven

Levi was grateful to be hanging out with his friends, because everything else was miserable.

But he wished they weren't giving him a hard time about the same old shit.

Dane looked at Elliot and Pussabo. "I need your help. He's not saying anything."

"There's nothing to say," Levi repeated for the zillionth time.

Pussabo said, "He doesn't want to talk about it."

Elliot agreed. "His mouth is a vagina and he's keeping his virginity."

Dane shook his head at Elliot and turned back to Levi. "Come on, man. I don't understand why you won't just tell us what your mom has been saying."

"Maybe you should go downstairs and have her make you some cookies. Then you can ask her yourself," Elliot suggested.

Levi was sick of this. His friends were supposed to be his safe space.

"Why the hell do you even care?" he finally snapped.

Dane flinched. "I'm sorry, man. Didn't mean to pucker your fucker."

And now the mood was ruined.

This shit usually went down between Elliot and Dane, when either Elliot took it too far or Dane finally had enough.

"Look guys, I'm not trying to be an asshole. I'm sick of talking about it, and I want it to stop." Levi exhaled and waited for his friends to start giving him shit.

No one did. At least not for the next hour. It was all eyes on *HardCorp* and an unprecedented string of wins for Pussabo.

"Welcome to the United States of Pussabo," he said, after his fourth straight victory.

The buzz was already fading from *HardCorp*. Levi wondered if any of them would be playing it by the end of summer. Probably not.

"Why don't we watch a movie?" he suggested.

"Because I'm winning," Pussabo said.

"And we're not gay," Elliot added a second later.

"Thanks."

Elliot winked. "Sure thing, Pussabo."

"I'm with Levi," Dane said. "This is officially boring."

"One more after this," Pussabo said, clearly desperate to hang onto his rare winning streak.

"Let's do something else," Levi pressed anyway.

"Yeah," Dane agreed. "Let's do something else."

"Just let me finish this one round. There only nineteen—"

Pussabo exploded into pixels, and a squadron of other *HardCorp* players made victory dances around him.

"And down goes Pussabo," Elliot said, then made a noise that was probably supposed to sound like a funeral dirge.

"Fine." Pussabo stood and dropped his controller onto the couch. "Whatdaya guys wanna do?"

"Got any pictures of your mom?"

"Fuck you, Elliot."

"You're right," he went on. "She's barely hot. Although I do appreciate the eighties era hair she has going on down there. I call it The Reagan and Bush."

"So what do you want to do?" Pussabo asked again, ignoring Elliot.

Levi wondered why everyone was so stupid. "I've suggested that we watch a movie more times than Elliot's farted."

"Not possible," Dane and Pussabo said together.

Dane kept going. "No one wants to watch a movie, man. Sorry."

"Why not?" Levi asked.

"Because movies take like two hours," Pussabo said.

"So what? You have somewhere else to be?"

"Two hours is a long time to sit in one place."

Elliot looked admiringly at Pussabo. "Pussabo has a point."

Levi yelled, "We've been playing *HardCorp* for almost three hours!"

"Exactly," Elliot nodded. "So let's just make it an even four and then call it a day."

"Seriously," Dane said. "If no one is home, then why don't we go into your mom's office. I bet I could get onto her computer."

Why the hell would Dane want to get onto Mom's computer?

"No way. Not an option. What makes you think you could?"

"It's a Hail Mary," Elliot said. "He's hoping he can delete the dick pic he sent her."

Ignoring Elliot, like everyone else in the game room, Dane said, "I don't. But what if I can? Aren't you curious?"

"Not at all." Levi shook his head. "But go ahead and try. My mom is only going to kill you if she catches you."

"Can I really?"

"No."

And now it was tense.

"Maybe we should watch a movie," Pussabo suggested.

"I'm not trying to be a dick," Levi said. "But she will go nuclear. You have no idea. One time I got Corban to sneak into her office, because it was off-limits. She. Went. Fucking. Ballistic. We were only nine, but even then my brother was a narc. He said I made him do it. That he *didn't want to bother Mommy's stuff.*"

Levi waited for the laughs, then continued. "And at dinner — *fuck.*" He visibly shuddered. "I've never seen her like that. He cried because he thought she was serious about putting him up for adoption."

"So you never tried again?" Dane was rapt, leaning forward, his mouth slightly open.

"Once." Levi was surprised to find that his heart was beating fast.

Even Elliot was silent.

"Remember last year when my mom was in New York for like two weeks with her agent?"

Nods all around.

"My dad was gone for a couple of days during that stretch too. I'd been curious for years, and that was my chance to see why she never let us in there. I was careful. I took pictures of everything, not because I wanted to keep anything, but because I wanted to make sure that I left everything *exactly* like I found it. I didn't want to leave anything up to my stupid memory. I found a pink box with a bunch of red journals inside it. All of them about the same guy. Someone she calls The Virgin."

"Now you're fucking with us," Elliot said.

"I'm not." Levi shook his head. He knew how he felt and could imagine his face. "I wish I'd never seen them. I erased all of my pictures."

"What did they say?" Dane asked.

"I don't want to talk about it."

"You're the one who brought it up," Elliot said.

"No I didn't. I'm explaining why I don't want to go inside my mom's office."

"So tell us about the journal," Dane said.

"I'm not going into details, but the dude is totally depraved." Levi remembered the horrors practically dripping off the page, this man's fascination with blood. Of course it couldn't have been a woman. Only a man could have darkness like that living inside him.

Because he knew they'd keep hounding him, Levi finished the story as best he could.

"It seems like one of my mom's patients was drowning himself in darkness so that he could figure out who he was. And all of his darkness was covered in blood."

Chapter Thirty-Eight

Why does a traffic light turn red?

If you had to change in front of everyone, you would, too.

Traffic was usually the enemy, but tonight it felt like solace to Adam. Every red light was another reprieve. Another chance to inhale and exhale and prepare for the inevitable.

He was out of excuses for staying away from home. But while heading out to the coffee shop to write some last minute one-liners for Anna Lies was fine, not showing up for dinner would be grounds for another fight.

Adam had expected to get the rough lines out in the first hour or so, then take a walk, maybe down to The Inside Scoop, seeing as it was only a couple blocks away from his favorite Hill of Beans. After his mind was rested he'd go back into the Bean and clean up his work.

But today he was a hack, and Adam's muse refused to meet him even halfway.

Every line was stupid.

Every idea fell flat as soon as he put it into words.

Every joke a cliché.

He usually found it easy enough to fuck with famous people, but for some reason the deep well of vapid celebrities wasn't filling his bucket. He couldn't focus, so Adam watched people instead.

Everyone bored him, until a redhead moved his thoughts elsewhere.

But that was no surprise, seeing as that was where they had wanted to go from the start.

And so he followed them out of the Bean and over two blocks to The Inside Scoop.

Or at least across the way, outside the Sugar and Slice. Adam could smell the pizza, the baking cheese alongside the chocolate. He always could while watching Poppy. He wasn't surprised to see her, knowing her schedule like he did. That might have had something to do with why he wanted to get his writing done in a coffee shop today, even though the noise and people were most often distracting. Deep down, he'd known that he wasn't going to be able to focus until he saw her.

Eventually he went inside to order his scoop.

She laughed at his jokes and he tipped her. She smiled and scooped as he imagined the blood leaving her body like strawberry syrup. She rang and revved him up, with no way of knowing that the man pressing his erection against his body to hide it was imagining fucking her bloody.

He threw his two scoops of bacon caramel maple sundae into the garbage, covertly adjusted his still-throbbing cock, then walked back to the Bean and finished his shitty one-liners.

Adam would have to go over them again after dinner. Right now they were worthless. An apology waiting to happen.

He was a mile from home. Guilty, resentful, pent-up.

He wanted to explode, and wasn't sure how he most wanted to do it.

But instead, he had to make nice.

My doctor said I needed to break a sweat at least once a day. So I promised that I'd start lying to my wife.

Things hadn't always been this way. They used to be better than he ever thought they could be. He kept telling himself he could get back there, work harder to improve things. But nothing he did seemed to work. Adam would start out with the best of intentions, and as soon as he opened his mouth, the conversation would circle the drain.

Before I tell my wife something important, I take both her hands in mine. That way she can't hit me.

He parked, then braced himself as he walked inside, prepared for battle. Hoping for a truce. And surprised to find Selena smiling as she approached him.

She was holding his book. *Their book.*

Adam wasn't sure he'd ever seen the red journal outside of her office. She fanned herself seductively, a southern belle about to swoon.

"I've penciled you in for tomorrow."

This was new.

A fresh arousal found him, sudden and different and new, despite it being so very old between them. She kissed him on the cheek and left his skin slightly wet.

"You're absolutely right. I have been ignoring you. This is all my fault, and I want to make it up to you. I'm sorry."

He didn't know what to say. Was afraid to utter anything that might destroy whatever this was.

"Come on," she said, taking his hand. "Let's go put this away in my office, and then I'll show you how sorry I am."

Adam could practically smell her excitement. But he

had to wonder, on his way to her office, if she was working so hard to make up because she genuinely wanted to help him?

Or had he made her suspicious by telling her too much about the woman with the blood-red lipstick?

Chapter Thirty-Nine

Selena didn't need to work out. Not after the way that Adam had pounded her.

But it felt great to be getting whatever this was out of her system. And besides, even though she hated exercise, Selena loved her AthletaTone.

She'd thought it was stupid when Adam ordered it for her, right after it first came out. She figured it was the sort of thing she would use three times and then leave to sit in their unused gym, with gorgeous bamboo floors that rarely had the chance to get scuffed. Now she sounded like a commercial for the thing whenever she got the chance to crow about it.

It really had been such a sweet gift. She hated to exercise, but he'd been right about it being the perfect solution, like he usually was about that sort of thing. She hadn't given his idea a chance.

She could be bad about that. And lately she'd been awful.

For so long, she'd been sure he was harmless. That their sessions were simply a way for her to participate in his fetish without sharing it. But now she was forced to wonder if he might actually be a serial killer, and she was the fool who had missed it.

She would be a laughingstock. The serial killer expert who didn't realize she'd married the very type of man she devoted her life to studying.

And it would be her own fault. She'd paid so little attention to her family, stealing precious time from them to fuel her career. She had to stop.

But right now life was a maelstrom, with Selena stuck in its center, seething and stirring and churning, struggling to parse beliefs from ambitions, fictions from facts, and family from the very future that she had been striving to create. A future that was starting to seem a fingertip out of reach.

How could she spend more time with her family when Sam was going to need her to give one hundred and ten percent to the show?

How could she justify holding back on the project that could ensure her family never wanted for anything ever again?

Worst of all, how could she make sure that Adam wasn't about to torpedo both by turning out to be the one thing she'd been certain he wasn't?

She had been wrong to put Adam on the back burner. They had to get back on track with regular calendar dates. She had to be sure he wasn't a danger to anyone else. To do that, she would have to set some boundaries with Sam.

She turned off the water, feeling a glow inside her.

Everything was about to get better. First at home, then everywhere else.

She dried off, got dressed, and felt truly fantastic for the first time in days. She would figure out this thing with Adam, and make sure that no matter how crazy things got with the show, she was scheduling regular sessions and time together.

It wouldn't be good for the show if she was going through a divorce.

Or if she failed to keep her husband's darkness in check.

Selena plucked the phone from its charger on her nightstand and checked the screen. Three texts from Sam:

Call me.

You're going to want to know this.

Then, *Knock knock.*

Selena smiled, satisfied with herself as she slipped the phone into her front pocket and started downstairs. She smiled again when it rang a few minutes later and she ignored the call.

But her smile thinned when the texts and missed calls wouldn't stop coming.

Curiosity grated and scraped against her, abrading her brain, making Selena want to surrender.

She didn't even make it an hour.

Hating herself as she did it, Selena slipped into her office, closed the door, and jabbed her thumb where it shouldn't have gone.

The phone rang twice, then Selena said, "What do you need, Sam?"

Chapter Forty

Corban watched his mother's car back out of the garage as he dialed Kari's number. Mom was suspiciously vague about where she was going and how long she'd be gone. But she'd promised to bring dinner home if he agreed not to mention her absence to Levi or Dad.

"So you want me to cover for you?" Corban had said, not because he cared, but because a guilty Mom could be negotiated with. And if she found out what he planned to do while she was out, he'd need all the leverage he could get.

It worked. He could tell by the way she pressed her lips together before she said, "I'm not asking you to lie, if they ask. But I'm trying to straighten things out with your father, and the simpler things are, the easier that will be."

Simple. Right. So he'd nodded and tried not to tap his fingers on the counter while she grabbed her purse and headed out the door.

"How fast can you get here?" Corban asked Kari.

"Twenty minutes."

She made it in fifteen, breathing hard from pushing

herself to pedal at top speed all the way. As soon as she got off her bike, he pulled her inside and locked the door behind them. Then he set the alarm, so that if Levi or Dad came home earlier than expected, they'd hear it beep as it was disarmed.

"I like your mom," Kari said, fast and frantic. "I don't want her to hate me, and if she finds out about this then she's going to hate me for sure. This is all private and if we—"

"It's the only way." Corban took her hands, then squeezed them gently until she met his eyes. "I already asked her to recheck the letters, and she said she was sure none of them were from the Almond Park Killer."

"We could ask her together."

"It wouldn't matter. We have to do this. For your dad."

She swallowed and nodded. "Okay then. You go first."

Now that she put it that way, Corban didn't know if he could.

He was mostly fine at the door, but something inside him disintegrated by the step until he found himself standing beside Kari in front of her office, his hand trembling as he reached for the knob.

"Corban, if you're scared, we don't have to do this."

Of course he was, but he couldn't let Kari think he was a coward.

I know when someone has been in my office, Corban. I know when someone has been through my things. If I ever, ever catch you going into my office without permission again, I swear that I will make you regret it for the rest of your life.

He gulped and turned the knob. Kari followed him into the office.

The air conditioning here was set fifteen degrees cooler than the rest of the house. Or maybe the fear made Corban clammy.

"Where should we start?" Kari asked.

He wasn't sure. The last and only time he'd been in here it looked different. Or his memory was failing him when he needed it most.

"She's changed things."

"But the letters will be together, right?"

Corban shrugged. "I don't know."

"How long do you think we have ... before we need to get out of here?"

Mom said she was bringing dinner home from Tequila Sunrise, and that was ten minutes each way. And she was clearly planning to do something else before hitting the restaurant. So, "Half an hour, at least."

"There's a lot of stuff in here." Kari sighed. "Maybe this was a mistake."

"I'll check over there," he pointed to a long row of cabinets, "and you check her desk. I'll set a timer for twenty-five minutes."

Kari quickly flipped through the papers on the desk. "This is a contract. Is that locked?"

She gestured toward a single piece of furniture behind the desk, a hutch made of rich-grained wood with a heavy brown wash. Naturally weathered, with the sort of fussy embellishments his mother loved. Plinth bases, crown molding, and fluting on the posts. It looked more like a work of art than office furniture.

"Might as well check it," Corban said.

It wasn't locked. But it didn't contain a stash of letters from serial killers, either.

Mom's cabinets were stacked with empty Apple boxes, manuals, defunct keyboards and hard drives. A lot of ugly old books. No letters.

Same for the space in the nook beneath the picture window, and the small empty closet.

"Any luck?"

Kari looked over. "Not so far. But your mom doesn't have a lot of patients. How long has it been?"

Corban looked at his phone. "Twenty-three minutes."

She didn't respond, just kept looking through the cabinet, without removing a single folder.

Corban was out of places to look, so he started searching all the same areas again. He wanted to help Kari, even wished that he had thought to start on the filing cabinet first. The buzzer was going to go off, and he didn't dare stay longer, for fear of being discovered.

With ten seconds left on the timer, Kari said, "I found something."

A pink box, about the size of a toaster.

Kari unlatched it. Peeked inside, then showed him the contents. A couple of small red journals.

"It was at the back of the last file drawer, hidden beneath a pile of receipts."

What was in it that Mom hadn't wanted anyone to find? He had to know. He'd find a way to sneak it back in here.

"We're taking it," he said. "I still haven't found any letters."

"Maybe she throws them away."

"I'd believe she sleeps with them under her pillow before I'd believe that."

Kari closed the file cabinet in slow motion, so it wouldn't make a banging sound. "We better get out of here."

"We still haven't found anything that'll help your dad," Corban objected.

"If the red journals don't help, maybe we can try again. We'll have to sneak this back in anyway."

After a quick check to be sure they hadn't left anything

out of place that might signal to his mom that someone had gone through her stuff, they retreated to Corban's room to examine the journals.

"Patient X," Corban said as flipped the pages and realized what he was seeing. "These are my mom's notes for her last book."

"The one that reporter asked about?"

Corban nodded as he skimmed another passage. "She also calls him *The Virgin.*"

"This one goes back more than ten years." Kari shook her journal. "Is it normal for someone to be in therapy that long?"

"I guess?"

How would he know? Mom had always kept him and Levi away from her work.

Kari slumped and leaned back against the headboard. "So Patient X probably isn't the killer."

"I'll keep looking for the letters," Corban promised. "She must've hidden them somewhere else. No way would she get rid of them."

Not the good ones, anyway. Which was an awful thing to say about letters from serial killers. But that was his mom.

"Wait …" Kari jumped off the bed as if goosed. "There was an entry in your mom's calendar for tomorrow. No name, just a time and the letter X. I thought maybe she'd gotten distracted and didn't finish whatever she was going to write. But if that's him, he's here in Almond Park."

"Then I'll ditch school and see who it is."

"*We'll* ditch school and see who it is," Kari corrected.

Chapter Forty-One

"I still don't get it, Pussy ..." Elliot shook his head. "Maybe you would be easier to understand if your parents were second cousins instead of first."

"Leave him alone, already," Dane said to Elliot.

Pussabo said nothing.

Levi wished he could ignore them all.

"It's true, right?" Elliot continued. "Your parents *could* be first cousins. Because how much could you really know about them? Maybe—"

"Shut up, Elliot!"

Now Dane was standing straighter, squaring his shoulders. He dropped his backpack on the ground.

"This is dumb," Levi said. "Both of you, chill."

"What am I supposed to chill out about?" Dane nodded at Elliot. "He's the one being the asshole. It's fucking old."

"That's two *fuckings* before the first bell. Maybe you need to get laid. Hey Levi, do you think your mom's home?"

Levi dropped his backpack beside Dane's and reached for Elliot.

"Shit ..." Elliot raised his hands and fell a step back. "I'm sorry."

Everyone was on edge. Had been for a while. Not just among their group, but the whole school. And really, the city.

The Almond Park Killer had murdered his town.

School was a jungle, and Levi was no longer immune — everyone seemed to have decided he was guilty by association. His mom was talking to the police and reporters, smiling for the cameras on a half-dozen stations. His brother was dating the number one suspect's daughter, whose wife had committed suicide rather than learn she'd been married to a serial killer. If this kept going, would his friends turn against him too?

The only thing that made him even the slightest bit better was challenging Decker to a fight after school. He'd abandoned Corban when his brother needed him, but he could make sure Decker never touched him again.

If he could make things right with Corban, maybe he could smooth things with Kari, too.

And when she finally got tired of Corban, like she eventually would, she'd realize who she belonged with.

And there it was again, another reason to hate himself.

Corban was his twin brother, and yet Levi always ended up competing with him.

"Were you born an asshole or do you have to recommit every morning?" Dane asked Elliot, interrupting Levi's guilty thoughts.

"It's really too bad that two-thirds of your dick went to your personality," Elliot said, ignoring him. "Your palm is really getting the shaft. Or not."

"I hope you die shitting."

"If your mom lies down and opens her mouth, then I might just give it a shot."

"I thought moms were out of this," Elliot said, looking genuinely wounded.

"Not yours." Dane glared at him, his shoulders still hunched.

Levi wondered if this was going to get seriously out of control. Corban had always been the buffer between them. Since he'd left the group, Dane and Elliot had grown increasingly obnoxious, and not just in their constant bitching at each other.

Elliot shrugged. "Then you should know that you were birthed out of your mother's asshole, because her pussy was too busy."

Eyes burning, Dane deadpanned, "I'm going to plant a tree in your mother's cunt and fuck your sister in its shade."

"Dude …" Elliot fell a step back.

Thankfully, the bell rang, interrupting whatever Dane would've said next.

Levi *had* to fix things with Corban.

Chapter Forty-Two

Corban still couldn't believe he was ditching.

Up until this year, he had liked, maybe even loved, going to school. And not for the same reasons as Levi. In that way, he had more in common with Dane. They both cared about how they did, because they saw higher education as an escape. The first rung on the long ladder to anywhere else. Dane had his eyes on Stanford, Corban was looking at Berkeley: their architecture school was one of the best, and close enough to come home when he felt like it, but not so close that his parents would be dropping in all the time.

Like his mom, Corban got lost in his work, and was grateful for a good school that gave him plenty to do. Homework distracted him from how crappy his life had become.

Kari waited for him a block down from the school entrance with her blue and yellow bike and a smile, even though he was running almost a half hour later than they'd agreed. She cleared her throat as he approached.

"Sorry," Corban said. "It was hard to get away because Mr. Jefferson was patrolling the front."

Kari rolled her eyes. "I have no idea why you walked all the way to school when you knew you were going to turn around and go back."

"I couldn't let Levi figure out that I was ditching. The way he's been lately, he'd text Dad."

"Now we only have a half hour to get home." She stood on the pedals, pushed, and started rolling forward. Corban jogged to catch up.

"We're going to wait outside my house to see who goes inside."

"Then can we go to a movie after that?" Kari asked. "Or the mall?"

"We should probably go someplace where we won't run into people."

Corban was starting to feel out of breath. He didn't usually jog one and a half miles home in summer heat with a fully-loaded backpack. "I've got to slow down."

Kari eased up, clearly reluctant. "If we miss him—"

"He's a regular patient. He'll be back."

They got there with seven minutes to spare, enough time to settle into their predetermined hiding spot behind the bank of planters, where they could see anyone approaching the front door. Looking out from behind the bright magenta bougainvillea overflowing their giant terracotta pots, Corban glanced at the windows of the second-floor study, in case Patient X was already there, but saw no movement.

His heart was pounding. He wondered if Kari could hear it.

"Nervous?" he asked.

"Maybe."

They waited in silence. Eight minutes felt three times as long.

"Do you think we were too late?"

"It's my fault we missed him," Corban said. Then, "What if I went inside?"

"Won't you get in trouble for ditching?"

"It'd be worth it, to catch the killer … I'll say I came home because I felt sick."

Kari nodded. "Take a picture if you can."

Corban ninja-walked on the sides of his feet to the front door, just like YouTube taught him. Then he quietly opened it, eased himself inside, and softly shut the door behind him.

Corban froze, listening.

The house felt empty, but he was never here at this time on a weekday. Maybe this is what it felt like.

He crept toward his mother's office, freezing again just outside it. He hadn't really thought this part through. What would be the best way to find out Patient X's identity?

Gathering his courage, he softly pressed his ear to the wood.

He heard murmurs. Mumbles and grumbles, nothing distinct. The tone seemed at times thoughtful, and other times hurried. Occasionally angry, then right back to thoughtful.

And then the sounds changed.

They became animal. Mumbles turned into moans, grumbles into grunting and growling.

His mother screamed in pleasure, a sound that would surely haunt him for life.

She was fucking Patient X?

No. That wasn't possible.

And besides, she wouldn't dare with his father's car right outside.

But she was definitely fucking someone.

Maybe that was why she stayed with Dad even though he'd cheated on her. She didn't care because she was cheating too.

Corban wanted to leave, but his feet felt cemented to the floor. He had to know what this was. He had to—

"Fuck me bloody!"

That time he heard her perfectly. She issued a final guttural scream, then the man in her office furiously grunted.

Corban did an about-face and ninja-walked as fast as he could without making a sound.

The door behind him started to open.

He ducked around the corner just in time.

Corban couldn't make it outside without being seen, but he could get to his room.

But then he couldn't see the man in her office, and would die if he didn't know.

So he waited to see who The Virgin might be.

He peeked around the corner.

It was his father.

Despite his disappointment, something relaxed deep in his chest. Patient X must've canceled his appointment, and his parents took advantage of the free time to mess around. Not that he wanted to think about them having sex, but that was better than knowing their marriage was crumbling.

They stood together in front of the door. Oddly, they weren't holding hands and there seemed to be no tenderness between them, despite what he heard.

His mother said, "Do you feel better after your session?"

His father's answer filled Corban with chills.

"I always do."

His insides were eating themselves.

This was impossible.

It didn't make sense, because it *couldn't* make sense. If it did, then everything else was a lie.

Yeah, his dad was annoyingly pleased with himself. He thought he was a lot funnier than he actually was. Maybe he was even a cheater.

But ... a serial killer?

NO. Corban refused to believe it.

Even though it made a sick kind of sense.

His mom spent her life studying serial killers. Nothing lit her up more than getting into the head of the sickest, most perverted people on the planet.

It was only logical that she'd fall in love with one.

The contents of her red notebook bled into his thoughts. His mother's steady script, gliding across the page in perfect penmanship, describing the monster she called The Virgin, and all of the darkest, most perverted fantasies Corban had ever heard.

The things he wanted to see and do.

Although, he had not done them yet.

Isn't that what was special about The Virgin?

Mom made her career with a book about how to stop yourself from becoming a serial killer.

Oh God.

He should read it. No, he couldn't read it. He'd know things about his father that he'd never be able to forget.

And his father would know he knew. He'd never be able to act like things were normal again. Because they never would be.

What was he going to tell Kari?

They'd been trying to prove that her father wasn't a

serial killer, and they'd accidentally proven that his father *was*.

Corban waited until his dad made a left at the end of the hallway and trudged upstairs before sneaking out of the house where his girlfriend was waiting for the horrible truth.

Maybe he shouldn't tell her.

Even though it meant her own father would stay in jail.

How could he ask her to endure the same horror that he was trying to escape himself?

Was he that much of an asshole?

When he rejoined her behind the planters, she took one look at him and asked, "What's wrong? What did you find out?"

"Not here," he whispered. "We need to leave, now."

She bit her bottom lip, but followed him back to her bike at the edge of the property. She swung a long leg over the seat and started to pedal, fast and then faster as Corban jogged behind her. They didn't stop until they were far enough down the road that his house was out of sight.

"So tell me everything," she said.

They were crying together by the time Corban finished his story.

"Do you really think that your dad could be the killer?"

"No." He shook his head, emphatic.

"No because he's your father, or no because that's impossible?"

He looked at her, sifting through multiple impossible answers. Because what could he say?

"I don't know … both?"

Corban was going to—

And then he did. Vomited everywhere.

"Oh my God! Are you okay?"

Corban was doubled over, clutching his stomach. He looked up at Kari, licked his lips. "How can I be?"

"What are we going to do?"

Corban shrugged and shook his head. "What *can* we do?"

"Um … tell the police."

"There's nothing to tell them!" Corban exclaimed, surprised by his own anger. "We don't know anything!"

"What do you mean *we don't know anything*? We just found out that your mom based all her research on a suppressed serial killer, and that that person is your father." And now she was practically yelling. "*What else do we need to know?*"

"We don't have a single fact, Kari. Not that I want to think about it or anything, but we might have seen something totally different than what we're imagining. What if that's just some sort of weird sex game that my parents play, where he pretends to be one of her patients, confessing all of his fantasies? Then she writes it down, because that's what she's supposed to do as his 'doctor' before they have sex."

Kari looked like she was trying to find a parking spot six miles away from *convinced.*

"I've heard of weirder fetishes," Corban added.

"Have you?"

Corban actually hadn't, so he shared in his silence rather than an answer. Then he finally said, "We can't tell anyone. Not until we have more information."

"What more do we need, Corban?"

"We need to *know* something. Right now we're just guessing."

"You mean like all the things the police *know* about my dad?"

He didn't have an answer for that. Kari was right, but

… just because her dad had been falsely accused didn't mean they should do the same to his. Not when there was still time to investigate.

Kari continued. "If the real killer gets away with this, and my dad goes to jail, then I won't have any parents."

Corban felt desperate, torn between trying to make this right with Kari, right with his family, and right with the world.

But the world had turned upside down.

"You're right," he said. "And I promise that we'll figure this out. Do you trust me?"

"Of course, but—"

"Then let me dig a little more. Once we have something concrete, we can go to the police together. Okay?"

The following silence was long and painful, finally severed by the most reluctant whisper that Corban had ever heard.

"Okay," Kari said.

Chapter Forty-Three

Adam tapped his digital pencil on the tablet's eraser and deleted all the garbage he'd spent the last half hour writing. Every word was terrible. The TV in the background had distracted him. He was hungry. He needed another session.

Who was he kidding? Excuses weren't going to solve the problem. Adam hadn't been able to make himself laugh in a while. Months, really. He was losing edge.

Maybe a different kind of writing might be easier.

He saw her in his mind. At first, her porcelain face was naked except for the lipstick, same shade of crimson as the blood that spattered her face as she flinched back in fear, her eyes widening with the knowledge that all of the life was leaving her soon-to-be-empty shell, spilling like syrup, bubbling onto the white tile floor, blood gurgling up from her lip and—

Adam's head spun toward the television.

No.

The anchorwoman looked grave.

"… The fourth murder. Another family was the target, but this time the brake line on their SUV was cut. Their home was at the top of the hill inside the Rancho Vista Community, the highest private point in Almond Park. The family's father, Benjamin Withers, managed to maneuver them down the hill well enough to save both his life and the lives of his two children."

The anchorwoman nodded gravely and her co-anchor took over.

Looking solemn, he said, "Unfortunately, Jennifer Withers wasn't so lucky. Her body was rushed to Almond Park Memorial, but the doctors pronounced her dead on arrival."

Back to the anchorwoman. "The police discovered an emerald green scarf with tiny yellow dots in the trunk of the Withers' family car, a vintage Mercedes. This is the fourth scarf found at the scene of what the Almond Park Police Department is calling 'the worst string of murders to ever hit this part of the country.'"

The camera zoomed in on the scarf. It looked familiar, but that was probably because it looked like one of Selena's. She sure as hell had enough of them.

He wished he could write. It didn't even have to be funny. Anything would do. Adam just wanted to empty his thoughts, and the words on the page at their best could do that. But there was something about these murders that bothered him. Burrowed into the depths of his mind, nesting in to fester and rot. There was something so wrong about all of this. They didn't trigger his fantasies, they triggered revulsion.

Adam stood and stretched, killed the TV and the commiserating anchors inside it, then went outside just to get the fuck out of his house.

He stood by the pool and thought.

Maybe he could go for a drive.

Then have a little adventure afterward.

Dinner, then dessert.

Except … things were better with Selena following their session. And he wanted to keep them that way. He had to find another way to defend against his urges.

His phone buzzed and he checked it, wondering if there was even a one-percent chance that whatever he saw on the screen might invite a smile.

It didn't.

Wayne was on *Really, Tonight?* and needed a few lines about the Almond Park Killer.

Is that purfect 4u or what?

Or what, asshole.

The request pissed him off. It was in poor taste. Why did he think writing serial killer jokes were perfect for Adam?

Because Adam was married to the one person in the world who seemed most pleased by the killings?

There was a time when he would've resented Selena for putting him in this position, but now he blamed Wayne for being an insensitive prick. People Adam had known for years were dying.

No thanks, Adam texted.

The killer was hitting closer and closer to home. What if he and his family were next? Adam's urges wouldn't protect them. If Selena didn't make a breakthrough soon, her expertise might not save them either.

A collision with death or worse seemed imminent, drifting ever closer until he could feel its hot breath curling the hairs on his neck. Whoever this—

Adam spun toward the TV.

The anchor said something that couldn't be possible. Adam *had* to be dreaming. Because if he wasn't, then everything was over for him, and everyone he knew.

The house filled with a bloodcurdling scream, and Adam knew that she'd heard it too.

Chapter Forty-Four

Selena was cooking, and she didn't even mind.

She had the ingredients from her BistroBox spread out on the table. Everything was washed and ready. *She* was ready, to cut and sauté and broil. As long as she could stay where she was, cooking while watching TV.

Selena was mesmerized. This was too much. Unlike anything she had ever seen. Especially in her own backyard.

Four families. Dead. In one city.

And whether Selena liked it or not, this was at least in some way all about her.

The scarves tied her to this, like a submissive's wrists to her master's whims. And here she was, trying to figure out why someone was trying so hard to flatter her with homicide.

Selena shouldn't feel so excited. But the heat felt good, warming her from the inside. She would do anything to keep it going, despite the danger.

But there was a big problem, looming and serious.

Something that could plow into their lives and total them, like an eighteen-wheeler careening into a MINI Cooper.

Now that there were four scarves, someone *would* put two and two together.

At first Selena believed that the third scarf would be tied to her, distinctive as it was, and eager as amateur sleuths tended to be. But after a few days passed without any attention — an eternity in awareness online — she felt safe enough to settle back into her skin.

But this new scarf ... emerald green with yellow darts? That one graced Selena's neck on the back of her latest book. It was impossible to believe that no one was going to notice that. And once they noticed this last one, the preceding three would line up single file to accuse her.

You were wrong about your research.

You were wrong about your husband.

You were wrong about everything.

Now people are dead, just like your career.

She knew Adam better than anyone on the planet. She hadn't just bet his career on his ability to control his violence, she'd bet her life, and the lives of her children. She *couldn't* be wrong about him. Their very existence proved it.

Unless he was just getting started.

Unless their sessions merely delayed the inevitable.

What did Selena *really* know?

Not nearly as much as she pretended in front of the cameras.

She doubted that the police would find any hard evidence at the crime scene. Not in the car, not in the house, not anywhere near Rancho Vista. This killer was too clever for that. And whatever they found on Ollie would be entirely circumstantial, like last time.

Almost as if it were planted.

226

It really could be him. Her Adam. But if she had been wrong all these years, and he really was sick, then …

No. She still couldn't think about it. Not until she knew for sure.

And even then, Selena would—

Her phone *buzzed*.

Then it *buzzed* and *buzzed* and *buzzed* and *buzzed*.

Her heart was an army of drums as she picked it up and looked at the screen.

LifeLyfe was exploding.

Because someone had leaked the truth about The Virgin.

And now her phone was ringing. The screen read: *Sam*.

Selena screamed.

Chapter Forty-Five

Corban had seen his mother's rage once before, but compared to now, that time seemed like a kitten lazily batting at a ball of yarn.

He'd heard his parents fight before, but never like this. And those fights usually happened in their bedroom, not her office. And he couldn't just go play a game with Levi like he used to.

Not that Levi would be any help at all right now.

Corban had learned about the leak around the same time as his mom. His phone was blowing up as she screamed.

She paced, listening to — then yelling at — Sam.

She paced, screaming at her husband.

She paced, upstairs, downstairs, inside, outside, and he had no doubt that she kept pacing behind her closed office door.

His mother was *livid*. But he understood. In his own way, Corban was equally angry.

He couldn't believe Kari had done this to him.

He had to see her. He couldn't wait to ride there on his

bike. And if Dad came out and found his Porsche missing, so fucking what? Maybe he could write about it in his diary.

He took the extra set of keys from the kitchen drawer, then went outside, climbed into the driver's seat, and raced toward Kari's, imagining all of the many things he was going to say. Because even though he loved her with all his heart, and had for a while, right now he hated her. She was responsible for the horror that had rolled into his life.

Corban looked at the speedometer, realized he was going over sixty in a thirty-five, and eased up on the pedal.

He couldn't afford a ticket, or anything else. Getting stopped by an officer now would be a disaster.

Do you know how fast you were driving back there?

Is this your car, son?

Hey, aren't you the one with the dad who confessed to being a murderer?

No. He'd confessed to having murderous thoughts. That wasn't the same thing.

Or was it?

He pulled up in front of Kari's house, saw that Ollie's car wasn't in the driveway — he didn't park in garages, because it changed a vehicle's natural temperature — and got out. Corban wasn't sure if it was a good thing or a bad thing that Ollie wasn't home, or if he was about to make the biggest mistake of his life, but the fury inside him couldn't be restrained.

If he had any future with Kari at all, he had to find out. *Now.*

He knocked on the door. Rang the bell. Knocked again harder when she still didn't answer.

He knew she was home.

He couldn't see her or smell her or hear her, but Corban could *feel* her, just like always, and with a sixth sense that felt helluva lot stronger than one he shared with his twin.

He pounded harder against the wood. Did she think he would give up if she ignored him?

Kari finally opened the door.

"What?" She didn't seem surprised to see him.

"How could you?"

Without blinking or flinching or drawing a breath, she asked, "What did you expect me to do?"

"KEEP YOUR WORD!"

This time, she did flinch, taking several steps back, leaving the door wide open.

Corban marched inside. He'd never been angrier.

"I'm sorry, I—"

"No, you're not! You know *exactly* what you did! You traded your dad for mine, even though you *promised* that we would wait! It hasn't even been a day!"

His breath came in hitches, catching in his throat. His eyes burned, and so did his skin.

"Calm down, Corban. You *made me* promise. That wasn't fair."

"But what you did was?"

"If you let me explain—"

"I hope you're planning to start with *I'm sorry.*"

"I'm sorry."

"No, you're not!" Corban words could blister the air between them. "If you were sorry then you wouldn't have done it!"

"I'm not sorry I reported what we found out, I'm just sorry that it hurt you."

"Then you're *not* sorry. You promised. And it's what *I* found out, Kari. I told you because I trusted you."

"I'm sorry I broke my promise, but you would have done the same thing! If your mom was on trial, either for real or in the court of public opinion, then you would protect her. I'm trying to protect my dad, because that's all I can do. I don't even have a mom to keep safe anymore."

"I stuck with you when *everyone* else—"

"Why should my father suffer when your father is the one *admitting* that he wants to kill people?"

When she said it like that, he knew that everyone was going to take her side. They'd been willing to turn on Ollie for being weird. Once they read what his own father had written, they probably wouldn't even bother to investigate. They'd take his fantasies as a confession and lock him right up.

Even if they didn't believe Corban had known, they'd see him as the son of a serial killer forever. His life was over, too.

He turned around, walked outside, got back into his father's Porsche, and drove with his hands shaking on the wheel, barely looking until he nearly collided with a rusty 90s era 4Runner.

The braying horn returned Corban to center. But a part of him wondered if it would've been easier if he hadn't swerved back into his own lane.

If dying would be easier than living.

He raced against the daylight as though night had sworn its allegiance to end him. But he couldn't go home. Not yet. How could he face his parents, now that he knew?

Now that they knew he knew?

Maybe his father was a monster.

Made sense, since it had felt like Corban was living in hell.

The images were nails and his memory a hammer.

Adam drowning his pancakes in cherry syrup at some roadside dive on the way to Vegas. He looked like Levi, the first time he saw porn. The way that Adam looked at their mother …

Adam laughing at a movie that Corban hadn't even wanted to watch, full of flesh, knives, and gory horror. He pointed to a pile of limbs and husks, covered in buckets of blood. "Anyone gonna eat that?" Then Levi laughed with him.

Adam saying to Ollie, just imagine all the blood!

Hey look, there's the body and here's the blood.

Imagine that instead of these quiet, silent deaths, the killer really went to town. Made McNuggets out of the family. Left their eyeballs floating in the soup. I mean, gruesome shit. Bloody. Well, no one could ever think that was you, could they?

Corban parked. But he couldn't get out of the car.

Chapter Forty-Six

Adam knew better than to ask, but somehow the question slipped out anyway. "Do we have to do this now?"

"Of course we have to do this now, Adam. This isn't a chore you can half-ass and pretend that you didn't, or a movie we can pause. This is an argument. It deserves your attention *now*. Asking me if this can be done later is the same as telling me that this isn't important to you."

"This is important to me, which is why I brought it up. But my side of this only got about a minute before we were back on The Selena Show and I was wishing for Tivo, because this is definitely a show I'd delete from my queue."

Adam didn't have an issue dealing with it, but he had a big problem with the way she was addressing him, and the entire situation. She wouldn't come out and say what she was thinking. Instead, she was unraveling, one passive-aggressive statement at a time. Just like her career. It seemed like she wanted to take him down with her.

But Adam wasn't about to let that happen.

"Just say it, Selena. If you want me to stay up here and talk to you, then fine. You either need to listen and help me, or say whatever is on your goddamned mind and stop forcing me to try and read it."

"I'm not forcing you to do anything."

"You're forcing me to stay up here in the bedroom with you, when it's obvious that we're not getting anywhere."

"You mean you're not getting your way."

"Not even close."

"What do you want from me?"

Adam threw up his hands.

"Are you kidding me?" He started to pace.

"Will you please stop being dramatic?" Selena practically screamed. He'd finally gotten under her skin. "What is it, specifically in this moment, that you want from me?"

"How about a little fucking empathy? How about you see what's happening around you, instead of waiting around for Sam to call and tell you. How about—"

"Is this where you just make a list of things to insult me?"

"How about you care about someone other than yourself for a change?"

"So, that's a yes."

"It's out there, and there's nothing we can do to change that. I don't care what Sam promises you, that cat already scratched its way out of the bag. I've been outed. The world knows I'm a killer."

"You're not a killer, Adam. Not even close."

"Close enough. I'm suppressed. This would have been the most earth-shattering event of my life even without the string of murders only miles away."

"*Exactly.* And what do you think that does to the credibility of my work? Of *our* work?"

"Absolutely nothing! What does one have to do with the other? Why are you making this about you, even after I keep begging you not to?"

"Because it's about me too, Adam. It's about all of us. It's about the future that we've invested in together. We can't afford this."

"What do you mean, *we can't afford this?* We're doing fine."

"Sure we are, in part because we're borrowing against a tomorrow that seemed all but guaranteed." She turned toward Adam, snarling, "And now you've gone and fucked that all up!"

"You always told me that I couldn't stop my thoughts, but I could always control what I did with them."

"And are you?"

Adam stared at his wife. Couldn't believe he was having this conversation.

"This is ridiculous."

"I agree," she said.

He looked at the door.

"You're not leaving until we're done."

"I'm not leaving?"

He sure as hell would be leaving. It wasn't like he had much of a choice. The police would surely want to have a chat at any moment. He had to start thinking about where he would go, and how he would survive on the run.

It didn't matter whether the police arrested him. Just as with Ollie, the questioning would be enough to ruin his life.

And unlike Ollie, Adam had said some terrible, terrible things.

What would happen to the boys, with their father on the run and their mother's career in ashes?

How dare she sit there and moan about how this was going to hurt her career when she should've been thinking about how this would hurt their family?

She finally broke the silence. "No. You're not. Let's finish this."

Great idea.

"Fine. Then why don't you just say whatever it is you haven't been saying? I'm sick of smelling it on you."

"Better than what I've been smelling on you."

More silence. Another glance at the door.

"Don't even think about it."

"Too late." If she'd *actually* talk about this — not at or around it, but really dig into it — he'd gladly stay. But this pretending … this, whatever it was, he couldn't be a part of it.

Adam wanted to throw up.

He shook his head at Selena and headed for the door.

He felt slightly better the second he was on the other side.

"Adam … Adam … ADAM!"

He ignored her all the way downstairs. He had to get out of the house. It didn't even matter where he went, just as long as it was away from this place.

But still, Adam knew exactly where he was going to go.

And maybe even what he would do once he got there.

If he could gather the courage.

Finally. Get the guts to spill hers onto the floor.

Into the kitchen and over to the fridge. He yanked the door like he was trying to unstick it. The thing flew open and the cold air that Adam had been craving started kissing his face.

Banish the thoughts. Before they took control and made him do one of the few things that would make his situation worse than it already was.

Adam closed the fridge, hesitating when he saw Dane in the living room with Levi and their friends. The other boys deliberately ignored him, but Dane turned around to leer at him.

Adam stared back. Without looking away, he opened the fridge again, reached inside, and grabbed a bottle of beer. Then he opened a drawer, pulled out a bottle opener, popped the top of his local craft, and took a swig.

It was easy to hold his smile with the things he was imagining doing to this little punk-ass pile of semen and shit. Adam would love to end him, and could merrily count the ways.

One: I'm going to punch you in the throat, then while you're choking on your few final breaths I'll carve a hole in the back of your neck. You'll be in shock, but quickly understanding that all of the blood will be leaving your body, and that I will use your empty husk to mop it up from the floor. I'm going to shove my fingers into that fresh hole and yank on your spine. Blood will rain when I disconnect tissues. Then I will puncture your organs, empty a one-gallon jug of gas into the hole, and drop a match.

Two. I'm going to—

No. He couldn't do this.

These thoughts would destroy him.

He nodded at Dane, almost pleasant, and walked toward the door with his beer.

He was worse than worthless, a total pariah.

His kids were never going to look at him the same way again, and it was all his fault.

He opened the door and looked back into the living room before leaving, wondering why Levi and his friends were downstairs at all. They practically lived in the game room. Maybe Corban was upstairs and they were all down here because he and Levi still weren't talking. They weren't even watching TV or playing a game. No one was on their phone. They were all just sitting around on the couch, staring at the coffee table in silence.

Dane nodded back at Adam. Slow, like it was some sort of threat.

Right. He was probably going to prison for the rest of his life for being a serial killer, but what really scared him was a teenaged piss-ant with an attitude.

Adam stepped outside and closed the door behind him.

He had suffered long enough, and everyone thought he was guilty anyway.

It was time to do what he'd been born to do, and yet denied all his life.

Chapter Forty-Seven

"He's gone," Dane said to the group, though it was mostly for Levi.

"About time," Levi said. "I still don't want to go upstairs."

For some reason the game room had started to feel like a prison. And he wasn't about to have his parents' bullshit keep him out of the rest of his house.

"I wouldn't want to either," Dane said. "Good for you."

Elliot raised his hand. "I would like to offer the counterproposal that Levi sucks, and that the game room is better than this stupid living room."

"I'm with Elliot," Pussabo said.

Dane laughed. "It's better than your living room. That place only looks good in the dark."

"I told you why I don't want to be up there," Levi said, sick of discussing it.

If they went up there, they'd start playing *HardCorp* and telling the same twenty stupid jokes, like nothing had changed, and *everything* had. He needed to talk to someone, and these three were all he had. They needed to talk about it too, even if they couldn't admit it.

His mom would say that they needed to do a better job of connecting, and she would be right, even though she rarely knew how to follow her own advice.

The other day had been rough. Elliot and Dane nearly tried to wipe the pavement with each other. Hard as it would have been to imagine that happening a couple of months before, it sure as hell looked like that was what would have gone down if they hadn't been saved by the bell.

The two of them always had more friction than anyone else in the group, but it used to be brotherly rather than adversarial. Sometime over the last few weeks that mood had shifted. The two were just *at* each other. He didn't want to lose either of them the way he'd lost Corban.

Because yes, Corban was a ghost. Levi hadn't seen him all day. Maybe he was living over at Kari's now. It would make sense, with her mom being dead and her dad being nuts.

Levi tried to smile at his friends, and was reasonably sure he succeeded. "Where do you think Corban is?"

Dane shrugged. "How would I know?"

"If he's still attached to his dick, which he probably is, then the better question might be, *Where is Kari's mouth?*"

Pussabo shook his head at Elliot. "He's probably taking care of her. You know, after all that stuff."

"Shows you exactly how fucked up my parents are," Levi said. "It's one thing for me to not know where he is, but right now neither of them cares. It's like they live on another planet from the rest of us."

"He's from Mars and she's from Venus." Elliot nodded knowingly.

"Do you think we'll colonize Mars in our lifetimes?"

Pussabo asked. "And if so, do you think we'll ever get to go there?"

Dane looked at Pussabo and gave him a look: *What the fuck, Pussy?*

Elliot said, "Maybe in our lifetimes. You're probably gonna die young from Stupid Question Syndrome."

"Seriously," Dane said, returning their conversation to center, "when do you think this will all blow over?"

"Blow over?" Levi laughed. "How can it ever blow over?"

"Everything blows over," Pussabo said.

Dane shot Elliot another look: *Don't you dare.*

"Have you really not seen the news? Or listened to a word I've been saying? My mom is probably going to lose her license. Her husband is a patient; that's a big fat strike one. But he's potentially a serial killer? And she didn't know? Or worse, she knew and did nothing? That's strikes two through a thousand."

"Shit," Elliot said, without a punchline to chase it.

"There's no proof," Dane said. "It's all hearsay ... right?"

"Well, sure," Levi agreed. "But perception is reality. She quotes her agent on that all the time."

Dane shook his head, empathetic and emphatic.

"This is all just a part of the story. If you're famous in this country, then you can get away with anything. And America loves a good comeback. Kobe raped some girl fifteen years ago, and tickets for his last game sold for twenty-five grand. The dude is a basketball legend and was up for an Oscar. But he put his dick in some girl against her will and everyone knows it. When this blows over, and it *will*, then your parents will have weathered the storm. They'll be stronger for it, and so will your family."

"Thanks." Levi put a hand on Dane's shoulder, grateful

for a friend who always helped him see the better side. "I'm not trying to be a downer about all this, and sure, my mom's deals have all disappeared just as fast as they showed up, and the network might cancel her show. Her agent thinks they will. He's seen this thing before. Her next book is on hold and, fuck, you guys, you don't know my mom. She can be a total bitch when she doesn't get her way."

Dane gave him a sour look. "Easy, man. At least you have a mom."

Fucking Dane.

It wasn't fair. Just because Dane had lost his mom, Levi was never allowed to bitch about his. And if there was ever a time when he deserved the latitude, it was now.

"Pussy has a mom," Elliot said. "He just doesn't know if she's really his."

The thing he couldn't say — the thing that hurt the worst? Levi had lost his hero. He couldn't remember when he *didn't* want to be a comedian just like his dad.

But his dad was a monster. And Levi had always wanted to be just like him.

Chapter Forty-Eight

It hadn't been a surprise when Adam arrived home to find Detective Sharpe sipping coffee with Selena. He'd been surprisingly polite, practically inviting him to the station for a chat.

What was the man thinking now? Adam wondered as he traced a scratch in the interrogation room's beat-up metal table.

Thankfully, the girl with the blood-red lipstick hadn't been working, even though it was her usual shift. Because Adam might have gone through with it, and now the guilt would be all over his face.

Adam agreed to answer any questions that the detective might have. Why not? He had bulletproof alibis for at least two of the murders. And he wasn't connected in any way to all four.

"Where did you say you were going … right before you got back to your place?"

"I told you. Out for a drive."

"Do you like to go out for drives? Is that something you regularly do?"

"Sure."

"When was the last time you just 'went for a drive'? You know, before today. Was it sometime last week? Like maybe last Tuesday afternoon? Maybe you went for a drive and wanted to see as much of this little burg as you could at once, so you drove up to Rancho Vista and—"

"I don't have the gate code."

Sharpe shrugged and nodded. "That's easy enough to get. Maybe you had a friend. The two of you might be working together, swapping kills and trading thrills. Maybe your kids are friends, so you've got that in common. Maybe in that light your alibis start making a lot more sense."

Adam shifted in his seat, working to remember what he promised his wife he would never forget.

Selena had given him a protocol, a specific way to behave both in public and private, a detailed procedure to follow that would keep his skeletons locked safely in their closet. But Detective Sharpe was sneering in the seat across from him, kicking at that closet door and using the bones inside it to rattle him.

"Ollie Harris isn't my friend."

"So, you're colleagues, then?" Sharpe grinned and waited for Adam to answer.

"No," he said through pursed lips. "We're not colleagues."

Sharpe studied Adam, ever so slightly nodding, now leaning back an inch in his chair.

But Adam refused to speak unless spoken to, because terrors were made in fissures of truth.

"Look, Mr. Nash. We know that you had something to do with it, but we also know that you couldn't have done any of this alone. So you help us and we'll be thrilled to help you right back. We just want to make sure this doesn't happen to anyone else. Your little confession? It looks good and bad. Bad for the obvious reasons. You're obviously a nutty pile of shit who wants to hurt people. But good, because it looks like you've been trying to do right by the world by keeping your crazy in check, which is why we're talking. So …"

And now he leaned forward.

"Do you want to start talking?"

"Not without my lawyer."

"A lawyer?" Sharpe repeated. "Why would you need one of those? I thought we were having a conversation?"

"This isn't a conversation, it's an interrogation. One where you've already decided what you want me to say. So no, I'm not interested."

Sharpe nodded. His eyes, face, and physical bearing were all suddenly so very understanding. The detective sighed and seemed to reset, settling down into his seat, his body now relaxed in what looked almost like surrender.

"Let's start over."

"You mean with my lawyer in the room? That's a great idea."

"Tell you what, why don't we finish our conversation, just you and me, for the next few minutes. I think we're close, and you know how it's going to look if you lawyer up. I don't want that for you or your wife or your family. People will talk. So what do you say, Mr. Nash? How about you give me another five minutes?"

Adam gave Sharpe a barely perceptible nod.

The man continued with a speech that seemed so rehearsed, Adam figured he'd given it hundreds of times already.

"I understand how this all happened, and if you're willing to cooperate, then I'm sure a jury will, too. You've been having these compulsions for years, but you've never acted on them. Your old lady doctor has done a helluva job keeping your monster locked in the attic. Maybe something happened before and maybe not, we're just getting started poking around Los Angeles. We'll see if there's anything back there that matches what we're seeing here. But let's just assume there isn't, and that this is all fresh. I still don't think that's you. Because regardless of all that shit in your head, I'm pretty sure you're a decent guy, Mr. Nash. You don't want to actually see anyone dead, you just like to think about it. But then you met Ollie Harris, a man who was willing to see things through. Maybe you couldn't help your curiosity, but then things ended up going a little too far. You couldn't pull it back in, and now it's everywhere. Like too much blood on the floor."

Adam shook his head. "If that's all you've got, then I think it's time to call my lawyer."

"You're saying that you had nothing to do with any of this? That you don't know a single thing that might help us solve this so that no more families end up dead?"

That was too much.

Adam wanted to stand, but instead he stayed put. "I would never want to see a family get hurt. Not *ever.* That's disgusting."

"Oh, right." Sharpe nodded in understanding. "Just young girls, got it."

Adam looked into the detective's eyes without flinching and hoped that Selena had simply lost the pink box. "That journal isn't even real. It's a lie that has now become a rumor, thanks to the efforts of Channel Five and you fine folks at the Almond Park PD. But the journal will never be found, because it doesn't exist. It's a hoax."

"I don't believe you."

"You don't have to."

"We can subpoena your wife's records. She has plenty."

"You don't know the first thing about my wife."

"I know more than you think I do. About both of you."
A knowing smile touched the corners of his mouth as the
detective held his stare.

But Adam knew this was only a bluff. "Then
charge me."

More silence. A game of chicken to see who would
break. Adam was in no hurry to go home, and it wasn't like
he could leave the precinct and head right over to The
Inside Scoop. He would be fine right here for a while.

"I don't want to charge you, Mr. Nash," Sharpe said,
his eyes and expression softening. "I just want to make sure
that the bad shit that's been happening doesn't happen
again. Can you help me with that?"

Adam shook his head. "No. I cannot."

Sharpe slid the folder toward himself, then he opened it
up and looked inside. He'd already done this several times,
and had to know the contents by heart. But he wasted a
few fat minutes with his eyes inside it anyway.

He finally set it back on the table and looked at Adam.
"Okay. Forget about everything. Let's just go back to that
first murder. The one with the fire and that pretty red scarf.
Was that first one premeditated, or did it just sort of
happen?"

Adam waited to see if there was anything more. But
there wasn't, because they had nothing. He might be guilty
of thinking like a monster, but he was innocent of the
deeds that the detective suspected him of committing.

"I'm not saying another word until I talk to my
lawyer."

Chapter Forty-Nine

Corban lay in his bed, mindlessly swiping through LiveLyfe, getting angrier by the image, but unable to look away from the posts that fueled his rage. People were cruel, and his classmates the cruelest.

He had never felt more alone. Corban was furious with his father, disappointed with his mother, disconnected from his brother, and devastated by the loss of Kari.

Looking through LiveLyfe was probably the last thing he should be doing to cope. But dealing with the anger over his classmates' postings was easier, or at least more straightforward, than facing the rest of his feelings head-on.

A knock on the door, then, "Corban?"

Adam said it softly, as though his name itself was an apology.

Go away.

Corban said nothing.

Another knock, then Adam repeated his name slightly louder.

Seconds passed. The door opened a few inches, just enough for Adam to poke his head inside. "You in here?"

Without lifting his eyes from the tablet, Corban said, "You know I'm in here."

Adam entered, walked to the edge of Corban's bed, and sat. "Mind if I sit?"

"I mind a lot of things."

"I'm sorry, Corban."

"I'm sure you are."

"But I haven't done anything *wrong* here. There's—"

"Are you kidding me?" Now he was looking at his dad. "*You haven't done anything wrong?* Do you even know what you're saying? You want to MURDER PEOPLE!"

Corban was up off the bed. He couldn't lie down, and he sure as hell couldn't sit there and listen to his father claim he hadn't done anything wrong.

"I don't want to murder people," Adam replied.

His calm, measured tone only made Corban's madder.

"I saw the notebook."

Adam flinched, but responded without hesitation. "Then you know that I've never actually done anything, Corban. I'm sorry I have these sick fantasies, I know they're wrong. But your mother has helped me for a long time, and I've never once acted on any of them, so —"

"Congratulations. You only *imagine* doing disgusting evil shit."

Adam slowly nodded. "I understand how you feel, but you can't help what your brain does. You can only help what you do with the information. And I try to do all the right things. I'm dealing with this the best way I know how."

"You're a real inspiration."

"What if I liked rape porn, Corban? I don't, but a lot of people do. Would you think I was a rapist if I did?"

"Probably. A rapist *and* a coward."

Corban couldn't take any more. He stomped downstairs, where he found Dane sitting in the living room, reading a magazine.

"What are you doing here?"

Dane looked up, closed the magazine, and dropped it on the sofa beside him. "Killing time, I guess."

"Where's Levi? Are they all upstairs?"

"No. Your brother's on some sort of *HardCorp* fast, so he's outside with Elliot and Pussabo. They're playing basketball. Or swimming. Who knows."

"Why aren't you with them?"

"I guess I'm just a little sick of Elliot's shit."

"Yeah." Corban nodded. "But why not just go home?"

Dane rolled his eyes. "Why don't you go to my house and see how long you can deal with my dad."

"Fine. Then you can stay here and deal with mine."

They shared a laugh. It felt surprisingly good rolling through Corban's throat.

Corban didn't mind Dane, now that he didn't have to hang with his brother at the same time. The two of them had always gotten along, until Corban's recent falling out with Levi.

"Your dad's not all bad, man," Dane said.

"You don't live with him."

"No, I don't. But I live with mine and he's worse."

Corban sat, because why not. "I never understood the problem you have with your dad. He seems like a nice guy."

"Sure, he's *nice* enough."

"Why are you saying it like that?"

"Like what?" Dane asked.

"Like nice is a four-letter word."

"It *is* a four-letter word."

"You know what I mean."

Dane shrugged. "My dad is a perfectly *nice* guy, but he doesn't give a shit about me."

"Sure he does."

"*No*, he doesn't. My dad doesn't even know who I am. Even the one thing we have in common, my going to Stanford, is a totally different thing for each of us. He doesn't know anything about me. And do you know why?"

"Why?"

"Because he never fucking asks. And when he does, he can't even hear what I'm trying to say. It's pathetic. He's been telling himself the same stories ever since my mom died. He can't get over it, and he has to drag me down with him."

Dane's face had soured. He exhaled sharply and shook his head.

"I'm sorry. I don't mean to be such a downer. I'm just trying to say that I get where you're coming from. Your dad can be annoying with the jokes and whatever, but you have it pretty good. You have an amazing mom, and at least your dad knows who you are."

"Yeah, he does. Which is why he's spent my entire life wishing that I was a little more like Levi."

Chapter Fifty

Levi sure felt a lot like his father.

By that, he meant out of control, or most of the way there.

Even on Saturday he couldn't escape what people were saying, let alone stop them. Memes were multiplying all over LiveLyfe, and now he was getting texts from numbers he didn't recognize, saying unspeakable things about him and his family.

After a lifetime of being Mr. Popular, being ostracized hurt like nothing else. The shunning hung on Levi like a shadow in winter. Even the last of the summer heat wouldn't warm the chill dogging him on his walk to campus. Even if his world was falling apart, even if he spent the whole day alone, he wasn't going to miss An Almond Summer, the school's annual carnival.

Every step filled him with ice. The guys had said they'd see him there, but would they? Or would they abandon him like he'd abandoned Corban?

Levi felt even worse, now that he understood how his brother must've felt these past months.

Now they were in the same boat, except that they weren't, because Corban had been in it longer, and he was trying to row in a different direction than Levi was, and … the stupid metaphor fell apart, like everything else in his life.

Levi had always tried to do the right things, and deserved for good things to happen. Good things like Kari. He couldn't remember the first moment he felt something for her as more than a friend, but he knew in his gut from the first second he did, that Corban beat him to it.

Why should she like Corban more than him? What made his brother so special? Or Levi so … so ordinary?

Levi stopped at the edge of the school parking lot and looked out upon An Almond Summer. It was impressive what the school managed to assemble: five rows of games and booths, a surprisingly large rollercoaster with a long line waiting to get on, and a giant moon bounce for the middle grade kids.

The bright blue sky, the scents of sweet caramel corn and spicy nachos, the determinedly-happy chatter — it made him feel sick to his stomach.

Right now, he felt like a monster lurking among humans, because while he had no interest in throwing baseballs at galvanized milk cans that were impossible to topple, there was a game that he wanted to play.

Levi was hunting for Kari.

He still wasn't sure what he would do once he found her, only that he would know the second he saw her, and it would be exactly what they both deserved.

Levi hadn't just lost something with this whole Virgin thing, it had been stolen from him. And while he couldn't prove it, Corban was the obvious candidate for *thief*. He was the one who'd snooped on their father's tablet and claimed to have found a cache of sick fantasies. It made sense that, when he couldn't get Levi to believe their father was such a pervert, he would've gone looking for more evidence. He must've found the same pink box.

But instead of giving Dad the benefit of the doubt and pretending he hadn't read them, Corban had fucking published them for the world to see. He apparently didn't care if he ruined his entire family's lives.

It felt like Levi's punishment, for not believing his brother.

But he would deal with Corban later. Right now his brother was at home, locked in his room like a little fucking baby. Which meant if Kari was at the carnival, she was here alone, and Levi could have her all to himself.

She couldn't deny him forever. Not here, in front of everyone.

His life was unraveling, and Levi needed something to hold onto. Why not grab it by the throat?

It was interesting, how fast love could wither to fury. Although he'd been annoyed by her melodrama in the past, Levi could barely stand his mother right now. He'd respected his father more, but that just made his betrayal hurt that much more. He was deeply attracted to Kari. He understood how Corban could love her so much that he'd doom his own family to save her father from prison.

So it didn't matter if Corban was the one revealing family secrets, it was still Kari's fault.

But even as Levi finally spied her across the carnival, alone and staring off into nowhere, her tongue stained blue by her snow cone, he felt angry, aroused, and entirely lost.

He had surrendered to something that had lurked inside him for a long time, something animalistic and ugly. It wanted to hurt someone as deeply as he hurt now.

It wanted revenge.

It wanted vindication.

It would take whatever it could get.

Before he knew it, Levi stood two feet from Kari.

She turned from the sky to meet his eyes. It felt like a dare.

Then Levi said, "So what's a girl like you doing in a nice place like this?"

"Not now, Levi."

"Should I make an appointment?"

"If you're going to be an asshole."

"Why would I want to be an asshole?"

She looked at Levi, her eyes as exhausted as her body. "I don't know. Why *would* you want to be an asshole?"

A pair of freshmen paused their walk just close enough to listen to the exchange. They were joined by a trio of seniors.

"I was just wondering why you were here," Levi continued.

"I have every right to be here."

Levi nodded. "I agree. And I was hoping to find you."

"Here I am. So when are you gonna tell me what you want?"

"I know what you did."

Kari looked at the growing circle around them, then met Levi's cool gaze with pleading eyes.

Please. You can't.

But he could.

Kari planted her feet, crossed her arms, and held his stare. Defiant. "I didn't do anything."

Levi whispered, in a rolling growl just low enough for her to hear, "You had your chance." Then, louder and mostly to the crowd, he fired the first shot. "Why doesn't your dad just admit what he did so that we can all get on with it?"

She said, "I could explain this again, but I can't comprehend it for you, so what's the point?"

A laugh at Levi's expense, a twittering from somewhere behind him.

She was going to pay for that. "Nice of you to fuck my brother. I was sick of hearing him beat off to that pic of you in a bikini."

She flinched. That got her. "You're a coward, bringing Corban into this."

"You're the one who brought my brother into this."

"And how is that?"

"Because it should've been us." They both knew the truth.

"I would never have been with you," she said. "*Ever.*"

"Why are you playing so hard to get when you're so hard to want?"

More laughs, but these were for him. He was winning.

"You're supposed to be identical to Corban. How'd you turn out to be such an asshole?"

Now there were twenty people watching, at least. Someone in the crowd had their camera. From their phone to LiveLyfe in real time. A few more admirers would be enough to put him back on top, and shove her back to the bottom where she belonged.

Because she was the reason his life was falling apart.

"Admit that you made up that shit about my dad."

"I didn't make anything up."

"Your father's the murderer."

"No. He isn't."

"You made it all up to get him out of jail."

"I didn't make anything up."

Adam lunged in for the kill. "We'll all celebrate the day he's convicted. Make it an official holiday."

Blinking back tears, Kari spat, "You're a tragic misappropriation of trace elements."

And in that moment he loved her.

But he hated her more.

"I'd call you a cunt, but a real pussy doesn't feel like ice."

"Fuck you."

The crowd was laughing and gasping.

But she wasn't beaten yet.

So Levi finished her.

"You're such a bitch, your mama killed herself to get away from you."

Chapter Fifty-One

"You're a coward, bringing Corban into this," Kari said.

Corban stood paralyzed by the hot dog booth. Levi was being a raging cock. Even though Corban still wasn't speaking to Kari for her betrayal, she didn't deserve the things he was saying.

"Why are you playing so hard to get when you're so hard to want?"

The mob laughed. Corban's skin heated with his anger, his frustration, his lust.

"Admit that you made up that shit about my dad."

"I didn't make anything up."

He had to do something. But all he could do was stare as his brother and the girl he loved publicly try to tear each other apart. Yeah, he was mad at Kari. But he was angry with Levi, too.

Maybe he didn't have to do anything.

Maybe they deserved what they were doing to each other.

A chorus of gasps dragged Corban back into the present.

He looked over at Levi just as his brother said, "You're such a bitch, your mama killed herself to get away from you."

Corban shoved through the circle of onlookers to the space where Kari and Levi faced each other.

Kari's face was void of expression. But Corban couldn't think of a single thing Levi could've said to hurt her worse. Her nostrils flared and her fists shook. Her entire body was trembling.

He resisted the urge to take her arm and lead her away. She wasn't his girlfriend anymore, and it wasn't his job to comfort her.

Corban moved to stand between them, nudging the pair farther apart with his outstretched arms. "Cut it out, Levi."

Levi turned to his brother, wearing a Grinch-like smile. "Hey Corban. Glad you made it." Then he looked from Corban to Kari and back. "Did you come to get some nuts on your nuts?"

"Fuck you, Levi."

"How about Kari fucks me instead? We already know she likes my body."

"How about you grow up and stop trying to steal my girlfriend?"

Kari looked shocked. Shocked that he was defending her.

Okay, he'd been cold-shouldering her for days. He had every right to be angry. But he didn't hate her.

Levi seemed to, though. His lip curled with disgust and he recoiled dramatically. "You're still fucking her? After what she did?"

Corban felt his face going cold and hard.

This is it.

Levi crossed his arms over his chest and waited for Corban to tear him a new one.

But instead, Corban punched him in the gut, and as Levi gasped for air that refused to come, Corban shoved him to the ground.

And spat on him.

The crowd went silent, watched as Corban stepped over Levi, took Kari's hand, and led her away without a backward glance. Elliot and Pussabo stared at Levi for a moment, then turned and followed Corban.

Chapter Fifty-Two

Selena seethed. When was Adam going to finally stop whining and grow a pair?

She wanted a husband. Not another psyche to fix.

She'd listened to him for a full minute or so without interruption, letting him spill out all the same bullshit, bitching that she wasn't giving him what he needed and hinting that if he lost control, it would be on her. So, blackmail. He took no responsibility for his urges.

And it was her fault. She'd so wanted the control that his neediness gave her, she'd encouraged the behavior. It was practically part of their mythos, that he was out of control and she reined him in.

Worse, no matter how she went at him, he wouldn't give her a straight answer. Selena felt like she was being given one piece of the puzzle and then told to *figure it out.*

But she didn't want to figure it out. She shouldn't have to.

Maybe finally spitting it out was the best thing Selena could do. Kick over the container with the cancerous question.

Did you do it, Adam? Are you the Almond Park Killer?

"You're acting like a fucking narcissist, Selena." He stood there glaring at her, no apology coming, despite that he'd just said the one thing he promised to never say again. "You're being a bitch because you're worried about your public image. And yourself. Not me, or this family."

"My public image has everything to do with this family, and you know it."

"Only because you won't allow us to live any other way."

"That's not true."

"It absolutely is. So if you don't say what's on your goddamned mind, then neither one of us is getting anywhere."

Fine.

"Did you do it, Adam? Are you the Almond Park Killer?"

Adam laughed. Shaking his head, he mumbled, "Finally."

"Finally what?" And now she was scared.

But maybe she didn't need to be. Adam's shoulders relaxed. He almost looked calm.

"Finally, you're taking me seriously."

Crap. "Is that a yes?"

"I thought you might be wondering, especially with that scarf bullshit the other night, but you were too cowardly to ask me then. Either that, or you were sure you'd emasculated me so completely that you forgot who I was when we first met."

"So you're mad at me because I wanted to believe that you didn't kill those four families."

She was terrified to hear his answer, that he might laugh again and tell her how wonderful it had felt to murder their neighbors. But if she ran now, she would never be Selena Nash, world's leading serial killer expert, ever again.

So she forced herself to look him in the eye and wait.

He looked positively euphoric, the bastard.

"What if I had? What if you could've stopped me?"

"Then *you* would've become a monster, Adam. If you think that would make me love you more, you're wrong."

"Well, since we're talking about monsters ..."

Selena didn't like this. He seemed almost ... condescending. "What's that supposed to mean?"

Sudden and bitter: "If I was a teenage boy, would you love me more?"

"Excuse me?"

"You know what I mean."

She did, but that didn't mean she was going to make it easy for him. Something inside her was clicking. The final few ticks before detonation. "What do you mean, Adam? *Say it.*"

"I don't need to say it."

"SAY IT!"

"You. Sleeping with one of our son's friends."

Fucking coward, still couldn't say his name.

Selena crossed her arms over her chest, trying for the same smug look he always wore while making a cutting joke. "I liked you better a few minutes ago when you were being an asshole. Now you're just being an idiot."

"So you deny it?"

"Of course I'm not sleeping with him. Fuck you for thinking that."

"Fuck you for thinking I would murder four families."

"*Are you kidding?* How many times have you sat in my office telling me about your fantasies?"

"That's different!"

"How is that different?"

"Because those are *fantasies*. Your office is the place where I can safely get them out. Isn't that what you've always said? And besides, do those murders look anything like what I've described to you?"

"Real life is different. It always is." Her voice cracked but she went on anyway. "Just ... tell me the truth. Whatever it is, we can deal with it. But I have to know."

"This is bullshit. I can't believe we're having this conversation. I thought that *if* you brought it up, then it would be a ten-second dialogue, because *WHAT IN THE FUCK?*"

He began to pace, like he did when he was about to start ranting.

"Adam—"

"If I was responsible for killing those families, then wouldn't that invalidate your bestselling bullshit? Is that what you're worried about?"

She shook her head, tried to figure out what she could possibly say next.

Because the truth wouldn't do, and anything else would just lead them both to further confusion.

Adam was smart, and he knew her well. He could clearly see that she was holding something back. And in this moment, she wondered if letting him believe that she might be screwing Dane would be better than the truth: that their entire relationship was based on a lie.

That she'd known he wasn't a serial killer. That she'd been using his blood fetish to manipulate him. That the killings made her wonder if she'd driven him to murder by letting him think he was capable of that.

He studied her, clearly unconvinced.

Adam's fantasies weren't there to relieve anxiety over predatory emotions like fear and abuse, or memories of neglect. His fantasies were only that, and his alone. Sex was hot because he was so excited. But there was no deeper connection with him through those fantasies, not for her.

She'd been using his libido to control him.

So what if there was a gap between his fictions and her facts? She helped him find a way to have a normal life and be himself, right? Helped him handle his guilt. More than that, she built a beautiful life for them. For their family.

Adam believed from the deepest parts of himself that Selena had saved him. That she taught him to control the poison inside him, when really his impulses were so much different from what she had led him to believe.

If he stopped believing that, what would they have left?

"I didn't take your treatment seriously enough. I didn't see that you were taking things to the next level. I thought that you were fetishizing the violence. How could I know that things were getting out of hand? I'm only human. It's not like ..."

Adam was shaking his head in disgust.

"What?"

"Even now, even as you accuse me of *murdering children*, which makes me wonder how we're ever going to sleep in the same bed again, even right now you can't help making this all about you."

"How am I making this all about me?"

"*I didn't take your treatment seriously. I didn't see it. I thought that you were fetishizing violence. How could I possibly know? I, I, I, I.* Fuck you, Selena."

"Don't talk that way to me. We're getting away from the point."

"Oh, we are? Should we circle back to how you're fucking one of our son's best friends?"

"I'm not taking anything from anyone, including you.

We've had sex less in the last month than we have at any time in our marriage, including after I had the twins."

Now it looked like he might hit her. He definitely wanted to.

"Maybe I don't feel like fucking someone who thinks I could do what you're accusing me of doing."

"I'm not accusing you, Adam. I'm *asking you*. So that I can *help you*."

"You mean so you can help yourself." Then picking up his previous thread, "And maybe I don't feel like fucking you, knowing you'll probably be thinking about some kid while I'm inside you."

"Maybe you don't want to fuck me because I'm not covered in blood!"

He grabbed her by the shoulder.

Selena sneered, "Sorry about menopause. Shit really went to hell between the sheets after I stopped coating your dick in blood every month."

He grabbed her by the throat. Pushed her toward the bed.

Selena was disgusted.

Who was this man she had married, so petty and jealous and obsessed with things that weren't even happening that he couldn't even look her level in the eye and tell her the truth?

She'd normalized his fantasies, but she had done so at the expense of her career, and now possibly her children's futures.

Selena wondered if this was it, if she was going to die.

Adam's hands tightened, and it was getting harder and harder to breathe.

This was all her fault.

With her life and career both crumbling around her,

Selena considered a final *maybe* that she never considered before.

Maybe it wasn't Adam that she had been lying to this whole time.

Maybe Selena had been lying to herself.

She looked up into his eyes, silently pleading with Adam to let her go.

His fingers relaxed, but there was still murder in his eyes.

And as he turned Selena around and yanked down her skirt, then followed with her panties, her suspicion felt like a certainty.

Her heart was broken, because she really did love this man.

Chapter Fifty-Three

She heard Adam slam the front door on his way out. It wasn't easy, you really had to throw your shoulder into the thing if you wanted to be dramatic. Adam wanted her to know that he was pissed, and out of there. Selena was glad.

The sex had been brutish and abrupt, and Adam had satisfied himself without trying to please her. For the first time in their marriage, he'd been using her, rather than the other way around.

She needed to figure out how to get control back. If he thought the only way to keep her attention was to become a serial killer in reality ...

She went to her nightstand and texted someone she had never texted before, though she was sure that his number would be in her phone.

It was, so she texted, *Can you come over? I have a favor to ask.*

Three seconds later, Dane texted back. *Be right there! Park at the side and I'll let you in through the back.*

The twenty minutes felt like an hour. Selena kept

worrying that Adam would return too soon. She was waiting at the door when Dane got there.

"Are you okay?" He eyed her up and down, because clearly she wasn't.

She nodded, trying not to think about the little bit of Adam still leaking out and dribbling down her inner thigh as she gestured toward the living room. "Mind if we sit?"

"Of course."

Dane followed Selena into the living room and sat in the love seat, across from her on the couch. She had no idea how to start.

"So what's up?" he prompted, trying to help.

"I need a favor."

He held up his phone with a smile. "You said that."

Selena smiled back. This felt wrong, but right now so did everything else in her life. "I need you to follow Adam."

Dane appeared surprised, but in no way displeased. "And why would you want me to follow your husband?"

"You drive, right?"

He barely nodded. Of course he drove. She just told him to park in the back.

"Then if it's not too much to ask, I'd love for you to follow him around for a day or two. This weekend. See if he's doing anything unusual, going anywhere weird."

"Anywhere weird? Can you be more specific?"

"I want to know if he goes anywhere near Ollie Harris."

A shadow fell across his face. "Why would he be around Kari's father? Is something dangerous happening?"

He'd be around Kari's father because Adam is smart enough to effectively frame someone else for his crimes.

She shook her head. "I wish I knew more, but I don't. I just ... I can't trust anyone else right now."

"Not even your sons?"

Selena swallowed. "Not with this."

Dane gave her what seemed like a wicked little smile. "What makes you think you can trust me?"

Trying not to cry, she said, "I don't have any other choice."

He moved from his loveseat to her couch. Sat six inches away. "Tell me what to do and I'll do it."

This felt wrong. She stood and walked toward the back door, and like a puppy, he followed. She held it open, suddenly wanting him to leave.

But Dane was lingering. Waiting for what, Selena didn't know.

Except that she did.

He was looking at her with hungry eyes that she had to ignore. Because she was *not* the woman Adam apparently believed her to be. She gestured outside, toward his Explorer. "Thanks again."

"Sure thing," he said, clearly wanting to say something more. Another few seconds of silence, then he asked, "Is there any place that you want me to start?" A bitter note entered his voice. "I don't mind being an errand boy, but do you know where he is now?"

"Of course," Selena said.

Then she gave him the address.

Chapter Fifty-Four

Adam sat in his Porsche outside The Inside Scoop, listening to *Blood in the Cut* on repeat.

He was sick and tired of waiting. He'd wanted to keep the cat in its bag, maybe drown it in the river, but now the feline was fucking his life with its bloody claws.

This wasn't his usual time, but it was the hour that chose him.

Adam preferred the midday shift, when the woman in the blood-red lipstick was usually alone. People wanted ice cream both before and after dinner, increasingly so as evening marched into night. Summer had taken the evening shift from two to three employees.

Hours later, the first of Poppy's coworkers had left, leaving her alone with one girl whose obnoxiously-long hair spilled down her shoulders almost to her waist. Her movements were swift compared to Poppy's slow and methodical scooping. The brunette appeared to be in a hurry, but Poppy seemed like she had nowhere to go.

Fate, or the devil it seemed, was definitely smiling.

Finally the last girl left, leaving Poppy to lock up alone.

Adam killed the radio and got out of the car, grateful for the shadows as he watched the glass door close behind the brunette.

After she turned the corner, he dashed across the street.

He opened the door and Poppy called out, "Sorry, we're closed!"

Then she turned around.

"Oh," she said. "It's you."

"It's me."

She didn't know what to say, and neither did he. The lights were mostly out. And in the silence and shadows the humming freezers sounded like thunder.

Adam wondered what he looked like. Was he drooling? Leering? Could she peer inside his mind and see herself as he imagined her, choking on her own blood?

"The register's closed and everything is put away. Is there something I can help you with?"

Yes.

You can make me whole.

You can make me a god.

You can be my sacrifice.

"Adam?"

His name sounded like a prayer.

What could he say? The impulse was killing him.

He'd expected this to feel right, but somehow it was wrong.

Was it because Selena had hobbled his inner killer?

Or because she was his first, and he'd been waiting a lifetime for this?

The door was open, and all he had to do was walk through it. The girl with the blood-red lipstick stood a few feet from Adam, awaiting her death by his hand.

He was aroused, but not hard.

Something was very wrong.

"I'm sorry," he stammered, not knowing what to say. "I shouldn't be here."

She looked almost concerned. "I can get you some water. Would you like some water?

"No. Thanks." He shook his head and closed his eyes. Tried to make this feel right.

He pictured her body, naked and sticky. Nipples erect, before they were severed.

But this time it didn't work. His dick was still soft.

This time Adam looked at the woman in blood-red lipstick standing behind the counter, staring back at him in worry or something worse, and he knew *exactly* what he wanted to do.

Despite the vivid images in his head, Adam didn't want to fuck *or* kill her.

He only wanted to *run*.

"I'm sorry … I … I gotta go."

"Are you—"

But Adam was already outside, walking fast toward his Porsche, feeling her watching him flee. He was hyperventilating. About to throw up.

Thinking about grabbing her, killing her, ending her life … it terrified him. Disgusted him.

Revolting, repulsive, repellent.

But why now? What was different?

Because something was obviously missing.

And then, like an anvil dropping on his head, Adam finally understood exactly what was missing.

Selena.

She had been a part of Adam's fantasies for so long, first listening, then talking him through them, and finally, roleplaying until they were sticky and panting. She was a part of the daydream, the cherry crowning his crimson-covered wish. But now she wasn't here and that left him nothing to hold onto.

Now he was empty, and thoroughly alone.

He thought back to all the horrible things he said, and wished he could take them back.

He didn't want actual blood, he craved the mutual fantasy of imagined chaos, that deep connection formed through their mutual fascination with violence, and their willingness to explore it without any judgement around their shared arousal.

She was the first person to accept him, when he revealed his darkest fears and fantasies. Instead of repulsing her, his darkness was an aphrodisiac. He helped her to stomach the same darkness inside her.

And that's why he loved her. He thought of their last session, when she'd thrashed back against his hardness, screaming for him to *Imagine the blood.*

His erection was back.

But this time Adam knew who it truly belonged to.

Chapter Fifty-Five

Dane couldn't believe what he was seeing. But suddenly, it was all adding up.

He'd driven directly to the address that Selena had given him. And sure enough, parked a half block away, Adam's car.

The Inside Scoop. A trendy ice cream chain with artisan flavors like carrot habanero, sweet cream and biscuits, and Dane's favorite, the spicy chocolate.

But Adam wasn't there to get ice cream. He was there to do something he wasn't supposed to.

Maybe he was fucking one of the working girls, waiting for her to get off so that he could too.

That theory turned out to be incorrect. Because even if the last girl was the one he was waiting for, she definitely hadn't been waiting for him. Dane had a clear line of sight right into the ice cream parlor. The window was a wide circle, so people could see the guys and gals slinging cream against the marble, to convince idiots it was worth the seven dollars.

She was surprised to see him. He fumbled around like

he was going to piss his pants, then skittered over to his bitchmobile like a roach.

Adam pulled away from the curb. Dane waited a few moments, then followed.

He tossed the red notebook onto the passenger seat and kept a couple blocks behind the man who was losing his secrets to the world. Dane knew the truth.

Before Selena confided in him (and he was glad that she had, even though she'd also sent him on this idiot errand), Dane knew all about Adam and his latest obsession. Half the internet had read the excerpts that someone posted from Selena's notes about him — the half that wasn't busy downloading GIFs of kittens in need of grammar lessons.

And there she was, the girl with the blood-red lipstick. She wasn't bad. Half of Dane wanted to follow her, see where she went and where that would take him. But the other half was dutybound to follow Adam. Since so many of his dreams and pretty much all of his future were wrapped up in what happened with Selena's husband, he let the girl go.

As he drove, Dane thought about one of the passages from Selena's journal.

Reading that, and realizing that Adam was the man behind those words, gave Dane what he now considered the happiest day of his life. Because now he knew that Selena could love him like he loved her. Her husband was so much darker than the face he gave to the world.

Just like Dane.

Selena would love him so long as he earned it.

Respect would come first.

And that's why he was following Adam now, disgusted as he was.

What was wrong with him? That sick fascination with

blood … it was filthy. There was a reason people got dizzy and fainted at the sight of someone else's blood. That was an evolutionarily appropriate response. Blood meant danger. If you were scared of the scent, then you were probably worried about being prey. Enjoying the sight, well, maybe that made you a predator.

So that's what Adam was.

And now Dane knew just what to do.

Chapter Fifty-Six

A knot of gnarled gray clouds hovered above Levi's home in what should have been a gorgeous summer sky. But it was even worse inside. Behind closed doors, the place felt like a funeral. Mom shut herself in her office, after a morning of monastic silence. Dad sat cross-legged on the couch, claiming to be writing new material for a gig, staring at his tablet like it was a window into a dimension where things hadn't gone to shit.

As for Corban, he hadn't come home. Levi wasn't sure if his parents didn't care that he'd probably slept at Kari's, or if they'd stopped caring what happened to either of their kids.

Levi was glad. He didn't know how he was ever going to look his brother in the eye again.

He didn't just feel embarrassed, he felt broken. Like he had snapped something inside himself while trying to do the same to Corban.

The look on his face. And Kari's.

The way Elliot and Pussabo had turned their backs on him and walked away — Levi couldn't tell if they'd abandoned him in support of Corban or out of fear that the crowd would associate them with his brother being a dick.

Only Dane had been willing to hang with him at the festival after Corban rubbed Levi's nose in his mistake.

Wanna hang? Dane texted, just when Levi had decided he couldn't take another second of silence.

Definitely. I'll leave the back open cuz fuck my parents and I'll take snacks to the game room. Meet u there.

Cool.

Levi went down to the kitchen and had barely opened the fridge when Dad showed up to ruin his day.

"Hey …"

Dad's best attempt to start a conversation.

Levi grunted. The best he could do, and really, the old man didn't deserve any better.

"Everything okay?"

Levi pulled a six pack of beer from the bottom shelf and slammed the fridge. *I dare you to give me shit about drinking.* "Are you kidding?"

Adam looked away, then back at Levi. "I know. I'm sorry. Is there anything I can do?"

Levi opened his mouth to tell his father to fuck off, but then realized he'd never seen his father's eyes so empty.

It was so unfair. Why was Levi aching inside when his dad had done something wrong?

"I'm sorry," Adam said, touching Levi tentatively on the shoulder. "None of this is your fault, but it's falling on you anyway."

Now it was Levi's turn to look away, thinking again of the horror in Kari's eyes, and the fury in Corban's. "Some of it's my fault."

"It's going to take time, but you're going to get past this." Dad nodded at the six-pack and surprised Levi with, "Why don't you start with one?"

NOLON KING

"Dane's coming over."

Something changed on his father's face. "Like hell he is."

"You were cool with it a second ago!"

"I was cool with your underage drinking, not with Dane coming over."

"Why do you care if my friends come over? Am I on restriction?"

"I don't want you being friends with Dane anymore."

He thinks he can pat me on the shoulder and mumble an apology, then take away the only friend I've got left? "What the fuck is your problem?"

"Don't swear at me, and yes, I'm serious. I don't want him in our home."

"Honestly, I don't give a shit what you want!" A deep breath. Levi didn't know if he should say it, but then *fuck it.* "Is this because you think he has a crush on Mom?"

Levi had never seen the darkness that twisted Adam's expression right then, something fierce and unholy, so close to violence that he nearly fell a step backward.

He'd never been afraid of his own father before.

Then Adam got the darkness under control.

"I'm sorry, Levi, I know it doesn't make sense to you. But I've decided. Dane's no longer welcome under this roof."

"Your house, your rules," Levi snarled. "By the way, what are the rules about ruining everyone's life with your serial killer fantasies?"

He should've felt righteous as he watched the blood drain from his father's haggard face.

He should've felt triumph as he snatched a bag of chips from the counter and stormed upstairs to the game room, fully intending to sneak Dane into the house whenever possible, just to prove that he could.

But all he could think was that he recognized the darkness in his father's expression when his true self came out for a peek.

He was sure it was the same darkness that everyone else had seen on Levi's face when he went after after Kari.

What if I'm doomed to become a killer too?

Chapter Fifty-Seven

Selena had already run three miles, read nearly a hundred pages of Gillian Flynn, and watched four episodes of *The Bloody Truth*. But nothing quieted the chaos inside her.

Her watch trilled. Sam. Where had she left her phone? The bedroom, maybe?

The ringing stopped before she had a chance to look for it. She used the app on her watch to make it chirp, then followed the sound. Definitely in the bedroom, but muffled. It wasn't under the scattering of papers she'd been sorting through on the bed. Or in her nightstand drawer. Or amid the clutter of miscellaneous things piled atop her dresser.

She pinged her phone again, and found it in her closet, right on the shelf where she'd been obsessively checking the news while changing into her workout clothes.

Is this what it would be like for the rest of her life? Half out of her mind with frustration and fear, unable to focus on anything for more than a few seconds?

Selena listened to the voicemail, expecting more bad news, but Sam's message surprised her with the first flicker of genuine hope she'd felt in days.

"So," Selena said after a single ring. "You have something good for us?"

"That's not what I said." Sam let out a polite laugh. She knew that particular sound. This news wasn't good or bad, it would be treading water at best. "But it is something."

"Tell me more. Will it get me out of Almond Park, even for a few days?"

"It's that miserable?" He didn't wait for her to answer. "But no, not really. You could tell your husband that it'll be more than a day, but I only need you tomorrow."

"For what?"

"A pitch."

"I notice you didn't say a pitch with Netflix or HBO. Who is the pitch with, Sam?"

"It's with a small production company called Trauma."

"I've never heard of them."

"They make smart stuff, mostly online. They're great at driving attention and traffic to the things that they make, most of which is on the darker side. It's a good fit."

"Sounds low budget."

"It is," he admitted. "But it's also the kind of project that can have exponential returns. You take this now, let things blow over, and the good stuff will be waiting on the other side."

It sounded to Selena like Sam was telling himself a story. "So, is it sleazy, or a shit deal?"

"Definitely more of a shit deal."

"How shit?"

"Not very, considering."

Selena sighed. "Okay. What's the project?"

"It's a show called *Murdering History*. You'll be profiling historical figures, identifying those who had serial killer tendencies. Imagining a *what if?* where they were killers who had to cover their tracks."

"That sounds colossally stupid."

"Hear them out."

"Did you? Or is this the only shitty offer we have left, so you didn't even bother to vet it?"

"Of course I did. It's not as bad as you're imagining. Their pilot episode is all about George Washington. Did you know that a lot of people close to him died mysteriously? And that he benefitted personally from many of them?"

"No, I didn't."

"Well, there you go."

"Seems thin."

"We don't want more than a season, anyway," Sam argued. "It's a web series with—"

"A web series?"

"Yes, Selena, a web series. But it has commercial potential, and if it does well, we'll get picked up. You can't forget that we're mostly starting over here."

It was a punch to the gut all over again, despite the fact that she'd known that.

"Fine, I'll do it. Should I even ask what they're going to pay?"

"No, because then you might talk yourself out of doing it, and we need you doing this so that you can land the next thing. I like this, Selena. It's the first time since all of this started going south that I can see a rebound on the horizon. Just take the meeting tomorrow morning with an open mind."

"Are you going to be there?"

"I can't. I'll be in New York."

"You mean this is too small potatoes, right? Because if we were meeting with Netflix you'd be on the next plane."

A long pause, then Sam said, "You're right. Do you want me to come?"

"Don't bother. I've got it."

Selena hung up without saying goodbye, then started to plan.

Her marriage and career were both in the crapper, but maybe they weren't over. She could do this. She *would* do this. If it went well, it wouldn't be long before everything would be back to the way it was.

She wished she could slink out of the house without telling anyone where she was going or why. Get through this without having to explain it to Adam or the kids. Get things back on track without the extra humiliation of letting them see her selling.

But she couldn't. Things were so bad right now, another mistake might destroy the little chance she had left of bringing her family back together again.

She called Tequila Sunrise and ordered at least one of everything on the menu that her family loved. At least three times what they could eat in a meal. The restaurant didn't usually deliver, but she offered the kid on the phone a hundred dollar tip to bring it all.

She had it all set up on the buffet a few minutes before everyone converged on the kitchen. But somehow, all that food looked ridiculous. Like she'd tried to throw a party and only three people had shown up.

No one wanted to eat dinner. Corban and Levi each loaded up their plates, refusing to look at her or each other, and retreated to other parts of the house. Adam barely looked at his food, skipping the street tacos and tamales — his favorites — for a blob of beans, a quesadilla, and one of the enchiladas verdes that he always complained were too spicy.

"There's queso if you want it," she said, scooping some

out of the Styrofoam tub not because she wanted some, but because she was hoping Adam would light up and say, *Thanks, I missed it.*

"Okay." He stared at his food for a moment, blankly. Then he picked up a section of quesadilla and shoved it into his mouth. Chewed mechanically. Swallowed. Put the quesadilla down again, his frown suggesting that he'd just remembered not liking them.

So much for winning her family over with a feast.

But she pushed on. "I'm driving to L.A. early tomorrow morning. It looks like I'm going to be doing a new show. It's called *Murdering History*."

"Okay." He pushed the beans around his plate with a chip.

"Sam thinks we can turn this around with a small win that gets me some positive word of mouth."

"Well, who am I to disagree with the all-knowing Sam?" Adam pushed his chair back and walked out of the dining room, leaving his plate full of food on the table.

Dinner was a stupid idea. So was expecting Adam to give a shit about her career right now. Doing a sensationalist show about how beloved figures of history might've been serial killers was the stupidest idea of all.

But Selena was going anyway. Because right now, it was the best idea she had.

Chapter Fifty-Eight

It was time to turn himself in.

Levi still couldn't believe that none of the people who'd watched his attack on Kari had reported him for bullying. Because that's exactly what he'd been doing. The principal should've called him in and suspended him. Or at least had a serious talk with his parents. Not that they'd care, but why was everyone letting him get away with it?

Were they all afraid that his dad would come after them if they said anything?

Or were they afraid of the same thing Levi was — that he was the same kind of monster his father was?

Knees bouncing anxiously, he shifted in the stiff-backed chair in front of the guidance counselor's desk. The school secretary said that Mrs. Michaels would be back any moment when she'd ushered him in.

What was he going to tell her?

He hoped that she'd already heard. That he wouldn't have to describe the incident over again. That she'd give him a stern look and tell him what he needed to do to make things right.

Because any punishment would be better than living his fucked up life a second longer.

The door opened and Mrs. Michaels entered, mug of steaming coffee in hand. She gave him a warm smile and sat behind her desk, leaning back, like he was a friend she'd been looking forward to hanging out with.

Crap. This was an awful idea.

He didn't want sympathy. He didn't want anyone to make excuses for him anymore, or to help him rationalize that he'd been right. He wanted someone who cared enough to tell him the truth.

"Nice to see you, Levi."

Was it nice to see a potential serial killer who'd already started ruining the lives of everyone around him?

But he needed her help, so it would be dumb to start off by being rude.

"It's nice to see you too."

"So, what can I help you with?" Mrs. Michaels asked, even though she probably already knew. When he didn't answer immediately, she smiled and took a sip of her coffee.

Levi squirmed in his seat, unsure of where to start. *I think I'm a serial killer.* The words stuck in his throat.

After a moment, she asked, "Would you like to talk about what's happening at home?"

YES. He flushed with shame, but it was time to grow a pair and tell someone the truth. "Everything's messed up. I might be the reason some of it's messed up. I'm messed up."

She nodded. "I'm sorry, I can imagine how hard it must be, what you're going through right now."

Oh shit, now his eyes were starting to water. He looked down, hoping she hadn't noticed. His friends, his brother, even his own parents hadn't tried to imagine what he was going through. Everyone was so wrapped up in their own shit, they had no time for his.

His voice wouldn't work, so he nodded.

Apparently, that was enough for her. "What's the hardest thing about it?"

Levi drew the deepest breath of his life and finally said it out loud.

"I think I might be like my father."

Chapter Fifty-Nine

Levi was surprised by how much better he already felt.

Mrs. Michaels hadn't laughed or scoffed or told him it was *just a phase* and that what he was feeling was *perfectly natural* for someone his age.

Instead, she'd nodded and listened as all of his craziest, most frightened thoughts poured out of him. How angry he'd been when Corban tried to show him their father's darkest fantasies. How isolated he'd felt as his parents' marriage fractured under the stress of Mom's career and Dad's murderous fantasies. How betrayed he'd felt when Kari turned their family into pariahs to save her father — and how everyone around him crumpled rather than fighting it.

Most of all, how much he hated himself for being just like his father, hated that he couldn't seem to help hurting everyone around him.

"I'm the worst kind of asshole," he'd told her.

"You've definitely got some apologizing to do," she replied with a smile that lifted his heart, because if she could listen to all that and think there was hope for him, maybe there was. "And you can't make people forgive you. You have to give them time. It's probably going to be hard for a while."

He could do hard, if that meant things would get better. "Where do I start?"

"Corban." She said it like it was the obvious answer. "He needs to hear you say that he was right."

"I already said that."

"You told him you were sorry you didn't believe him when he was snooping on your father's tablet?"

Uh . . .

"No, not that."

"That's what started the original fight, wasn't it?"

She was right. This had been going on for nearly a year now.

"Okay." He smiled, for the first time in months.

Mrs. Michaels smiled back at him. "If you want to come back and tell me how it went, I'll be here."

But what seemed so simple in her office was harder in practice. Corban avoided him at school, and when Levi cornered his brother on the way to gym class, he'd shunned him, acting as if he couldn't see or hear his twin.

Now, as he stood in the open doorway of Corban's room, Levi wondered what he could do to make his brother listen.

"I'm sorry," he said again, for the dozenth time.

"I don't care that you're sorry. Fuck you *and* your sorry. Fuck you and Pussabo and Elliot and Dane. Fuck everyone. You're just like him!"

"Who?" But Levi knew.

"You only care about yourself, and what other people think about you. You only care about being funny, not who you might hurt along the way. Get out of my room."

Levi winced. Corban wasn't wrong, that's exactly how he'd been. But he wanted to be different.

If only he could make Corban talk to Mrs. Michaels. He'd left her office feeling hopeful. And heard. She hadn't forced him to do anything, she'd just listened to his words and acknowledged his pain. She hadn't told him what to feel or think, or …

That's what he had to do.

"You're mad at me," he said.

Corban gave him a *have you not been paying attention?* look that could have fried an egg, before pointedly returning his attention to his phone.

"You're so mad that just seeing my face makes your insides feel like they're on fire."

Now he had Corban's full attention.

"Mom and Dad let you down, but it's easier to forgive them. No one's parents really get them."

Corban eyed Levi like he was a snake about to strike. But he was listening, and that was enough.

"When you found that stuff on Dad's tablet, you expected me to believe you. Instead, I dumped all over you because I was afraid to hear it. You were freaked out, and if I read it, I would have to freak out too."

The muscles at the sides of Corban's jaw bulged, but still he said nothing.

Levi took a deep breath. "I'm your brother. I should've believed you. You have every right to be mad."

"Fuck you." Corban looked like he wanted to jump off the bed and smash Levi's face in.

"If you want to be mad at me for the rest of our lives … I'd hate it, but I get it."

"I was *right*. Our father is sick, and I knew it, and we might've been able to do something about it if …" He looked down at his phone, blinking hard. "I should've gone to the police. Maybe those people wouldn't have died."

"No, if anything, that's on me."

"I found it first—"

"No, I already knew. I just didn't want to admit it."

"What are you talking about?"

"Months before you—" He'd been about to say *snooping.* "—before you realized something was wrong with Dad, I went into Mom's office, when she wasn't there."

Corban's jaw dropped. "You what?"

"I found this box with a few red journals in it."

"You knew?" Levi's brother leapt off the bed, fists clenched. "You knew Dad was The Virgin?"

Levi raised both hands as if in surrender. "I had no idea who Mom was writing about. Or that Dad was one of her patients."

"But when I found what Dad wrote—"

"I still have nightmares about some of the stuff I read in those journals. The idea that Dad might be sick that way too … I couldn't take it." Levi lowered his hands, held them out toward his brother in supplication. "If I read the stuff you found, I'd have to believe it."

"Why didn't you tell me about the journals?" Corban was blinking again.

Levi pretended not to notice. "I should have."

"*I* would've believed you."

"I know. I'm sorry."

"You're sorry." Corban took a deep breath. "I don't know if I can forgive you for what you did to Kari."

"It was inexcusable."

"Yeah, it was."

"I'm going to apologize to her, for everything. In public, where everyone can see. So she knows I mean it."

And … "She doesn't have to accept it, but she deserves to see me grovel."

"Yeah, she does." Corban sighed. "Get out."

That was it? "But—"

Corban was off his bed and marching toward the closet. He flung it open, rooted around inside, and emerged a few seconds later holding a bat. And then he screamed, "Get the fuck out of my room *right now*!"

"What the hell is going on in here?" Their father was suddenly standing in the doorway, looking stern. As though he had the right.

Corban raised the bat over his head, and for a moment Levi actually thought he might charge their father. But instead he lowered it without a word and stood there snarling like a bull, staring at the man in the doorway.

Levi cleared his throat. "We were just figuring a few things out."

"I could hear that. Wanna talk about it?"

Together, the twins said, "No."

Dad continued, trying to make something better when he was clearly only capable of making everything worse. He turned to Levi.

"If this is about Kari, Corban has a right to be upset, so maybe you should—"

Corban interrupted. "Are you kidding?"

Dad looked almost comically surprised. Levi had to stifle a laugh, despite the tension. Or maybe because of it.

"What do you mean? I'm trying to help."

"You're not helping anything," Corban said. "It's too late for that."

"But—"

Corban looked at Levi. For support?

He could do that. "Get out of his room, Dad."

"This is my house."

Levi walked over to his father, looked him in the eyes without any apology, and slammed Corban's door in his face.

Then he turned to his brother and dissolved into laughter as Corban dropped the bat and flopped backward onto the bed. Laughing with him.

For the first time in what felt like forever.

"Can you believe him?" Levi asked, desperately clinging to whatever this was.

"Haven't been able to for a while." Corban looked as uncertain as Levi felt. *What now?*

"Do you want me to go too?" Levi asked.

His brother hesitated, then shook his head. Although he didn't say he wanted Levi to stay.

But he did.

Levi was afraid that he might do something stupid to pop this brittle, beautiful bubble. "Can you believe we were raised by The Virgin?"

"Ugh. I *hate* that word, at least in that context."

Levi looked at his brother, almost didn't dare to say it, then decided that they weren't going to get back to where they needed to be unless they started sharing again. Preferably something positive.

So he asked, "But you and Kari … right?"

For the first time, Corban's face cracked into a wide and unrestricted smile. "Yep."

"And?"

Corban laughed. "You know."

Levi laughed too. He did. And that was enough for now.

Chapter Sixty

Adam had to get out of this house before it ate him alive and spit out his bones.

His reputation, ruined. His wife, gone. But his sons no longer respecting him hurt more than anything else. They might never be willing to call him father again. He couldn't blame them.

This is it. This is what rock bottom feels like.

He stumbled outside. Into the Porsche. Engines on, windows down, Tom Petty's "Free Falling" on the speakers.

Out of the driveway and onto the road.

Sunshine nearly blinding him as it bounced off the bathtub body's gleaming silver hood. Trees whipping by in a blur of serenity. The hum of tires zooming over asphalt.

Everything would be fine. He just needed to keep driving. Eventually he would get somewhere better.

Adam drove faster.

He was nearly down the hill. Once there, it was left or right, or nothing.

If he chose nothing, it would be the last choice he ever made.

A right would take him into town, and a left toward the river. There wasn't much of anything if he went left, and that was probably the smarter choice. Choosing right meant choosing to continue, choosing *her* instead of his family.

He was done with that. Forever.

The girl with the blood-red lipstick. The murder fantasies. All of it. Right now and until the end of time.

Even if it meant he had to be locked up to keep from being a danger to the people he loved most.

He turned left, toward the river.

It was where he'd taken the boys to ride the bike trails and skip stones and fish.

It was where they'd celebrated most of their birthdays, at least until the boys became video-game-obsessed teenagers.

It was where they'd spent their happiest times as a family.

Now it was the place where Adam would figure out how to keep his inner serial killer from murdering any chance he had of getting his family back.

He made it a mile before his phone rang. *Private caller.*

He answered more out of curiosity than anything. "Hello?"

"Hello, Adam."

A familiar voice, but nothing he could place. "Who is this?"

"Give it a second. I'm sure you know."

The caller was right. Fuck. "What do you want, Dane?"

"I thought that maybe we should talk."

It took everything Adam had to temper his rage. Through gritted teeth he said, "What about?"

"A few things. I think we should meet in person."

Great idea. In person was the best way to get his hands around this little bastard's throat. "When and where?"

"Do you know where I live?"

"I don't. Probably because you're always at *my* house."

"943 Hidden Trails. I'll be there in twenty minutes."

Adam hung up.

Chapter Sixty-One

Selena had been sitting in her chair long enough to know that she had seriously underestimated Sam.

He was right, this web series could blow up. If the thing hit even a fraction of its potential, it could get picked up by someone big. Web series were the new pilots. *Broad City*, *Ugly Americans*, and *Adult Video* — all of them got their start as web series before becoming the next big thing. HBO was paying attention, Netflix was paying attention, whatever was coming next was paying attention too.

Why hadn't Sam made *this* argument yesterday? Selena would have felt much better about the whole thing. Instead, she was getting it from April, Paul, and Tyler, the trio from Trauma, who were selling her hard. Not that they had to. She was loving every word from their mouths, and the feeling seemed to be mutual.

"Really," April continued, "the show is yours. We feel really lucky to have you, assuming we're going forward."

Selena laughed. "Why wouldn't we? After what happened, this is exactly the right move."

That was another thing she loved about them. They didn't care that her life was a disaster.

"We can work with what happened, turn it into a great story," Paul assured her. "Our marketing department is already on it."

"So then," Tyler took over, "just tell us how *you* see the show, now that we've given you a bird's eye view of what we're thinking."

"I love the George Washington angle for sure, and I've already been looking into that. There's lots of great stuff there, and I'm surprised I've never heard of any of it. I'd love to do Thomas Edison. He had the power and the means to hide his life as a killer, plus there's that whole thing with Louis Le Prince."

"Louis Le Prince?" April repeated.

"You've never heard?" Selena said, even though she was sure that at least one of the three of them hadn't. "We all know that Edison was responsible for the first motion picture camera, but few people know that Louis Le Prince was on his way to America to demonstrate his single-lens camera, and the short films he made with them nearly a decade before Edison built his cameras. Le Prince boarded a train from Bourges to Paris. But the train arrived in Paris without him, despite numerous passengers swearing to his presence. His luggage disappeared along with him. Same for the camera and movies. The disappearance was investigated by his family, Scotland Yard, and the French authorities. But Le Prince was never found, and they declared him dead seven years later in 1897. The same year Edison patented his Kinetograph."

She shivered with excitement. Selena could *see* this show.

"So what if Edison murdered Le Prince? What if he murdered the original inventors for most of his patents?"

"Maybe *many* of his patents," Tyler suggested. "Most might be a bit much."

"Or many," Selena agreed. "Whatever. Point is, history is full of stories like this!"

Paul smiled. "That's why we're here."

Now came the tricky part. Selena licked her lips before she spoke. "So, I was thinking of an interesting angle."

"Oh?" Paul raised his eyebrows.

"We all know what a shit-show things are in Almond Park. After all, that's why we're here." She smiled at Paul. "But maybe we can use what looks rotten to make something fresh."

"Keep saying things like that," April said.

"My husband ..."

"Yes ..." April was leaning ever so slightly forward. So were Tyler and Paul on either side of her.

"He's not a killer."

"Of course not," April said.

Selena swallowed. "But that's because of our work together. Hard work for sure, but work that can be done."

She took a breath, then a sip of her water. It felt nice, drawing this out while they hung on her every word. Being wanted.

"What if some of this country's worst killers had been given similar treatment? What if we could identify these people before they succumb to their worst impulses? What if we made it safe to do so? Like admitting you're an addict, then getting the help you need?"

"Go on ..."

"Jeffrey Dahmer, Edward Kemper, and Ted Bundy. They were all geniuses, and they all should have been studied instead of destroyed. We did the world a disservice. But that's another show."

She laughed, enjoying their attention.

"What if we did what you're wanting to do with the historical figures, but in reverse. We could take a guy like Bundy, and imagine who he would have been, and the things he could have done."

"It's dark," April said, clearly meaning it as a compliment.

"Terrible," Paul agreed.

Tyler nodded. "Much better than what we had."

"If we're going there," April said with a coy little smile, "then can we talk a little more about Almond Park?"

Selena nodded, knowing what was coming. Then April said it:

"What do you say to people who think that your husband could be the Almond Park Killer?"

"It's ridiculous. I do feel terrible that his imaginings are out there like they are. It really is unfair to him, the way that happened. Can you imagine if the same thing happened to one of you? Your spouse accidentally unleashing your most private thoughts onto the world?"

Interesting. Paul and Tyler made sympathetic faces, but April squirmed in her seat.

Selena continued. "But since they are out there, then anyone can easily see that he doesn't fit the profile at all. He could have been a brilliant filmmaker. Adam is *extremely* visual. And he has hematolagnia. Yes, that's a blood fetish. But that's *all it is.* He's aroused by the sight or thought of blood. The Almond Park Murders have nothing in common with my husband's fetish."

All three of them nodded, but she could tell from their expressions that none knew where she was going.

"If we look at the six phases of the serial killer cycle and apply them to the Almond Park Killer, we get a specific profile that has nothing in common with my husband. There is no Aura Phase because we have been openly discussing his imaginings for twenty years. We're home together all the time, there was no wooing. Capture and murder are all about emotional climax, and as ugly as it might be to say out loud, what we're looking at here would do nothing to satisfy my husband."

Selena paused, holding her breath, trying to gauge whether they were interested or being polite. What she was about to propose would be an amazing show, a way to get where she'd been trying to go before everything fell apart.

And Adam was going to hate it.

But she couldn't pass up the chance, not when it might mean the difference between getting back to life as usual or ending up homeless.

Paul wanted more. "Go on, please."

"That leaves Totem and Depression, and while Adam is depressed these days, I think we can all agree that he has every right to be. But the Totem sure doesn't fit. There's nothing bloody about a scarf. Nor sexual. Not these scarves. If anything, it's ..."

But she couldn't say it, because that would make everything true.

"Ms. Nash?" April looked concerned.

Maternal.

Oh God. How had she not seen it before?

"I've gotta go."

"Go?" Tyler was standing, a second behind Selena. "You can't go!"

"I need to leave. I forgot something really, really important."

"But—" tried one of the guys, it didn't matter who.

"I'm on board, we'll talk tomorrow, I'll call you."

If she was still alive tomorrow.

She sprinted to the elevator, hitting Adam's contact entry and getting voicemail.

Down to the parking garage and behind the wheel of her Mercedes.

Corban didn't answer. Neither did Levi.

Resisting the urge to scream as she hit every streetlight on red, then barreling up the highway on her way to Almond Park, she called them over and over again. No answer.

If her family died, it would be her fault. She'd hadn't just made them targets, she'd practically invited the Almond Park Killer to be part of their lives.

Selena floored it.

Chapter Sixty-Two

943 Hidden Trails.

This couldn't be the place.

Adam hadn't thought so when he'd entered the address into his phone and it showed him one of the newer neighborhoods where lots were still being filled with custom McMansions. He was pretty sure that Dane's father wouldn't be able to afford a place like this.

But he really thought it was the wrong address when he pulled up to a new — just finished — home with a SOLD sign in the yard. Goddamn kid was playing games. Good thing Adam was in the mood to play back. Dane was going to regret ever coming near his family.

The lawn was lush, fresh sod that sank underfoot, beside a paved walkway of sand-colored stone. The concrete driveway and parking area outside it didn't have a single speck of dirt or drop of oil.

Adam went around back, just to make sure. The gorgeous built-in grill had never been turned on. He looked in the windows and saw that the inside was just as pristine, with not a single stick of furniture.

He went back around front and knocked on a freshly-painted door that had surely never been knocked on. Again, just in case. No one answered.

His phone rang and Adam jumped a little, embarrassed that this idiot kid had him on edge, and hoping he wasn't watching from the shadows and laughing.

He looked at the screen, saw it was Selena. *Decline.* He turned the phone off — didn't want it going off again while he was sneaking up on Dane — and slid it into his pocket.

Adam tried the door. Unlocked. He went inside.

"Hello?"

The little shit was in here somewhere. The question was what the asshole wanted, and what Adam would do when he found him.

"Dane?"

There was a dripping, coming from the hallway.

Adam flipped the light switch. The lights actually came on.

Through the kitchen and down the hallway. Maybe the master bedroom? He followed the dripping.

"You here?" Then under his breath, "You little fucker."

The dripping got louder. Halfway down the hall Adam smelled something rich and metallic.

That scent used to excite him. Now it made him want to retch.

He reached the end of the hallway and stood in front of a white door, about one-quarter ajar, with a single crimson streak running across it.

His heart pounded. Sweat erupted from every pore.

This wasn't a trick, it was something else. Something terrible.

Adam did not want to see what Dane had left in the empty bedroom, but he had to look.

A fallen ladder, too old and rusty to have had any part in finishing this house. It had to have been brought here, just like the girl draped across it.

And not just any girl. It was the girl with the blood-red lipstick. The first time he'd seen her without her perky smile, unless Adam counted the gaping aperture at her throat, the wound through which her blood had poured onto the plush, creamy carpet below.

That wasn't even the worst part.

Adam clutched his stomach, doubled over, covered his mouth and swallowed hard to keep from polluting the crime scene with vomit.

That's what the police would call it once someone reported it.

His stomach convulsed again, trying to force its contents up his throat. He couldn't stand to look, but he had to.

Because what if he was imagining this?

Maybe he was stuck in one of his sick and twisted fantasies?

What if he had finally snapped himself into a living nightmare?

This was how it would be now. His nightmare made permanent.

So Adam looked back, saw the impossible, and lost it again, dry heaving this time, losing himself to a full body shudder, disgusted by the reek of death and the sight of blood, horrified of who he was and had believed he might become.

The reality was nothing like his fantasies.

The girl with the blood-red lipstick held something in her hand. It looked like Selena's red notebook, and sure as shit it probably was. On the floor next to her he saw Selena's missing Dr. Who scarf looped in the shape of a heart, surrounding the word *Virgin* written in blood.

Adam grabbed Selena's scarf and managed to stand.

That little shit framed me.

He'd probably already called the cops. Adam had to get out of there.

Oh hell. He'd left fingerprints everywhere.

Chapter Sixty-Three

Adam's phone kept going straight to voicemail.

Selena kept calling and calling and calling, hoping and wishing and even praying, but no matter what she kept getting the echo without an answer.

Same for Levi.

Ditto for Corban.

She even tried Kari, not that Selena expected the poor girl to give her the time of day.

What have I done?

And who the hell am I?

Pity could come later. Right now, Selena needed help.

She considered calling Dane. That might be her best play.

Or was it? So far, her judgement had been pointing due south. He'd left clues like breadcrumbs, and she'd been blind to them all.

Right now Selena couldn't trust herself. So calling Dane was out of the question.

There was someone else she could contact.

So Selena dialed him instead.

Chapter Sixty-Four

Corban watched as Kari's expression shifted from suspicion to uncertainty, and then from uncertainty to acceptance.

"I accept your apology," she said to Levi, and for the first time since this whole thing started, Corban felt like life might get back to normal.

No, not normal. Better than normal.

But then Dane came over, uninvited.

He wasn't exactly acting like an asshole. It was weird, Dane was a brooder in general, but today his pouting felt almost vicious, and instead of being like his usual darkly funny self, he seemed downright mean.

Levi kept trying to make it better. "Dude, we'll call Elliot. He'll bring the weed. Then you can chill the fuck out."

"Don't call anyone," he growled, glancing at Kari. "She shouldn't even be here."

What was his problem with Kari? Corban was about to tell him to go fuck off when he asked again, "Where's your mom?"

"He told you," Corban said. "She's in L.A."

"Why is she there, and when will she be back?"

Levi took the ball. "We told you, she's there for some show or something, and she'll probably be back tonight. She's been trying to call, but we agreed that neither one of us would answer. Maybe there's a voicemail, I haven't checked."

Dane took out his phone and looked at the screen, then glanced up at the wall clock, looking uncharacteristically, and unnecessarily, nervous.

All of a sudden, his expression changed. "Let's go play a game."

Corban looked at Levi: *What should we do?*

"What do you want to play?" Levi asked.

"Anything. *HardCorps.*"

"But you hate *HardCorps*," Corban said.

"Let's just go to the game room."

Now Levi looked at Corban: *Something's not right.*

Kari spoke their minds. "Why do you want to go to the game room so bad?"

That was the wrong thing to say. Dane's face twisted into something ugly, lips sneering, eyes going dark. "We're going to the game room."

This time it didn't sound like a suggestion.

Levi looked around the living room, then he gestured at the couch, where three of the four of them were comfortably sitting. "I think we're all good here." Then he tried again. "Maybe you don't want to see Elliot. Why don't I hop on over, then come right back with the weed?" A smile. "You'll still get to chill the fuck out."

"I don't need to chill out. Now let's get upstairs."

Dane's expression twisted into something even uglier.

What the hell was wrong with him?

Corban put his arm around Kari's shoulders, gave her

a protective squeeze as he pulled her close and whispered, "I think you should go home."

She gave no sign that she'd heard him, but a moment later, she checked her phone and said, "Whoa, just got a text from my dad, I better go."

Dane stood and reached for the small of his back — holy shit, he had a gun! It looked nothing like the big purple bazookas in *HardCorps*. It was small and black. He held it in a way that made Corban think it was heavier than it looked.

"Duuude," Levi said, raising his hands like he was being robbed in a comedy sketch. "If you wanted to get your ass kicked at *HardCorps* that bad, you just had to say so.

Dane pointed the gun at Kari's face. "Now. We go. Corban, Levi, Kari, in that order."

What. The. Fuck.

They trudged up the stairs. Corban longed to turn around, see that the other two were still okay, but he was afraid that Dane might lose it and kill Kari. Then Levi.

Once they made it to the game room, Levi said, "Okay, we're here. Tell us what this is all about."

Dane switched the gun to his left hand and held out his right. "Unlock your phone, then give it to me."

Levi shook his head. Dane shifted the gun toward him. Aiming right between the eyes. Levi swallowed and delivered his phone.

Dane turned to Corban next. "You too."

Corban didn't argue.

He didn't ask for Kari's. Instead, he sent texts, first from Levi's phone and then from Corban's.

"What did you do?" Kari asked.

"What had to be done."

Then Dane closed the door, and they heard the hall

tree being dragged across the floor, then anchored against their exit to keep them prisoners inside.

Oh shit. How did he not see it?

"What the hell is happening?" Levi asked.

"Don't you get it?" Corban said. "Dane is the Almond Park Killer."

Chapter Sixty-Five

Going over ninety the entire way, Selena was nearly to Almond Park.

She'd be grateful for flashing sirens in the rearview. Let them follow her home. She could explain that it was life or death, and thank the officers for their help once she got there.

Her family was ignoring her, and she deserved it. So Selena was surprised when her phone buzzed on the passenger seat. Twice, with twin texts.

She asked her phone to read them out loud.

"One text from Corban," announced the blandly feminine voice. "Hey mom emergency at home get here fast."

"One text from Levi," it continued. "Help we need you."

Neither message sounded like her sons. It was Dane, doing his best to grab her attention again. Selena did the only thing she could. She drove even faster.

Where's a cop with a radar gun when you need one?

She teetered on the edge of an unfamiliar abyss, knowing that panic waited at the bottom. Because even though she'd *thought* she understood the darkness, in truth she was a fraud. And that self-deception had put her family's lives on the line.

If she was reading the situation right, she had a little leverage with Dane. Because he was infatuated, and had been for a while. She had just been too stupid or self-absorbed or selfish to see it for what it was, too busy luxuriating in the attention to recognize the peril. She'd thought he was a normal teenage boy crushing on her, the MILF he'd happened to fixate on.

She'd been ninety percent right. He *was* fixated on her. But he'd been expressing his crush by murdering innocent families — because what better way to woo a serial killer expert than to give her a new case to solve?

It was a relief to see her house still standing as she drove down their street. On the trip home, she'd struggle to block out images of Corban and Levi inside, passed out from smoke inhalation while the house burned down around them. It had happened before in Almond Park, and not long ago.

But that didn't mean they were safe. Each of Dane's murders had been executed differently. Who knew what she would find inside?

Dane's Explorer sat in the driveway. Selena parked next to it, then got out and glanced in the garage. Adam wasn't home.

Maybe that was best. If she could use their connection to manipulate Dane, she might convince him to leave them alone. Or leave, long enough for Selena to get the boys to safety.

She took out her phone, set her dictation app to record, and slipped it into her purse's mesh outer pocket, screen facing in so Dane wouldn't see that it was on.

Then, hand on the doorknob, she braced herself for

the worst and prepared to do whatever had to be done to keep her family safe, even if it meant surrendering herself to Dane and doing whatever horrific things he surely had in mind.

Dane was waiting in the kitchen with a smile, alone and unarmed.

Her heart raced, but she couldn't let him know she'd figured out that he was the killer. So Selena smiled back, pretending that she was on TV and playing for the most important cameras of her life, setting her purse on the counter, mesh pocket aimed at her foe.

"Where is everyone? I just got texts from the boys that asked me to come home right away, so I didn't even stop for groceries."

"They're up in the game room, having fun."

She had to lower his defenses and keep him talking. "Why aren't you with them?"

"It's the game room. They're playing games. But none of that *HardCorp* shit. They're playing analog. I think they're having an air hockey tournament or something."

"You didn't want to play?"

"No." Dane shook his head. "I wanted to wait here for you."

It was chilling, the way he said it. His smile was crooked and his eyes were flooded with the shadows of emotion — she'd been assuming it was the pain he carried around from the loss of his mother, but now she recognized it for what it was. Dane's body language was too relaxed for the mayhem that was surely inhabiting his mind.

With a roiling stomach, she took her voice low, almost purring. "And what were you waiting for?"

His smile straightened and his eyes got brighter. "I thought that maybe we could talk."

"About?"

Dane looked thoughtful, and paused before answering. Not too long, maybe twenty seconds or so, it was hard to know for sure. But standing there across the counter from Dane in her kitchen, like she had so many times before, pretending that nothing had changed, terrified that her family was in imminent danger, it sure as hell felt like forever.

He finally answered with a question of his own, and one Selena was glad that he asked.

"What do *you* want to talk about?"

She already knew the answer. Not the one that she wanted to give, but the one that Dane needed to hear, maybe the only one that might open the door for a negotiation. As seductively as she could manage, Selena said, "Let's talk about *us*."

As she hoped, this seemed to ever so slightly relax him.

Selena perched on a barstool, making a coy moue as she touched the corner of her mouth, drawing his attention to her lips.

"What about us?" He licked his lips.

Ha. Gotcha.

She'd established a connection and caught his interest.

Now to move the charade along, see if he would open up.

"Everything, silly." Her laugh sounded natural enough, but it was pouring acid into her stomach. "I think there are some things that you've been waiting to share with me."

Selena leaned forward, made her voice conspiratorial, and ever so slightly sexy. With a peek down her blouse, of course. "Is there something you want to tell me … maybe about Adam?"

That last part hurt the worst, but it was the prompt that Dane had been waiting for.

"He's not the right guy for you."

"Oh?" Selena smiled, as if it had occurred to her too, but she needed Dane to say it out loud. "What makes you say that?"

This is your chance to say all the things you've been bottling up since you met me.

"He bores you."

She nodded like he'd made a good point. "I can't argue with that! But he's my husband, Dane. We have a life together."

"I could give you an exciting life." He leaned forward too, until they were nearly nose-to-nose across the counter.

If she kissed him, would he be easier to manipulate? Or was keeping the tease going more likely to work?

But he drew back before she could make up her mind. "You have a decision to make."

She made her face curious, because she had to ask, couldn't stand not knowing for even one second longer. "The house is so quiet. I don't hear anyone up in the game room."

But that was the wrong thing to say. His smile fled. He wanted it to be all about him, and here she was bringing up her children.

"Quiet as a tomb. Have you *ever* heard us up there with the door closed?" Now his smile was back, and more sinister than she'd ever seen it. "No, you haven't. Because I'm sure you would have objected to some of what you heard."

He laughed. A hateful, hellish cackle.

This was going in the wrong direction. Selena had to do something.

"I want to check in on them, Dane, and then we can finish this conversation. We can do *whatever* you want." She looked up at him, pouting a little. His eyes went back to her lips. He wanted her, and it made him forget how angry he was for a moment. "But first, I need to know that they're safe."

Selena could see it immediately. She shouldn't have used that word. *Safe.*

She had showed her hand, and now Dane was showing his.

She expected a knife, so the pistol surprised her. He held it casually, like a bottle of water. But then he turned it toward her.

"What makes you think they're not safe?" And again he laughed, just as nasty.

"I want to talk about this," Selena said.

"We were talking. You're the one who suggested we stop. So what do you want to talk about now?"

"Let's start with the gun. Where did you get it, and what makes you think you need it?"

"This thing?" Another laugh, this one tiny. "It's my father's. This hasn't exactly gone as planned."

"What was your plan?"

"I think you know."

Selena shook her head and in a sultry voice she said, "I don't. Will you please tell me?"

But this time he didn't buy it. She should've suggested they go somewhere — anywhere he wanted — anywhere that her children weren't.

"You had your chance, Selena."

"My chance for *what?* Just tell me what you want, Dane. Maybe it's what I want too."

"I doubt that."

"*Please.* Just give me a chance. Tell me what I can do to make you happy." And then, a spark of inspiration. Or maybe a roll of the dice. Because if she said the wrong thing now, everything might end.

"I want to hear about the murders." She poured every ounce of genuine curiosity into her voice. "I want you to tell me *everything*. How you did it, why you did it, and how you were smart enough to not get caught."

And there it was, the truest smile she'd seen all day.

This was what he wanted. It was more than attention or acknowledgement. Dane wanted recognition for his brilliance, for executing four families with surgical precision, then casting suspicion on others, and walking away unscathed. He wanted to prove that he was the best.

She could play that game; she'd used it before to get serial killers to talk. But this time, everyone she loved depended on her ability to play it and win.

"The first one was easy," Dane admitted. "They got easier after that."

"Easy how? You mean in actually doing it, or do you mean in not getting caught?"

He shrugged, then answered with a word. "Both."

She whispered, "Did you want to get caught?" Then, even more softly, "Did you want me to catch you?"

Dane considered. His jaw moved. It looked like he was tasting the answer on his tongue. "I didn't *want* to get caught, but I guess I always knew that I eventually would, and I was hoping that you would figure it out before anyone else."

"Did I?"

This laugh sounded disgusted. "Not exactly?"

Her heart might have stopped beating. "Who else knows?"

"Your family."

She swallowed hard. "Who in my family?"

"All of them."

She fought the dizzy sensation of stepping off the edge

of a cliff. *All of them*. That meant all of them had to die, for Dane to believe that he'd succeeded.

Selena said, "No one's going to believe any of them. Who's going to believe Adam, after reading my notes on his therapy sessions? And if Levi or Corban say anything, well, they're just trying to protect their father."

He wasn't buying that either.

She had to give him something realistic. Something he could easily believe. If Selena promised that they could run off together, then he would see through her like a ghost.

"I know how the police think. I know exactly how to throw them off y—"

"I'm an adult, Selena. I won't be tried as a minor. I'll go away for the rest of my life. I can't take the risk."

She laughed like that was ridiculous. "Oh honey, that's not how this works. You of all people should know that. I thought you were a student of this stuff. Getting you off will be the easiest thing in the world."

Another slinky lilt to her voice and Selena could see his response to the innuendo. The flush in his cheeks. The shiver of anticipation that made his gun waver. The hint of a bulge at the crotch of his jeans.

She had him. Now she just had to get him out of the house.

"Do you have an idea?"

"I do," Selena said, practically purring.

Unfortunately, it meant sacrificing herself to keep Adam and the boys safe.

Dane exhaled as if he'd been holding his breath. "So tell me what you're thinking."

As Selena opened her mouth to speak, Adam came charging in.

Chapter Sixty-Six

"Selena!"

Adam stormed through the front door, stampeded inside, and stopped dead in his tracks in the kitchen entrance.

Dane held a gun on his wife, and Adam had no doubt that he'd shoot. Whether his eyes were open or closed, he saw the blood everywhere. Smelled it. Tasted bile. As he remembered what Dane had done to the girl in the blood-red lipstick, he could easily imagine him doing the same to Selena.

"Adam," Dane said, perfectly calm. "Did you enjoy your present?"

"Present?" Selena repeated.

"I got him something special. To celebrate his coming out as The Virgin. Something like that really should be commemorated." Then, Dane turned back to Adam. "So, did you like it?"

"What is he talking about, Adam?"

He swallowed, looked from his wife to the killer. "The girl, from the ice cream parlor. He killed her."

Pure horror stretched Selena's face. "No." She swayed, grabbed the edge of the counter.

Dane laughed. "Someone had to do it."

"You're a monster," Adam said.

"Takes one to know one." And then Dane winked.

Selena pulled herself together. "Dane, we can fix this."

What the hell was she talking about? Adam wished Selena would stop talking, so that Dane would focus on him.

"You're right. We're both monsters. But my family is innocent."

"There are no innocents," Dane scoffed.

Adam swallowed. "Neither of us wants to go to jail. Let's talk about how we keep that from happening."

"You've *never* wanted to talk to me," Dane said.

"I do," Selena said. "I always have."

Oh shit.

She was trying to manipulate Dane, talking to him like he was one of her patients. And that was fine for a therapy session, but didn't she care that the wrong words would earn her a bullet?

Dane turned to Selena. "Tell me what you love about him."

She looked trapped. Every answer was a guaranteed wrong for someone.

"I love Adam's mind."

"What *about* his mind? Be specific."

Selena stuttered, then managed, "I ... I love his imagination. It's probably a lot like yours."

Dane scowled and shook his head. "Don't patronize me. I'm not a child."

"I'm telling you what you already know. That's why you're here, isn't it? Because you know violence gets me hot."

"I know what you're doing."

"Of course you do," Selena said. "Why wouldn't you? But that doesn't mean that it isn't true."

Dane's scowl turned to confusion. Adam was also perplexed. What was she up to?

"You asked what I loved about Adam for a reason," she continued. "You *really* want to know what I love about my husband that I could also love about you, or what you might be missing that he has. Isn't that right, Dane?"

To Adam's surprise, the boy nodded.

"I love his fantasies, and I love that he confesses them to me. The release is more than sexual. Isn't it, Adam?"

Selena looked to him with pleading eyes. *Go with it.*

"Yes," Adam admitted, hating to reveal even the smallest part of himself to this little shit who was trying to steal his wife. "I can't live without it."

"But you've been living without that release," she said to Dane. "You don't have to. Tell me about your imaginings. *I want to hear them.*"

Adam didn't want to hear this, but he couldn't plug his ears any more than he could close his eyes and miss the moment when Dane's attention finally slipped. When Adam's moment to disarm him would come.

And come it would.

Dane exhaled and a weight seemed to leave him. Smiling, he said, "I think about the ripple effect. It isn't just the deaths that delight me, although they absolutely do." He smiled wider. "I think about the misery those deaths leave behind. Echoes and stains … right, Selena? Isn't that what you called them? Death is only the end if you assume it's about you."

Adam had monstrous thoughts, but he wasn't a monster. He'd lived with the guilt and the horror of who he might be ever since the first fantasies intruded on his teenage mind. He'd spent most of his life afraid that he was a demon walking the earth in its human shell, waiting for the devil to one day maybe set him free.

But the fiend standing before him seemed to have no guilt at all. He embraced his evil. Relished the darkness.

He peered at Adam and asked, "Is death only about you?"

"No." Adam shook his head, not knowing if that was right. Because everything felt so very, terribly wrong.

Dane turned back to Selena. "Is that the best you can do?"

"Okay Dane," she said. "You win."

Chapter Sixty-Seven

You win.

That's what he needed to hear, and so that's what Selena said.

Every second she kept Dane talking was a second closer to finding a way out of this.

Adam, thank everything that was holy, had followed her lead. Trusted her to understand what Dane was thinking and navigate the conversation toward a chance for escape.

She loved him.

"You win," she repeated, hoping he would understand what she was about to do.

"What do you mean?" Dane asked.

He was smart enough to step around her trap, if he saw it, but infatuation could be even blinder than love. She could make him dance, if Adam steered clear of the conversation.

"Exactly what I said: *You win.* You're more of a man than my husband ever was, because as good as he was at *imagining*, he's never followed through."

She licked her lips, took a small step toward Dane, praying he wouldn't shoot her.

"Do you know he's been talking about getting a show on TV for over ten years? And talking about making his first kill for more than twenty?"

Another step, this time with a deliberate sway of her hips.

"Not you. You're a man of action, Dane." A smirk twisted his lips.

This was it. So she went in for the kill.

"But you also fucked things up for me. Because thanks to these killings my career is in jeopardy." She took a chance, raising her voice and putting one hand on her hip, playing both mother and temptress. "How did you think that would go over? I know you're not that fucking stupid!"

Dane flinched. "I—"

"Why couldn't you have just come to me? Confessed your feelings?"

Selena softened her voice as she shot a disparaging look toward Adam. Was he truly jealous or was he acting for Dane's sake? She couldn't tell. She focused on the boy.

"You already knew he wasn't working for me. You could see it every time he interrupted us talking."

A knowing look from Dane.

He wanted to believe it, even though his brain was telling him this was a trap.

Selena let her expression swell with regret. "None of this had to happen."

For the first time, Dane looked uncertain.

And in that moment, she dared hope that they were going to make it. That *their family* would make it. She glanced at Adam, not daring to give him more of a hint.

He didn't nod back, because Dane was watching him too. But Adam didn't need to. Selena could tell from the set of his jaw that he understood. And her husband was ready.

"There's a way out of this, for all of us. It isn't too late for us. For you and me, Dane." She let the promise linger in the air before adding, "But I want to see my children first."

"I don't believe you." His gun wavered again.

"Seriously, you can have her," Adam said, sounding disgusted. "I want out."

He couldn't afford to send her a signal, nor did he need to. This was his confessional voice. She had never heard it outside of her office. His way of saying, *I got this.*

"You're lying," Dane said.

"I'm not." Adam shook his head. "The only thing that my wife and I agree on right now is that we both want to see our children safe. Think about it. When's the last time you saw us being affectionate?"

He wasn't trying to hurt her, but that one felt like a blade between her ribs anyway.

Their marriage really had been falling apart.

Maybe now, in the midst of this disaster, they could find what they needed to stitch themselves back together.

Adam said, "Tell me where the children are and you can have her."

"It's too late. You both know what I did." Dane shook his head and waved the gun. "What I'm doing now."

"It isn't too late," Selena assured him.

"Finally." Adam gave her a dirty look, and Selena did her best to look stricken, for Dane's benefit. "Something we can agree on."

"I'm not going to prison."

Selena said, "You won't have to. I can help with that."

"But you won't."

"I promise I will," she lied, adding exactly what Dane

needed to hear. "Genius like yours should be protected. There's only—"

There was a clattering from somewhere outside.

"What was that?" Dane thrust the gun closer to Selena, even though she clearly hadn't made the noise.

"I don't know," Selena said.

He turned his weapon on Adam. "What did you do?"

Adam shook his head and raised his hands. "I've been here talking to you this entire time."

"I'm sure it's nothing," Selena said in the voice she'd used when the boys were little and were waking from a nightmare. Her *Mommy's here, everything is going to be all right* voice. "Probably a bird or a raccoon."

"It was too loud for that," Dane protested.

She laughed and changed gears again. "How did you do it, Dane? Evading the police is easy enough, people do that all the time. But I didn't see it and I *know you.* So—"

"You didn't see it because you didn't notice me!"

"Is that why you killed the girl?" Adam asked.

"That was a present for you. So that you could see what it looks like to follow through and finally execute."

He laughed at his joke like a maniac, but he was using her language, and that was an excellent sign. It meant that he'd started buying into the assumptions she was using to frame their conversation.

Dane circled the counter, coming around to Selena's side.

"Please, Dane." It took everything she had to focus on his face instead of the barrel. "Put the gun down. You're making me nervous."

He seemed to consider, then lowered his weapon. Another good sign.

"Why did you kill the girl?" Selena asked.

"I made your husband's fantasy come true."

Selena hoped that Dane wouldn't look over at Adam. Not now, when he was so close to the butcher block and all of those knives. She used everything she had to turn her face into something that resembled exhilaration, or maybe arousal. Hard to tell with all this adrenaline screaming through her blood.

"What did you do?" she asked, making sure that it sounded like a riveted query rather than an accusation.

"I—"

Adam drew a blade from the butcher block and charged.

Dane heard him coming, spun around, and aimed his gun at Adam's heart.

No!

Adam dove behind the counter.

Selena tackled Dane, ramming her right shoulder into the small of his back and losing her balance as he fell forward onto the tile floor.

Dane's gun went off, so loud that Selena panicked for a moment, instinctively clapping her hands over her ears. Before she could recover, Dane shoved her off and scrambled to his feet. He kicked her hard in the stomach, growling, "Stay down!"

Behind him, Adam vaulted over the counter, the blade of Selena's favorite Santoku glinting silver as it arced down toward Dane's back.

He whirled, barely dodging the knife, bringing the gun up again to shoot at Adam, who was forced to duck behind the counter again.

The Santoku clattered to the floor behind Dane, too far for Selena to reach before the kid pulled the trigger.

So she reached for his ankle, hoping to trip him, but the hem of Dane's jeans slipped from between her fingers as he retreated. He spun back around and shot her.

Pain exploded in her shoulder. Selena screamed, curling into a ball as the world seemed to slow all around her. Ears ringing. Hot blood surging out with every pound of her hammering heart. Where was Adam? Hiding behind the counter. And now that she could barely move, there was nothing to distract Dane from chasing him into the open and shooting him too.

Then the boys. If Dane hadn't killed them already.

"Come out," she heard him say, as if from a distance. "Don't you want to watch your wife bleed out?"

"Fuck you," Adam replied.

Good. She needed him to live. Someone had to save the rest of their family from this asshole.

Selena's shoulder was on fire, but the rest of her felt icy. Like all the heat in her body was draining out through the hole where the bullet had entered her.

"Suit yourself." Dane came back into view, standing over her. Still clutching that damn gun. Still wearing that ugly leer. "This is really more your thing than mine, though. All that blood. This is your last chance to share a boner with her."

Adam crawled out from around the far corner of the counter. Scrambled over to Selena. Said something she couldn't hear as he tore off his t-shirt and pressed it hard enough against her shoulder to make her scream again. Something hot and wet dripped on her face as he said *no* over and over again.

If it'd been Adam bleeding out, she would've been cursing every atom in Dane's body, wishing him to hell, except hell wasn't awful enough for someone like him.

And what did that make her? Someone who'd spent her life fascinated by men like Dane. Yes, she'd helped stop several of them from killing more people. She'd justified her career as a service to society. But deep down, she'd also admired them for their cunning resourcefulness and their ability to stay a step ahead of everyone else.

She'd never hated herself more.

"Soon as she dies, I'm going to kill you," Dane promised Adam. "Then Levi. Then Corban. No, then Kari. I'll make Corban watch her die before I kill him. That's more romantic."

Adam bellowed and lunged for Dane's knees. Another shot sounded, and Dane went down, Adam clinging to his shins in a bear hug.

Please please please tell me he missed. Levi and Corban needed at least one parent to take care of them until they could survive on their own.

Adam pushed himself up on all fours, grabbed the knife he'd dropped earlier and buried it in Dane's chest.

Dane wailed like a toddler with a stubbed toe. Adam punched him, once, twice. He stopped making noise.

Detective Sharpe entered the kitchen, gun drawn. Soon as he saw Selena, he pulled his cell out and called for an ambulance. Then he knelt beside her, grabbed the bloody shirt Adam had dropped, and shoved it against her shoulder.

She screamed.

The room went blurry. Her body was frozen, and there was nothing she could do.

Except make sure that the blame for all this landed squarely where it belonged. On Dane.

"Phone," she whispered as the darkness swallowed her whole.

Chapter Sixty-Eight

Adam stood as a doctor in blood-stained scrubs entered the waiting room. He looked sweaty and exhausted. It was hard not to see both despair and relief in his expression. Probably because that was all Adam had been feeling for the past few hours while waiting for Selena's surgery to be over.

Levi and Corban jumped up too, rushing to meet the surgeon who'd been operating on Selena.

"Is our mom okay?" Levi asked.

"Can we see her?" Corban added.

"Your mother is recovering, and the nurse will let you know when you can see her." The doctor nodded at Adam. "Can I speak with you alone, sir?"

Adam pulled a twenty out of his wallet and handed it to Corban. "Would you two please get me a coffee from the cafeteria?"

"There's a machine right over—"

"I need cafeteria coffee."

Corban sighed and elbowed his brother. "I'm hungry anyway."

Once the boys were on their way to the elevator, Adam turned back to the doctor. "How bad is it?"

"Your wife was extremely lucky."

Adam couldn't help his exhale of disbelief.

"The bullet nicked the brachial artery, but the internal bleeding was light. If the hole had been a millimeter to the left, she would've died in the ambulance."

"Will she be able to use her left arm?"

"She'll need reconstructive surgery and months of physical therapy, but yes."

The tightness in Adam's chest loosened a little. "Can we see her? Just for a minute? I think the kids need to know she's okay. They had quite a scare."

Who was he kidding? He needed to see her chest rise and fall, to touch her hand and feel its warmth, to hear Selena say his name. To prove to himself that Dane hadn't won.

"It'll be an hour or so before she wakes up. The nurse will bring you back then."

"Thank you, Doctor."

The man didn't even say goodbye, he just marched back through the double doors, his lips pressed into a tight, thin line. Back to save the next dying person in the queue.

He slumped back into his chair, weak with relief and ashamed that he couldn't be stronger for his sons. The two had spent the last few hours huddled together in their chairs, whispering to each other. Adam hadn't even tried talking to them. Maybe he should have, but how was he supposed to help them deal with the discovery that one of their best friends was a serial killer?

He didn't know how to deal with that himself.

The boys were back much sooner than Adam expected — Levi carrying a cardboard coffee cup in each hand, Corban sipping from an enormous cup of soda and a paper bag that turned out to be filled with snack-sized bags of potato chips, mixed nuts, chocolate covered espresso beans, and bite-sized cookies.

Corban tossed Adam a bag of cookies. "We need to talk."

They did. Adam braced himself.

"When we heard the gunshots, we had no idea who Dane had shot," Levi began. "But we realized—"

"—we didn't want it to be either one of you. You or Mom. And I'm sorry—"

"—we've been such jerks—"

"—for ... for saying you weren't my dad," Corban finished.

"And I'm sorry I told you to fuck off," Levi added.

"I'm sorry K—" Corban made a choking sound. "—sorry about the journals getting leaked."

"If you want to put us on restriction until we're thirty, we'll understand."

Levi raised his chin, clearly being brave. "We won't complain. We deserve it."

Relief hit him again, this time so hard that Adam was glad he was already sitting. He didn't understand how it happened, but the boys had managed to rip out whatever wedge had been driving them apart this past year.

But that wasn't the only thing that needed fixing.

"I'm sorry, too," Adam said, gruffer than he meant to. His throat felt full of razor blades. Should happiness cut like this? "I haven't been the father I should've been, not for a while. I'm not going to make any excuses, because you deserve better than that."

He'd been about to say more, apologize for being so broken, and for the pathological urges that had nearly ruined their lives. But before he could, Levi said, "I still can't believe it was Dane. He fooled me. He fooled everyone."

"Even Mom," Corban added.

"She figured it out in time." Adam wasn't quite sure how she'd realized it, but he was grateful she had. If Selena hadn't been there, Adam would've barged in and Dane would've shot him. No small talk, distractions of flattery, or hope. No reason for Dane to delay his spree.

It was awful watching Selena try to seduce the boy, to convince him that they could run together and that she would help him stay ahead of the cops, even though he'd known it for a ruse. That had been his nightmare for weeks. Selena leaving him. Deciding to start over with a younger man who didn't share the same sick fantasies. Humiliating him by choosing that little shit because she knew Adam couldn't stand him.

He should've known better. From now on, he would.

If there was a *from now on*.

For all he knew, this would be the straw that snapped the back of their marriage.

And if Selena was done with him, what would he do?

Chapter Sixty-Nine

Selena woke with a sweet, metallic taste at the back of her throat.

Why didn't someone turn off whatever kept beeping?

She blinked into the blurry glare, which slowly sharpened into a white-tiled ceiling.

She tried to turn her head, but didn't have the energy for such an impossible effort.

She willed her eyes to cut left and saw a translucent tube dangling from a saline bag on a metal rack.

I'm in a hospital.

That explained why she could barely feel her body. Painkillers. Or anesthesia?

She eased her eyes over to the right, saw a nurse in purple scrubs passing the open door. Then a doctor, in a hurry. Then a woman with a small, crying child.

"Hello?" she croaked.

No one heard her.

She swallowed, the walls of her painfully-dry throat sticking together, making it even harder to call out. Where was Adam? Where were the boys? Did they all hate her so much that they wouldn't come to see her, even if she might be dying?

Was she dying?

She remembered Dane's smirk as he shot her in the shoulder.

Adam's horrified attempts to stop the bleeding.

Dane, about to kill Adam too.

Adam, on top of Dane, with her favorite knife.

Then what?

The beeping got faster — her pulse racing, she realized — as she struggled to remember who had won.

It must have been Adam. Dane wouldn't have called an ambulance to save her, not after she'd clearly taken her husband's side.

Unless he got spooked after killing Adam. If Sharpe interrupted Dane, that could explain why she was still breathing.

But the thought that Adam might not have survived was too awful to contemplate.

Because this was all her fault.

She should've seen what Dane was up to, and turned him over to Sharpe long before anyone had a chance to leak her journals online, exposing Adam and ruining the boys' lives.

She should've realized it after the first murder, and stopped him before he could kill ten other people, including that girl whose only crime was becoming the unwitting focus of Adam's fantasies.

She should have recognized the signs of Dane's sickness well before it drove him to his first kill. She'd been mothering him since his own mom died while he was still in grade school. She should've known he was a potential serial killer before he realized it himself.

But she'd been so terrified of becoming a failure. It

made her self-obsessed. The people around her — not just her family and friends, but the very killer she'd been profiling — stopped being people to her. She'd been treating them all like stepping stones to the career she craved.

In doing so, she not only lost her shot at that coveted line of work, Selena also lost her family.

Because she had to tell Adam the truth. Even if he forgave her selfishness, how could he forgive her for lying to him all these years about what he was?

She'd let him think he was a monster, because otherwise she would've had to publicly admit that her bestselling book was based on a mistake. To sacrifice all of her professional credibility in a single stroke.

If Selena could go back and do it again, she would have told the truth.

Because no career was worth losing the one person who understood her better than she understood herself.

Adam never hesitated to call Selena on her bullshit.

He'd sacrificed *his* professional dreams to make hers happen.

Most important of all, he'd proven that he'd do anything to protect their children. Even kill for them, and prove to the rest of the world that he *was* the person he'd spent his entire life trying not to be.

She didn't deserve him.

"You're up."

Adam.

She tried to sit up, but barely managed to lift her head off the pillow.

You're here, she couldn't say, because her parched vocal cords would only make a raspy wheeze.

He appeared in her peripheral vision as he approached her bed. Set his coffee on the bedside table, picked up a cup with a straw poking out of the top, then carefully lowered the cup until he could slip the straw between her lips.

She sucked, and a cool, delicious stream of water burst onto her tongue, wetting her throat as she swallowed.

Several gulps later, he withdrew the cup.

"The boys?" Selena whispered.

"Safe. They're staying with Elliot."

Thank God. "Dane?"

"Staying with Detective Sharpe."

The relief was intense enough to spin the room. Or maybe that was the drugs.

She tried to reach for him, but her arm wouldn't move. "Are you—"

"Visiting hours are over, but I bribed a nurse to let me come back for a few minutes anyway."

"My fault. Adam, I'm so sorry—"

"Enough. You need rest."

"You're not a serial killer."

He didn't look surprised.

"I know. When I saw what Dane did to that girl … I could never do that. Whatever I am, it isn't that."

"Hematolagnia."

Adam looked confused.

"You have a blood fetish," Selena said.

"There was blood everywhere when I found her." He grimaced. "More than I'd ever imagined."

"The association between blood and sexual arousal," Selena paused to catch her breath after stringing so many words together, "probably formed when you saw Charlotte die."

"I have a new association with blood now. You, dying on our kitchen floor." Adam shuddered. "And I'm done with that."

But she wasn't done apologizing. "I've been a terrible wife."

"This isn't the time—"

"You're right, I put my career first." Another gasp for air. "I neglected you. And I neglected our sons."

"You did."

"I was terrified I'd be a failure—"

"—because then both of us would be."

That wasn't what she'd meant to say. "A lot of people would kill to be a successful comedy writer."

And that wasn't how she meant to say it.

But he burst out laughing.

He stopped, and she tried again. "Please forgive me. Because I've been so obsessed with being right, I did everything wrong."

"You're not the only one who needs to apologize. I put everything on you. Made it your fault when I couldn't control myself. Expected you to save me from myself."

"If I'd been honest with you—"

"I'd still have needed a foot up my ass to make me see I've wasted years wallowing in self-pity. *I'm* sorry."

The nurse in the purple scrubs stuck her head into the room. "Shift supervisor's coming back from her break in ten. I need you outta here."

Adam smiled and scooped up the hand with the IV attached to it, carefully lifting it to kiss her palm. Selena couldn't feel the pressure of his hand on hers, thanks to all the drugs, but she could feel a ghostly warmth where his lips touched her skin.

"I'll be back tomorrow," he promised. "Someone named April left about fifty messages on your cell about a meeting you apparently walked out of. She wants to know where to send the contracts."

What? They still wanted her to do the web show?

"Also, I want to bounce some book ideas off you."

Selena's head was spinning, and this time she didn't think it was the drugs. "Book ideas?"

"I've been pissing and moaning about how I don't have the stage presence to make it big." He looked embarrassed and happy in unison. "But I'm a comedy *writer*. And I've been writing for everyone but myself."

She couldn't believe she hadn't thought to suggest it to him before. "I'll tell Sam. Whoever he recommends to rep comedy will be the best."

If her career was over, at least she could help him with his.

Chapter Seventy

Adam signed his name with a flourish and handed *I Am Patient X* to the last fan in line, a heavily-pierced, blonde twenty-something whose psychedelic skull tee was neatly tucked into black leather pants. "I hope you enjoy it."

The girl squealed a nearly incoherent thank you, blushed, and ran off to join her boyfriend, who'd been watching the exchange with feigned indifference from the bookstore café.

He suppressed a smile as he capped his blood-red Sharpie. He could've shrunk away from the whole Patient X thing, but he'd decided to embrace it instead. His memoir mixed brutal honesty with a heavy dose of gallows humor. Because that's what people would talk about anyway. Better to take control of the conversation, have it on his terms.

He'd expected the sneers of those who felt that his memoir glorified violence, the emails from people who considered him human garbage for being able to think such things. But he'd been surprised at the fetish community finding something valuable in his musings. Fans turned up at every signing, confessing to thinking they were alone, that they were crazy … monsters even. Thanking him for shining a compassionate light onto a seldom-discussed topic by sharing his experience.

Knowing that he'd helped people made last year's humiliating ordeal … not better, but something he could live with, even if he never lived it down.

Now that he'd gotten the book everyone expected him to write out of the way, he was free to focus on his secret project: a darkly-comic novel about a sociopath in love. It was biting and raw and wickedly funny — at least, that's what Selena had said. He'd rewritten it twice, based on her feedback, but he couldn't tell if he'd made it better or worse.

Maybe it was time to take the standard advice to set it aside and write something else. Get some distance so he could look at it more objectively.

Someday he would be known for his writing, not for the blood fantasies in his old journals.

As he tucked his spare pen and the few remaining bookmarks into a duffle bag, he saw Selena heading toward him.

"How'd it go?" she asked.

"Sold out." He couldn't help grinning at her as he held up his hand, twisting the fingers into a claw for "signer's cramp."

She grinned back. "I'm so proud of you. Your first book's sold more copies than all of mine put together."

It didn't matter how many copies he'd sold. Only that she was proud of him.

"I have news." Selena bit her lip. "I wanted you to hear it from me first, before we talk to Sam and the others."

Uh-oh. Was some whack-job suing them over something he'd said in his book? Or had the deal with those big shot producers fallen through? Maybe Sam had called to say they'd been put off by something in his memoir. Maybe he'd been too honest. He didn't care for himself, but the thought that his book might hurt Selena's career made him sick to his stomach.

"I'm sorry—"

"Trauma's interested in your book," she blurted.

He blinked. "That's good news, isn't it?"

"Not your memoir. Your novel. I mentioned it to Sam last week."

The bottom dropped out of his brain. "Okay, I'll write up a synopsis—"

"I sent him the draft."

Holy shit. "It wasn't ready."

She bit her lip again. "I knew that's what you'd say."

"So you sent it to him behind my back."

Selena nodded, managing to look ashamed and defiant at once. "He loved it. He thinks Dominic and Melinda Shelly will love it too. If you're willing to turn it into a series."

If he was willing to turn it into a — was she kidding? It was a dream come true. And she'd just handed it to him on a silver platter. Okay, a silver platter of mild betrayal, but the sting of knowing someone had read his novel before he'd been sure it was good enough was already fading. *Sam loved it.*

Sam, who only took on the best of the best as his clients, loved his first novel.

"I know it's not the career you've always wanted. It won't be you in front of the camera, making people laugh. But it'll be your ideas. Your words."

Did she really think that mattered to him anymore?

"A wise woman once told me that I should know who I

am, without ever limiting myself to anyone else's idea of who I should be."

Selena smiled at hearing her own words quoted back at her. "And if you still *do* want to be on camera, there's something else."

"You're finally ready to make some amateur porn?" he joked, because he hated the idea that she'd managed to get him a pity gig doing standup. Yes, he'd held the career he couldn't have over her head when they'd fought in the past. Clung to the idea of being the next George Carlin long after it was obvious that his talents lay elsewhere.

It was time to move on.

"The Shelleys have asked if we'd like to do a show together. A lighthearted look at the psychology of serial killers. Some serious in-depth analysis, but presented with humor."

"You know I don't have the charisma for stage work."

"You wouldn't be there to make jokes, you'd be there to represent an educated viewer's perspective."

"So you wouldn't want me to be funny?"

"I'd want you to be yourself. It would be you and me, having an insightful conversation about a case. Be as witty as you want to be. Or you can punch me up and I'll be the comic relief."

"Sam was on board with this?"

"Sam suggested it."

"After you hinted that you wanted it?"

"After he read your novel. He said it was clear from your characters that you have a deeply-nuanced understanding of human nature that would make the show more accessible to the layperson."

Never in a million years would Adam have ever thought this could happen. He'd always seen Selena as the one who belonged in the spotlight. Seen himself as someone who'd been relegated to the shadows. Someone meant to play a supporting role.

But why couldn't he be both?

"So … what do you think?"

"You and me, working together?" Adam grinned. "I think we're going to *kill it*."

What To Read Next

When down-on-his-luck actor Orson Beck receives a mysterious invitation it might be the chance to revive his career … or kill it forever.

As his newfound fame and fortune grows, will Orson destroy everyone he's ever loved to keep it?

A Quick Favor ...

If you enjoyed this book, please take a moment to write a review on your favorite bookselling platform so other readers can enjoy it too. It would mean a lot to me.

Thank you,
Nolon King

About the Author

Nolon King writes fast-paced psychological thrillers set in the glitzy world of entertainment's power players with a bold, insightful voice. He's not afraid to explore the darker side of human nature through stories featuring families torn apart by secrets and lies.

Nolon loves to write about big questions and moral quandaries. How far would you go to cover up an honest mistake? Would you destroy your career to protect your family? How much of your soul would you sell to get the life of your dreams? Would you cheat on your husband to keep your children safe? Would you give in to a stalker's demands to save your marriage?

Also By Nolon King

Cold Vengeance

Cold Vengeance

Cold Reckoning

Hidden Justice

Hidden Justice

Hidden Honor

Hidden Shame

Hidden Virtue

No Justice

No Justice

No Escape

No Hope

No Return

No Stopping

No Fear

Once Upon A Crime

Once Upon A Crime

Twice Upon A Lie

Three Times a Murder

Dead For Good

Dead For Good

Left For Dead

Dead Of Night

Wake The Dead

Dead For Life

Stand Alone Novels

Pretty Killer

12

Blown

Miserable Lies

The Target

Secrets We Keep

Close To Home

Heat To Obsession

A Simple Kill

Tell Me No Lies

Red Carpet Black

Fade To Black

Victim